On Scent

Cherie O’Boyle

Other books and stories by Cherie O'Boyle

***The Estela Nogales Mystery Series*:**

"Intelligently written, with well-drawn characters, lots of humor, and mystery plots that will keep you guessing."

—Ian Wilson, author and book reviewer

Fire at Will's

... a body discovered, a shocking secret revealed ...

Iced Tee

... the community freezer is opened, revealing the frozen corpse of an elderly neighbor ...

Missing Mom

... what's happened to Nina's knife?

Deadly Disguise

... bodies are falling ...

The Boy Who Bought It

... some say he got his just desserts ...

Back for Seconds?

Free short story prequel!

One
First on the Scene

At the halfway point, Jody Murphy made the turn and headed back the way she'd come on her six-mile conditioning run. Glancing over her shoulder, Jody saw her companion, Flag, a black-and-white border collie, take the opportunity to pause and lift her snout to the early morning scents along the river. If Flag had been a human exhibiting the same behavior, Jody would have assumed she was thinking. But what, she wondered, was going through the dog's consciousness? Anything more than a cataloging of the smells? Flag looked over her shoulder at Jody, and dropped her ears to make that canine facial expression that looked so much like a smile. Then she too turned, and loped to catch up. Absently, Jody reached down and ruffled the soft fur on the dog's head.

Her footfalls thudding on the dirt trail, Jody went back to memories of the pair's last search and rescue mission. She recalled how Flag had tugged at the end of her eight-foot leash, pulling Jody gently away from the decaying body. Flag had been on scent all morning, drawing ever closer to the lost hiker, but by the time they found her, both Flag and Jody saw it was too late to help the woman.

If only the district ranger had called Jody and her canine squad in sooner, before dozens of searchers had trampled the rocky trail and filled the air with the scent of too many humans. With a clean trail, Flag would surely have found the woman sitting among the rocks thirty feet below the trail in time to save her.

The woman's belongings scattered about told the end of her story. The shiny plastic of a full water bottle glinted in the noonday sun, wedged between rocks ten feet downslope from where it had escaped her small pack. A dark stain on a boulder to her left showed where her head had likely made initial contact, and yet the body sat upright. She'd regained consciousness long enough to get herself into a seated position. Her pack was pulled into her lap, but a whistle rested inside, untouched. None of the searchers on the trail above had heard her call or seen any signs or signals of her presence below. At the same time, she must have drifted in and out of consciousness for days before she died.

Once Flag had drawn Jody to the find, and Jody had radioed in, she sat to await the arrival of law enforcement. She'd filled Flag's folding water dish and watched as her thirsty dog lapped.

Quenched, Flag dropped to lie on the rock, her back turned to the body, and gazed over the forest below. While she sat, Jody resolved to talk to the district ranger about requesting her canine teams earlier in the next search. The next time a hiker went missing, the dogs and their skills would get the respect they were due and get called first, not after the trail had already gone nearly cold and everyone else had given up.

Jody turned her attention back to the trail ahead. She glanced down at Flag, who was not even breathing hard. Time to step it up for the final mile. Jody leaned forward and broke into a sprint. What she loved about any kind of focused physical exertion was how all of the thoughts of what should have been, the regrets about choices not made, and the sadness about lost loved ones, vanished completely, for a time.

***

For a split second, the squeal froze Matthew Tolliver's heart in panic. Had Cecily already torn off the duct tape? No, his ex-wife couldn't have managed that. Her hands were taped behind her back, and he'd rolled layers of tape around her head and mouth. She could still breathe. It might take her a couple of hours to get the tape off her arms, but he would be long gone by then. He had no intention of hurting her. He only wanted to take his son and spend a weekend with the boy in the mountains. That wasn't too much to ask. But Cecily was so damned uncooperative, and that mother of hers was worse. The plan was to leave Cecily in her car in the storage garage taped up while he escaped with Jayden for some fun. He'd bring the baby back. Then Cecily would know what it was like not to have enough time with your own child. Matthew knew other dads who'd taken their kids. The court couldn't do much if the kids were brought back, safe and sound.

Leaving Cecily alive, working to get the tape off for a couple of hours inside the garage, that would give her time to think. As usual, though, she had infuriated him.

Matthew pulled hard on the garage door again and it gave another loud screech as it slammed closed. He snapped the padlock, pulled the baseball cap low over his face with a shaking hand, and strode toward the exit of the public storage yard. Lifted a hand to shield his face from the too-curious attendant in the office window. Tried to steady his breathing, slow his racing heart.

That whole thing, taking Cecily, wrapping her up, that turned out to be much harder than he'd anticipated. At five-seven, he wasn't much taller than his wife, and she probably outweighed him. He'd twisted her arm, hard, but she kept fighting. And she must have hit her head on something because her nose was bleeding pretty bad, splattering it everywhere.

Still a half mile from his own car, his legs started to tremble, and he felt faint. He wanted to stop, sit for a minute, but decided it wasn't worth the risk. Anyway, he'd finished the first part of his plan, getting Cecily out of the picture for a couple of hours.

Second step, back to Cecily's mother's house to find his little boy and take him. Luck was with Matthew when he got there. Gamma appeared to be getting ready to go shopping. She was leaning over the open trunk of her car, while his little boy was trying to crawl into his car seat by himself. Matthew pulled alongside and made quick work of snatching Jayden around the middle and placing him in the passenger seat beside Matthew. He gunned the engine and they raced away together.

Matthew hummed tunelessly as he sped through California's central valley. From his perspective, the plan to grab Jayden had come off almost without a hitch. Another couple of hours and he would turn off the interstate and head toward Shaver Lake, where he'd camped as a Boy Scout. They could set up their tent there for a few days and have some fun. So far, the bags of treats he'd packed had been a hit, and now the kid had finally fallen asleep. A rest stop came up and Matthew took the exit, carefully locking Jayden inside while he used the facilities. A couple of nosy biddies were peering in the car window and tapping when Matthew came out. They scolded him for leaving Jayden in the car. He shooed them away, calling them busybodies, and backed out, but the confrontation left his hands shaking again.

Merging onto the freeway, he tuned the radio to a local station, hoping for some soothing country music. Instead, he caught the opening of a news broadcast. With growing horror, he realized the broadcast was about him. The newscaster described the make and color of his car and gave the license number. It was called an Amber Alert. Everyone on the highway was supposed to call the highway patrol if they saw his car. His mother-in-law must have reported him, the old witch.

Matthew escaped off the next exit and started east, toward the Sierra Nevada mountains. Not sure what was ahead, he only knew he had to find someplace to hide the car. Miles of winding two-lane roads later, through small towns with off-brand gasoline stations, he kept going. Jayden woke several times, whined and squirmed and cried for food. Matthew bought them take-out at a podunk cafe and they ate in the car.

Late in the day, he tuned the radio in again. Finding mostly static, the signal from a Modesto station finally buzzed into clarity. Matthew listened, then stopped breathing. He let the car drift to the shoulder where he stopped, still listening. The newscaster said a woman had been found dead in a storage garage. Matthew knew that had to be Cecily. Cecily was dead. They said she'd been found in her car inside the storage garage.

At first, Matthew couldn't believe it. Cecily was alive when he'd left her. Sure, he'd been forced to get a little rough with her. Sure, she'd hit her face on the dashboard, but the worst injury she'd gotten was that bloody nose. She couldn't be dead. People don't die from a bloody nose. Then he got angry. It was a trick. They were lying, trying to trick him into taking Jayden back. He knew guys, friends, who'd kept their kids longer than the courts allowed. Their wives were pissed, sure, but afterwards, the wives had a better attitude. Dads had rights, too. Cecily was playing a trick on him, she and her mother, and they wouldn't get away with it. He'd take Jayden back when he was good and ready.

Then Matthew thought about the layers of tape around Cecily's mouth, and how securely he'd taped her hands. He pictured the blood clotting around her nose. He flashed on the manager's face watching him through the window as he walked out of the storage garage. What if Cecily really was dead?

A battered pickup came up over a rise in the opposite lane. The old guy driving slowed and peered at him as he passed. Matthew watched in his side mirror as the pickup slowed, started to turn back. The guy was probably just going to ask if he needed help. Or he'd recognized Matthew's car from the alert. Matthew's mind spiraled in panic. All he could think was that he had to get out of there, find a place to hide the car, take Jayden and disappear. The rear tires of Matthew's car spit gravel as he peeled out and headed farther up the narrow mountain highway.

Two
Smoke Spotter

Although Charlie Benson kept the television at a low drone a good deal of the time, it was mainly for the company. He didn't pay much attention to the news. From his post at the base of the remote fire lookout tower, most news didn't concern him. He'd been seeing the Amber Alert on the local broadcast for a couple of days or so. One day kind of ran into another up there on the mountain. The kid was a cute little blond tyke, but still, not anything to do with Charlie.

What concerned Charlie that morning was the wisp of smoke to the south-east. By ten o'clock, he knew the smoke meant a fire. What began as a barely visible trail across the blue sky had become a streamer of gray drifting to the north-east. He'd been at this smoke-spotting business too long to mistake the dark serpent for anything but smoke from a fire. Not much bigger than a campfire, though. He took a last long drag on his cigarette and held its toxic fumes in his lungs as long as he could, letting them do their damnedest. He released the blue haze, crushed the butt under a heel and dropped it into the tin can at the bottom of the fire lookout tower stairs.

Already breathless, he started up the fifty feet to the glass-walled cab at the top of the tower. The day he could no longer make that climb would be the day he turned in his badge. Charlie pulled himself to the next step, waiting for a stabbing pain in his chest, anything that would mark the end. He topped the last flight of steel stairs and unlocked the door to the cab at the top.

Taking a moment to pull out a handkerchief, he wiped the sweat from around his eyes and oriented himself to the waves of forest spread out below. Steep ridges of granite, scoured clean by massive glaciers eons ago, were now spotted with Jeffrey and whitebark pines. Patches of low-growing manzanita and the brush called mountain misery covered the shaded northern slopes. Bunchgrass and willow saplings grew on the flats along creeks and around springs. Far below and out of sight, Charlie knew songbirds flitted, and small animals scurried, eyed by hungry hawks. The lookout tower perched near the summit, and had a view out over Lake Nell, nestled between two ridges. The lake shimmered a placid indigo that morning.

Charlie stepped to the Osbourne Fire Finder device that would allow him to pinpoint the location of the smoke. In the center of the sun lit room, the flat circle of the fire finder displayed a map of the surrounding forest. He spun the scope to point at the place on the horizon where the spire of smoke climbed into the troposphere. The smoke was several miles to the south-east, far across the lake. He focused the device, creating a lighted line across the topographical map. Typing in the coordinates, he read the calculations. The fire finder located a spot 12.23 miles from this location on bearing 110 degrees south-southeast. He locked in the point and a red dot appeared on the map. He stepped closer to read the details.

The smoke climbed out of an area of steep granite ridges cut with canyons, threaded with creeks, and scattered with high altitude forests. The red dot clung to the bank of Turtle Creek, surely a misnomer, as the creek ran fast and deep this time of year, full of late spring runoff.

He considered his options. He could place a call that would set in motion a completely automated wild land fire response, launching multiple air tankers and helitack crews into the area. One phone call and a whole variety of agencies would roll into action to put out what might turn out to be the end of a smoldering campfire on the banks of an overflowing creek. With his years of experience, this smoke did not appear to be in any hurry to grow. The barometer held steady, and the humidity sat at a sticky 82 percent. A breeze wafted from the west at less than two miles an hour. Even as he watched, the smoke seemed to dissipate. A full-scale response would be overkill, and might result in serious damage to the fragile forest ecosystem.

On the other hand, being the kind of guy who'd rather be safe than sorry was what had made Charlie an excellent smoke spotter all these years. Deciding whether or not to launch an all-out attack was not his call to make. His job was to call in the smoke and let the district fire management officer handle it from there. Charlie radioed in his findings, his connection going straight through to the dispatcher. In precise language, Charlie read off the coordinates of the smoke and local weather conditions. The dispatcher said he'd relay the information to District Fire Management Officer Cullison.

Charlie flipped on the speaker so he could keep track of the response to his report, and stepped to the glass wall. Squinting, he could almost convince himself the smoke curling upward was in his imagination. After ten minutes of nothing but static from the radio, Charlie began to wonder if he should also give the district ranger, Cullison's supervisor, a heads-up on the smoke. In some circles, that might be considered an end-run around Cullison's authority, and would almost certainly get Charlie into hot water.

Really, there was no sense in causing a ruckus this close to retirement. Then again, he should make sure his message had gotten through. If he called the district ranger station directly using his phone, he'd likely have a chance to catch up with his friend Roxie, the district ranger's administrative assistant. Hadn't talked with her in a good long time. Charlie figured he could keep the call private by making it on his cell phone. That way, he'd also keep the radio channels clear.

As he reached for the phone, the speaker on his radio came to life. According to dispatch, Cullison was delayed, out on the remains of a fire last night deep in the forest at the far north-eastern corner of the district. Dispatch was asking if District Ranger Russell had someone he could send out to get a closer look at Charlie's smoke. Dispatch apparently agreed with Charlie that a small smoke occurring during mid-spring under conditions generally unfavorable to the growth of a fire did not warrant the full pre-planned response. At least someone should try to get a better look first. The coordinates placed the smoke directly on the boundary between the wooded canyon along Turtle Creek and a designated wilderness area above the canyon. In the wooded part of the forest dotted with cabins, the fire would be attacked. In the mostly granite wilderness area, it would not.

***

At the same time, but a hundred miles away, Jody was easing her weight by fractions to the left, stretching upward, reaching. The only possible grip lay inches beyond her grasp. She took a long slow breath and searched the sheer wall for a crack, an uneven surface, anything to hold, and found nothing. The fiery pain of a cramp in her quads had given way to a trembling numbness. The toes on that one foot would not bear her full body weight more than a few seconds. She didn't dare glance back at the ground far below. She had to find a way up.

Relying now on only the stickiness of the dried sweat on her skin, she embraced the rough wall, pulled one knee up and out, gripping with the side of that leg. Her arms outstretched, fingers splayed, she clung to the too-smooth surface. She imagined an evil shadow reaching for her foot, intent on grabbing her. Using the last reserves of strength in her quads, by fractions she breathed her body upwards. Every muscle, every sense focused ahead. As though levitating, her toes lifted off the one purchase she had, and for a fraction of a second she defied gravity through the sheer force of will.

Scrabbling hard against the surface, the fingers of her left hand reached out for a hold, caught it, and she pulled her right knee up and out. Before her body could slow and drop, she lunged again, upward, and caught another foothold. A half second to take a deep breath, then she pushed off, using the last of her oxygen, every sinew, and all the raw desire her body could summon. She reached the top of the wall.

A ripple of applause broke out below. A small group had gathered at the base of the climbing wall to watch Jody make the nearly impossible climb. She raised her hand in a weak wave and called for the belay down.

She thought about getting on a treadmill, but decided she had time to take Flag on another road run instead. As an on-call search and rescue dog, the border collie needed to stay in top condition, too. And a run would leave Jody just enough time for a shower and quick lunch before starting her shift at the fire station.

Tossing her damp towel and pushing through the exit, she caught the photo of a baby on one of the overhead television monitors. An Amber Alert up in Sacramento. That would be under the jurisdiction of the California Highway Patrol. The car was described as a light blue sedan. No sign of the kidnapper or the baby. The news report said the two might have gone south, to Mexico, or possibly east into the mountains.

Again, Jody wondered, why couldn't she and her canine search teams get called in first on a mission like that one. The dogs could find that baby before it was too late. She huffed in frustration. Too few opportunities to prove the dogs' skills presented themselves, and here was another one where they had not gotten the call. Not that she wished any family such a loss. She only craved the excitement of the search, and the chance to prove what her teams could do.

Three
Amber Alert

District Ranger Thomas Russell pinched the bridge of his nose while he listened to the dispatcher's radio call, then ran a hand over his thinning gray hair. Sitting at the front desk, Roxie fiddled with the tuner, bringing in a clearer signal. Russell stepped to the laminated topographical map of the district covering the wall of the U. S. Forest Service district ranger station. After several seconds spent locating the coordinates, he stabbed one finger at a spot, and reached the other hand behind himself, toward Roxie. Without a word, the administrative assistant stuck a small red paper dot to Russell's finger. His heavy belly pressed to the wall as he placed the red dot on the map.

"Right there," he muttered, tapping the spot for good measure. "Cullison's been out on that Buck's Lake fire for at least two nights. Probably won't be back before noon. Who've we got out that way to go take a look now?"

Roxie glanced at the sign-out board. "We've got Greg Gardner, that new fire prevention technician. He's patrolling those cabins over near the dam at Lake Nell. He might already be on his way back here by now."

"Yeah, okay. Tell dispatch to give Greg a buzz. Tell him ... " Russell located the dam on the map, and followed the thin line that marked the road going east from there with a finger. "Tell him he should probably drive out N301 about six miles east." He went back to studying the map. "See if he sees anything from the road. Also, ask dispatch to confirm this trailhead here. The Eagle Meadow trailhead," he read. Russell poked at the map again. "If they have to send a ground strike team out, I think this is our staging area here, at Eagle Meadow. And tell dispatch to get Cullison in the loop as soon as they can." Roxie picked up her radio handset, ready to reply to dispatch, but Russell spoke again. "Don't we have a backcountry ranger out there already?"

She put the handset down and moved to the other side of the map. "Um ... no, that backcountry ranger should be more like over here, on this ridge." She pointed to the east. "That's about four miles east of the smoke, and on foot. I think Greg could get into position more quickly. Anyway, we won't hear from the backcountry ranger until his regular time to report in at one o'clock."

"Unless the smoke is more visible from his position than what Charlie saw."

"Yes, unless it's a bigger smoke, or there's a fire burning closer to his backcountry location."

"Okay, well, I'm not going to get all worked up over a smoke even Charlie isn't sure about. Tell that new guy to get out there as soon as he can. We'll wait and see what he finds."

***

The season's new fire prevention technician, Greg Gardner, was chatting with a cabin owner on the shore of Lake Nell when his radio started up with a blast of static. The dam and the water behind it in Lake Nell were owned by the city of San Francisco, almost 200 miles to the west, but the U.S. Forest Service watched over the surrounding countryside. Part of the fire prevention technician's job was to advise cabin owners on brush clearance and safety precautions around their vacation homes. Greg had just handed over his inspection report, and the cabin owner was locking up, getting ready to head out, when Greg's radio came to life.

Greg gunned the engine on the small truck as he entered the highway from the unmarked dirt road leading back to the cabins. He slowed as soon his tires hit asphalt and he no longer had an audience. The trip took him nearly forty minutes on the narrow mountain road. Hugging the western-facing flank of the ridge, he never saw enough of the sky to see any smoke. At a wide place in the road, he turned the truck and headed back the way he'd come. Even on this second pass, he almost missed the unsigned turnoff into the trailhead parking area. He jerked the wheel right and rolled to a stop in the small gravel lot. Dead ahead sat another vehicle, a late model but dusty light blue sedan.

Greg pondered the car. Hadn't there been something on the news the last couple days about a blue sedan? Seemed like there had been an Amber Alert. A two-year-old baby kidnapped from a parking lot up in Sacramento three days ago. Greg couldn't remember much more than that. He had a two-year-old himself, which explained why he remembered the alert. Greg wasn't a law enforcement officer, but he was a parent. He knew what he would be feeling if anything like that had happened to either of his kids.

Vaguely, he remembered something about the Amber Alert from dispatch the other day. He flipped through the batch of dog-eared papers on his battered clipboard. Today's weather report and fire conditions topped the report, then toward the bottom were messages and alerts from other agencies. Three or four pages in, Greg found the Amber Alert, issued by the California Highway Patrol, and sent out by dispatch as a "be on the lookout" notice. CHP described a ... he placed a finger beside the item and read out loud, "a light blue BMW, 2011, sedan, license number 6SXW448." He looked up at the plates on the sedan, read those out loud too, and checked the report again with growing excitement. This was the car.

He glanced around the lot, wondering if there might really be a kidnapper nearby. From inside his truck, he searched the ground near the surrounding trees. Someone could easily be hiding under the shadows there, although he didn't see anything moving. He read the Amber Alert again. It described the kidnapper as "possibly armed and presumed dangerous." Taking a deep breath, Greg eased open his door and slid to the ground. Searched his surroundings again, turning slowly. He walked to the sedan, and contemplated the driver's door handle. Pulling his shirt sleeve down to avoid leaving fingerprints, he tried the door. Locked. A child safety seat took up the middle of the rear, and a few spilled Cheerios were scattered on the floor. This was definitely the car.

If he had found this car as a member of the public, off on a day-hike or something, Greg would immediately have called the CHP and reported his discovery, but as of last week, he was an official employee of the U.S. Forest Service. There was a chain of command to follow. Greg tried to remember the plan. If he saw a fire he would call his immediate supervisor, DFMO Cullison, but this was not a fire. The person who'd sent him off on this mission, to try to get eyes on that reported smoke, was Cullison's dispatch officer of the day, and he seemed like a friendly enough guy. Probably Greg should call this in to dispatch anyway.

Greg went back to his truck and picked up the radio handset. Then he keyed the radio off and stared through his bug-spattered windshield. The question was, should he use his phone and keep this call private, or call on the radio and have the whole forest service, local law enforcement, plus a few looky-loos monitoring radio traffic all in on the situation? Greg sighed, dug in his shirt pocket, and pulled out his cell phone. Dispatch could decide how far and wide to spread Greg's message.

***

Dispatch took the information and disconnected to run the license plates through the state system, then relayed the Amber Alert find immediately to the CHP station in Jamestown. Next, he notified the county sheriff's department and the one U. S. Forest Service law enforcement officer. Those calls all went out over the radio for everyone to hear.

***

Six minutes later, two CHP vehicles fishtailed off the lot in Jamestown and hit Highway 108, sirens wailing, racing well over the limit. Even then, they were probably two hours out from the remote trailhead location.

Less than an hour away, a county sheriff's SUV with two deputies aboard made an illegal U-turn on a deserted stretch of Highway 108 and sped past the ranger station on its way toward Lake Nell on N301. In Sonora, the local radio station got a call from an amateur radio operator who'd been monitoring law enforcement frequencies. The Amber Alert find was big news, and word spread fast. Across the region, reporters and camera crews hopped into vans and cars and headed out, global positioning systems programmed toward Lake Nell. No one wanted to miss the excitement.

***

Standing next to the blue sedan, Greg sniffed the morning air, searching for a hint of smoke. Nothing. A sign posted just beyond the lot identified his location as Eagle Meadow. An arrow below indicated the trailhead to Lake Nell. He could hike out to the ridge overlooking the creek and try to see the reported fire from there. With luck he wouldn't run into the guy who'd left the BMW. He didn't want to depend on luck. He'd wait in the parking lot until someone with more authority, and more firepower, arrived. About the most lethal thing Greg had with him was a wild land firefighting shovel. He couldn't see any smoke. The only fragrance he smelled was a crisp pine scent with just a hint of pungent mountain brush. Really, he thought, his best bet would be to wait for law enforcement. Just to be on the safe side, he climbed into the truck bed and took his shovel off the rack. Hefting it in one hand, he returned to the driver's seat and locked himself inside.

Four
Helicopter

District Ranger Russell stood in the parking lot of the ranger station gazing into space. Inside, Roxie monitored the radio, waiting for the backcountry ranger, who was currently patrolling several miles east of Lake Nell. He was due to set up his radio transmitter and make his daily check-in at one o'clock. If they didn't hear from him until then, that would mean he'd not seen any smoke. So, in this case, no news was good news.

Nothing came over the radio from Greg either. That was harder to interpret. It could mean Greg wasn't seeing anything. Or it might mean Greg had gotten distracted, lost, or entangled in some other situation. That young man was not all that dependable. Russell decided he would allow Greg another fifteen minutes, then have Roxie give him a jingle on the phone. All this waiting around for news to filter through layers of bureaucracy could give a guy ulcers.

Russell wondered why dispatch hadn't at least mobilized a helicopter to do some aerial reconnaissance. Even without more smoke reports, that would seem prudent. For any fire burning in a designated wilderness area, protocol would be to let it burn, but still, making that decision before anyone had gotten eyes on it seemed premature. Russell gnawed on a loose hangnail and mulled over the possibility of buying himself a drone. Realizing he'd still have to be on that ridge to launch and navigate the device, he set that idea aside.

Three of the seasonal firefighters currently washing and folding hoses could start out for Eagle Meadow. Maybe Greg had gone into a ditch or something, and anyway, it wouldn't hurt these young people to have something to do this afternoon. On the other hand, they'd have a long hike in, even after the hour's drive to get to the trailhead. No sense in sending someone else out on what looked likely to be a wild goose chase. He'd wait to hear what Greg had to report. Half the time these smokes in the high country blew back on themselves and burned out. Really, it was DFMO Cullison's call. Where had everyone gotten to this morning anyway?

Just as Russell stepped inside, the radio squawked. Dispatch calling in CHP on a law enforcement issue. Something about that Amber Alert in Sacramento. Roxie pulled the printout of the alert to the top of the pile on her desk and waved him over to have a look. Dispatch went on and on, calling in the sheriff and forest service law enforcement.

Russell read the be-on-the-lookout notice. "So that's here in the forest somewhere? Or driving through?"

"Yes," Roxie said. "Well, no, not driving through. I didn't really catch it all. The call went out to CHP and the sheriff."

"Yeah, okay. Could we get some clarification on that? Get dispatch on the phone, possibly, instead of the radio?"

Russell's words were interrupted by a squeal of tires on the asphalt in the parking lot. The official law enforcement officer for the U. S. Forest Service, wheeling in fast. He ran directly from his white SUV through to the restroom in the lobby and slammed the door. Russell and Roxie exchanged eye rolls. The law enforcement officer's full-of-himself's attitude had not earned him any friends. He emerged a few moments later wiping his hands vigorously on a length of paper towel, then took a shot at the wastebasket across the room. The wad ricochetted off the edge of Roxie's desk and landed with a damp plop on the floor. He left it there, moved around Roxie at the front counter, and stopped in front of the map.

"Any more word on that Amber Alert find?" He put his finger on the red dot.

"Uh, not while you were ... indisposed," she said. "Nothing more."

"Okey dokey. Well, I'm headed out there now. Be in touch." He pushed through the glass front door and was gone.

Russell's brow furrowed, and he grumbled. "Headed out where? That dot is the smoke Charlie spotted. Why is law enforcement going out there?" Roxie opened her mouth, but a cacophony of chatter on the radio interrupted. She fussed with the tuner, trying to keep the frequency clear for the backcountry ranger to report in on if he spotted a smoke. A blast of static announced the beginning of a transmission coming from him. She glanced at the clock. He was reporting in almost an hour early. He gave coordinates for a smoke to his west, exactly where Charlie had reported it. Said he'd seen only a wisp, but enough that he thought he should call it in. Any kind of smoke in the forest had to be taken seriously.

The backcountry ranger's report settled it for the dispatcher, who made the radio call seconds later, executing the pre-planned procedure for responding to a smoke at that location. Dispatch's radio transmission went to the U.S. Forest Service helicopter base at Bald Mountain.

***

Three minutes after they got the call, two figures dressed in fire-resistant khaki jumpsuits ran from the hangar at the helitack base, climbed into the red-and-white Bell 407 light-duty reconnaissance copter, and hurried through their pre-flight checks. They were in the air within seven minutes.

The bird rose to about sixty feet, dipped once, and turned southeast, chopping over Highway 108. The co-pilot keyed in the coordinates from Charlie's smoke report, and they were on their way. Flight time estimated to be about ten minutes. They were almost on top of their destination when the pilot pointed to the thin stream of smoke riding the bottom of the high pressure at the same altitude as the copter. They were coming up on it sideways, so what would be clearly visible from the ground as a wide band, looked thin, like the edge of a tapeworm, from where they hung a couple hundred feet up.

The pilot dropped altitude and pointed again, this time at a tiny blackened circle in the middle of a flat area beside the creek. Looked like a backpacker's campfire had not been fully extinguished. She dropped the copter lower and circled back around to return through the canyon carved into the granite by Turtle Creek. Cruised past the campsite again. She slowed and steered around a couple of tall snags along the bank, then dipped so the co-pilot could see the circle and black thread where the abandoned campfire had burned through vegetation away from the creek. They didn't see any flames.

***

Below them, as the air warmed with the morning sun, a light breeze had pulled the fire back into a small side canyon and up onto the western-facing flank of the ridge. The fire struggled below, occasionally finding a deposit of dry leaves caught in a crack, or a stunted bunch of yellowed grasses, but mostly burning out as it hit only granite. More than an hour had passed since Charlie made his first report, and the dark smoke formed only a faint haze in the back part of the tiny canyon. The wind from the rotors on the copter bent the tops of two nearby pines, fanning one thin tendril of flame below.

***

The pilot let the bird rise on the third pass. As they drew alongside the smaller canyon, they could see one sickly-looking pine that had burned earlier, its struggle to maintain life on the rocky slope now over. That was probably the main source of the smoke Charlie had reported. Neither the pilot nor co-pilot spotted any additional smoke rising out of the canyon.

Another copse of trees grew farther up the slope, vulnerable to stronger breezes and the burning embers they might carry, but at least for now, the tiny fire appeared unlikely to live that long. The co-pilot picked up the radio and called in a report. They could head over to the lake, hook up their small Bambi bucket, and dump a couple of buckets of water on that flank. Even that seemed unnecessary. If the fire encountered enough fuel to eventually blow up onto the rocks, it would never threaten human life or property, and the odds were low that it might find a way to turn and come downstream through the canyon toward the lake. On the other hand, one could never be certain with a wild land fire. Anything could happen.

Five
Indecision

District Ranger Russell rolled his chair to the window, staring at the slice of forest visible there. The helicopter reconnaissance crew had recommended a wait-and-see stance on the small, possibly already extinguished fire. More for the practice than anything, they had offered to do a couple of water drops on the area. From their report, it sounded as though the fire may have been caught at the back of a dead-end canyon in a thinly-forested alpine landscape. On the other hand, with even a small amount of fuel the fire could grow larger and spread to the adjacent flank, or a wind could come up and push the fire over the top of the ridge into new territory. Russell checked, but the flag outside hung limply against its pole.

He scratched his head, adding the Amber Alert situation to his considerations.

"Roxie! Anything more on that Amber Alert thing?"

"No, sir, nothing on the radio. Let me call my friend in the forest supervisor's office and see if I can find out something from her."

Russell sat impatiently in his office, listening to a series of ohs, mys, and uh-huhs from Roxie's end of the conversation. That was the trouble with telephones. They were a good way to avoid radio traffic, but only two people could hear both sides of the conversation. Roxie disconnected and stepped into his doorway.

"So here's the scoop, sir. According to my friend in the supervisor's office, that fire prevention tech you sent over to try to get a look at that smoke report, Greg? Well, apparently he found the BMW the highway patrol issued the Amber Alert on a couple of days ago. The vehicle in question is parked at that trailhead. So, CHP is en route and a couple of deputy sheriffs have just now pulled in. It's like the Amber Alert says, a guy who kidnapped a baby in Sacramento. These deputies think the kidnapper is out in the forest with the baby."

Russell lowered his head into his hands. "Ooh, boy," he said. "Is the kidnapper armed?"

Roxie referred to her notes, flipped through the pages on her clipboard. "Well, the first report on the Amber Alert says ... this kidnapper is a white male, in his early thirties, brown hair, blue eyes. No photo or anything. The baby is a boy, twenty-three months old, taken from his grandmother's car parked in front of her apartment in Sacramento. No photo of the baby either, but I saw something on television the other night. Cute little nipper, lots of blonde curls."

"So, is this guy dangerous?"

"Well," Roxie said, "he is a kidnapper. He's described as 'possibly armed, presumed dangerous.' It says, 'law enforcement only' and 'approach with caution.' Also, and this is from the latest alert, the kidnapper is now listed as the father, a Matthew Tolliver. Nothing about the mother. Like I said, the baby was taken from the grandmother. Those details are sketchy." She offered the papers to Russell, but he waved them away.

"If you want," she said, "I can keep trying to get Greg Gardner on the phone. Talk to him myself."

Russell added this new information to his considerations about how to react to the reported smoke. Pre-planned responses kind of went out the window when real-life complications intervened. He didn't want to put the lives of the Forest Service helicopter crew in jeopardy by having them haul buckets of water over a possibly armed and dangerous kidnapper.

Cullison would doubtless want at least one strike team sent in on the ground after that smoke, even if the fire had already extinguished itself. They could stage at the Eagle Meadow trailhead, a little more than a two-hour hike from where the copter crew had seen the burn scar. The strike team would need to be onsite by this evening. As the air cooled, down-canyon drafts would start, possibly pulling any remaining embers into the Turtle Creek drainage and toward Lake Nell. That all assumed ideal conditions. An armed kidnapper on the scene did not make for ideal conditions. Russell had the safety of the fire crew to think about. If that kidnapper proved to be as dangerous as law enforcement feared, sending unarmed firefighters tramping all around that canyon would be ill-advised, if not downright negligent. Someone other than him, CHP or possibly the county sheriff, had jurisdiction over locating and arresting that kidnapper.

And someone had to be thinking about the kidnapper's victim, the baby. Who might be responsible for finding the baby? Russell tried not to think about what might be happening to the poor little guy. Someone else could catch the kidnapper, but the baby was lost in Russell's forest. He should get a search team out there. They could be ready to deploy in the event the sheriff found the kidnapper. If the baby was not with the kidnapper, someone would need to find him, and fast.

The last few cases of people lost in his forest were disasters, every one of them. That old guy whose friend dropped him off with a fanny-pack full of chocolate. The friend said his buddy had gone on a day hike, but it later turned out he'd recently been diagnosed with dementia. Russell suspected the guy had intended to get himself so lost he'd never be found. Good plan too, if that's what it had been, because it worked. Search teams combed the area for weeks and never found so much as a candy wrapper. Russell had finally called in the dog search teams in what by then had become a recovery rather than a rescue. The dogs tracked the guy and within four hours, they'd found his partially eaten remains stashed in a crevice between granite boulders about a hundred feet off the trail. Truth was, the find proved a bit anticlimactic because circling turkey vultures had been pointing out the location of the body since the day before the dogs found it. All things considered, if

Russell had gotten the dog teams in there when the missing reports first came in, the story might have had a different ending. That case woke Russell up to the importance of getting dogs in early on a search.

The most recent failed search mission in his forest gave him the most grief, and was the one that convinced him he had to get dogs on the search first, rather than last. A woman had gone off on a hike one morning, slipped off the trail on wet granite worn smooth by hiking boots, and hit her head when she landed on the rocks below. The medical examiner said later she'd probably drifted in and out of consciousness for the three days she'd lain on the rocks before dying of thirst and exposure. Searchers scoured the trails, passing a few yards above where her body sat curled beside a rock, but she never called out, and they never saw any sign of her. A tracking dog brought in five days after she went missing couldn't isolate the woman's scent. Too many other people, too many other smells, had traversed the trail in the search. It took an air-scenting dog to pick up the hiker's scent early one morning when odors lay close to the ground. The dog and handler worked along the base of the cliff, staying off the trail entirely, and found the woman's body in plain sight at the bottom of the rocks within two hours. If he'd deployed either of those dog teams earlier, they might have found that woman in time to get her out and save her life. He didn't want to make that mistake again.

Six
Enemy Soldiers

Charlie stood at the glass wall in the fire lookout as the distant helicopter passed over the canyon carved by Turtle Creek and dropped behind the ridge. Seventeen years ago, when he'd first taken this job, he'd backpacked through all of the countryside he could see from up here. The elevation hadn't gotten to him then the way it did now, and hiking hard through the forest had taken his mind off the death of his wife, off the cancer they said he gave her with his second-hand smoke. Climbing endless mountain trails and slipping through narrow canyons helped him forget his boys, both of them long since grown. They were wrapped up in their own lives now, too busy, or maybe too angry, thinking he'd killed their mother. Except for the occasional holiday card, Charlie hadn't heard from either of his boys since the funeral.

He stepped to the catwalk, lit another cigarette and drew deeply, picking off a bit of tobacco stuck to his lip. He gazed across what, after seventeen years he considered his forest. The smoke had come from high up in Lake Nell's watershed. On maps, the Lake Nell Trail wound along the north side of the creek, but there were no signs on the ground. The trail started in a parking lot up on the ridge at Eagle Meadow, accessed off route N301. From there, the trail came north across the ridge top, through a narrow pass, and then down a granite-covered hillside by switchbacks to a shallow gravel ford across Turtle Creek. After crossing the creek, the trail broadened and meandered west to the lake. The whole trail ran only six or seven miles, leading hikers to a pretty campsite along the lake's edge. Once across the ford, though, a hiker would have to come west, toward the lake, as the trail didn't go far east, ending at an impenetrable granite ridge. The creek passed over the ridge there in a tumbling waterfall, blocking access.

Only a faint haze of smoke remained now in the rising late morning air, just beyond where Charlie saw the copter emerging. The fire must be close to those falls, he reasoned. Why would a backpacker hike east from the ford to the dead end of Turtle Creek canyon?

***

Russell asked Roxie to try Greg again, but she couldn't raise him on the radio. The district ranger gave a disgusted grunt. He didn't want to be forced to start the drive out there himself. "Try Cullison again," he said. "This is a job for fire management."

Roxie felt the need to defend this season's newest fire prevention technician. "Greg's probably left his truck and is out on the trail. You asked him to get eyes on that smoke, and he wouldn't be able to see anything from the trailhead at Eagle Meadow. His only radio is the one in the truck. I could try his cell, but in that canyon he may be behind a rock or some place else where he wouldn't receive."

***

Greg wasn't on the trail. Until just before Roxie's radio transmission he'd been sitting vigilantly in his truck, gripping the handle of his shovel and nervously watching the shadows under nearby trees. The sound of another vehicle pulling into the trailhead lot startled him, and he got out of his truck when the two county sheriff's deputies emerged from their SUV. They all walked around the abandoned sedan for a bit.

At the moment Roxie's radio call came in, the three of them had wandered a couple hundred feet out along the trail. They were peering under the tree cover for any kind of movement, and wondering if the child described in the Amber Alert might be easily located there. No one wanted to venture too much farther without more information about the kidnapper and how much danger he might pose.

***

A quarter mile to the east but still on the ridge top bordering Eagle Meadow, Ted squatted on his haunches on a rounded chunk of granite over-looking Turtle Creek. He shifted one leathery bare foot to move a sharp sliver of rock, scratched the red sore on his stubbled cheek. He surveyed his domain. He was hungry, as usual. He was also annoyed with all the activity in his canyon. The occasional enemy soldier disguised as an innocent-looking backpacker he could tolerate. Sometimes they even gave him food. More often they left their food unattended long enough for some of it to go missing. But for the past few days there had been too much activity for Ted's comfort.

Two days ago, there'd been that enemy soldier with the little boy. After four tours of duty in Afghanistan, multiple near-misses with roadside improvised explosive devices, and shrapnel and bullet wounds suffered during skirmishes with local hostiles, everyone in Ted's world was an enemy soldier. Unable to cope in a landscape crowded with people, Ted sought refuge on the edge of the wilderness in the remains of a long-abandoned and disintegrating cabin. The stone hearth and fireplace of the cabin formed his home, well off the trail. The stone provided a sturdy shelter and would suit him well through the coming summer months, he'd thought. Now he wasn't so sure.

That enemy soldier had walked right up to Ted's stone hearth a few days ago. He'd pawed through some of Ted's stuff, and didn't even seem to care that Ted wasn't far away. Ted had pulled his heavy stick closer, prepared to defend his home, and stepped threateningly into view. The enemy waved his own weapon, not a gun, but a red club-like thing. Then the soldier looked at the child, shrugged and moved on.

The part Ted had trouble understanding was the little boy traveling with the enemy soldier. Hardly more than a baby, the boy called the soldier Daddy. What soldier brings his baby into combat? In spite of his young age, the soldier made the boy walk on his own, and carry a big paper sack. The poor little thing cried quietly, and put the sack down several times. Ted kept his eyes on that sack as the pair made their way over to the trail, the soldier pushing the boy ahead of him. They reached the pass through the rocks. At that point, the enemy soldier picked up the boy, and they started down the switchbacks to the ford across the creek. Ted watched.

Once on the other side, they disappeared into the trees. No opportunity had presented itself yet for Ted to get his hands on that sack, but there would be time. The pair headed east, and Ted knew they couldn't get out of the canyon on that end, so they'd be back before too long.

Now, this morning, a helicopter buzzed over the creek, searching for something. Possibly looking for that soldier and the boy. More likely checking out that smoke farther up the canyon. Ted had seen the light from the small campfire two nights ago. Must have been the enemy soldier's fire. No one else had gone out that way. Now, this morning, smoke curled up. Any fool could see the smoke was blowing to the east, and there wasn't anything to burn out that way. Ted absently scratched that sore on his cheek again. Yes, there had been altogether too many people invading his territory lately.

Seven
Misery

If Jayden had been old enough to be capable of abstract and complex thought, he might have been thinking about how to escape his present dilemma. Instead, his consciousness was filled with a blooming, buzzing confusion of sensory perceptions and emotions. And his emotion in that moment was abject misery. Hunger gnawed at his middle, and his eyes ached from exhaustion. Trying to sleep next to Daddy on the ground made him miss the soft mattress of his crib. Trickling sweat made dirty tracks, matched by dried tears on his cheeks. The skin on his heels was broken and bleeding where his shoes had rubbed it raw. The top of his head bubbled with sunburned blisters. Legions of hungry mosquitoes had taken advantage of his tender and exposed skin. Itchy red welts pocked Jayden everywhere. He'd scratched open a painful bite on his scalp, and a few drops of blood matted in his blond curls. Soggy pull-ups stung the angry rash inflaming his thighs and bottom. Every square inch of him cried out in pain from one insult or another. And what wasn't injured was being pricked by the bark of the tree Daddy had lifted him into and told him to stay. He'd tried to pull his sneaker from where it was wedged under him, his leg twisted at an uncomfortable angle, but he only succeeded in popping the sneaker off and into the dirt far below at the base of the tree. He looked at the ground, gave a helpless sigh, and went back to weeping quietly.

Jayden had only a vague memory of a few days ago, when he'd been doing his best to climb all by himself into his car-seat in Gamma's car. He'd gotten one leg up, and pulled for all he was worth to get the rest of himself onto the seat. Momma would never have let him try, but Gamma didn't see him. The next thing Jayden knew, Daddy's car drove up, and Daddy grabbed him, whirling him through the air—the way big people always did, and dropping him into Daddy's car. Daddy yelled at Gamma. He told her Momma and Daddy were taking Jayden camping. He told her they were going to pick up Momma next. Daddy and Jayden sped away. Gamma yelled back, and a thump shook Daddy's car when she hit it, but Daddy kept going. A few minutes later, Daddy's car stopped hard. Jayden's belt was not buckled and he fell off the seat, bumping his head, leaving a big knot on his forehead. He cried a lot.

Decorated now with a mosquito bite, that bump still hurt. Gently, he poked at it. After that fall, Daddy had buckled Jayden into his car-seat, gave him a bag of crackers, and started driving again. And drove and drove for a long time. The crackers were long gone when Daddy lifted another bag, this one with small cubes of cheese, over the seat back and handed it to Jayden. After a while, Jayden got so bored, he took off his shoes and peeled the socks from his feet, just to have something to do. He tried to throw his socks at Daddy, but they only fell somewhere on the floor below, out of sight. Even without having words for it, Jayden knew better than to throw his shoes. Much later, Daddy gave him a bag of Cheerios, but Jayden couldn't get that one open. After a while he chewed a hole through the bottom and fished out few of the tiny snacks. Most of them flew out and disappeared. Finally, after a long time and after wetting his pull-ups, Jayden fell asleep.

Jayden woke up again when they stopped someplace with lots of big trees. Daddy changed Jayden's pants, but the rash had already broken out. Daddy wasn't nice when he put Jayden's shoes back on, and didn't take the time to find the socks. He gave Jayden a big bag to carry and said to hurry up. Daddy said he would take Jayden to a cabin. Daddy made it sound like the best thing ever, so Jayden carried the bag and walked. It was almost dark. They stopped, then he and Daddy slept on a big blanket in the dirt. Jayden cried and Daddy said to shut-up. He was cold, and Daddy said to stop squirming.

In the morning, they walked more. Daddy found tall rocks, like Jayden's Legos. Daddy got so mad. He wanted a cabin, not rocks. The more Jayden whined and cried, the angrier Daddy acted, which made Jayden cry more. Daddy finally put his big bag way up in a tree, and picked Jayden up.

Daddy carried him over scary rushing water and walked and walked more, to where there were only rocks and the crashing creek. Daddy yelled about finding a place to hide. He put a blanket on the ground and told Jayden to sit on it. When the sky turned night again, Daddy picked up some sticks and made a fire on the ground. He put a can by the fire, but the beans didn't get hot, so Jayden and Daddy ate cold beans and juice in boxes.

When morning came, Daddy said they would look for a safe place to stay. At first he made Jayden walk, but there were too many rocks and bushes, so Daddy gave Jayden a ride on his back. They walked and climbed all day, but Daddy never found a safe place. When they got hungry, they went back to the blanket. and Daddy made another fire.

Jayden's tummy hurt when he woke up in the morning, and he had made a big mess in his pull-ups. Daddy said he couldn't carry Jayden any more. He said that took too long. He told Jayden to stay on the blanket while he went to look for a place to hide, but Jayden got scared and ran after him, so Daddy came back, but he was mad. He told Jayden he would tie him to a tree if he didn't stay on the blanket. That made Jayden cry even more. Daddy looked at him with a very angry face. Then Daddy gave him a tiny white candy to eat. The candy did not taste good, but Daddy gave him a juice box and that made it better. Daddy told him a story until he got sleepy.

Jayden saw black sky again when he woke up, and Daddy told him to go back to sleep until the sun came out. In the morning, Daddy took him by the creek and washed him in cold, cold water. They had dry Cheerios for breakfast and Daddy gave Jayden another candy. He put Jayden in a tree where the branches made a flat nest. Jayden cried when Daddy told him to be quiet or something would eat him. Jayden felt so tired he didn't even scratch at his mosquito bites. Daddy stomped around when he came back, and yelled more. They ate tuna out of a can, like Momma's cat did at home. After a while, Daddy rolled them both up in the blanket on the ground and told him to sleep. Jayden wanted to tell Daddy he always slept in his crib, but Daddy didn't understand. Jayden didn't know how many days had passed that way. Every day he felt sicker and sadder. Today was the worst day. Jayden whimpered quietly for Momma.

Eight
On Call

District Ranger Russell rolled his chair back to the desk and sent a message through to the helitack crew, now parked on a wide spot at the edge of Lake Nell. He wanted them to stay put there near the confluence with Turtle Creek until Cullison could break free from that fire up at Buck's Lake and get back here to assume the role of incident commander on this fire, if it was a fire. Given the kidnapping situation and the missing baby, the district's entire management team would need to work together on this one, but probably it would be best if water drops didn't begin until the search teams and the kidnapped baby were well out of the area. The kidnapper was on his own.

On his way through the office, he asked for an update on Cullison's return. Roxie cradled the desk phone under one ear and dialed her cell with the other hand. The radio at her elbow crackled static, peppered with short transmissions. She gave Russell a bewildered look, shaking her head. She hadn't heard from Cullison.

He hadn't gotten more than two steps out the door when Roxie called him back to the office.

"It's about that Amber Alert, sir. Came in from dispatch just now. FBI says the dead woman found the same day the baby was kidnapped was the baby's mother. They're seeking the kidnapper as a person of interest." Roxie shook her head, tears pooling on her lower lids. "So sad. I'm going to tell Greg to be really careful."

Russell walked out to the steel corrugated building that housed the district's firefighting vehicles. He stood for a moment, thinking. Should he round up the three seasonal firefighters and send them out there? The young people would be excited to be deployed on a fire so early in the season, and raring to go. He corralled them to explain the situation. It would take them an hour to get to the trailhead. He instructed them to follow the directions of law enforcement as to the possible dangers at the scene, and not to deploy to look for any fire unless it was safe to do so. "Wait until you're released by law enforcement to search for that fire. Once it's safe, you are to proceed to its reported location and use hand tools to ensure full suppression." With a final request to report back when they arrived on scene, Russell gave them a wave, then had a last thought.

"And I might send some dogs out there to search for that missing child," he said. "Try not to mess up the scent trail for the dogs. And be careful!"

He wandered back to the office where Roxie continued to try to get more current information from the CHP or the sheriff's department about the Amber Alert situation. There were, at that time, just two county sheriff's deputies on site, plus Fire Prevention Technician Greg Gardner. The only information Roxie could get was relayed from the deputies on the scene through the sheriff's dispatch office. Word was, the car was empty. The deputies were speculating that the kidnapper and small boy may have hiked into the remote canyon on foot. If that's where they went, it was reported, they would most likely be on their way to the shore of Lake Nell, possibly to one of the cabins there. Roxie said that hypothesis didn't make a whole lot of sense to her, since those cabins were more accessible via four-wheel drive on a rough track going north from the dam road than they were from the backcountry trail. In any case, no one else had any additional information. The CHP units were still on their way to the scene.

Russell flipped through the worn cards on his ancient Rolodex. Names, numbers, and notes in pencil and every color of ink imaginable were scrawled across the cards. If dog teams were to be first on scene this time, then he wanted the best, even if he had to call someone from outside the local region.

Like many in law enforcement, he had started out not one hundred percent convinced dog teams could perform a search better than humans, but his experience had taught him that, more often than not, they could.

Russell knew the canine teams were all volunteers, and covered their search-related expenses themselves. He felt some reluctance to ask for a team from outside the county. On the other hand, he knew the local county had only a few search and rescue volunteers and no canine teams. Might as well see if he could get that woman he knew from the last search.

The district ranger read the number for Jody Murphy off one card. From the area code, it looked as though she lived at least two hours from the search site, but she also led the best-trained canine search and rescue team he knew, and she handled Flag, an amazing air-scenting dog. Flag was the dog who had found that woman's body last fall. With Jody's name and number in hand, Russell placed a call to the California Office of Emergency Services to make his search and rescue mission request. He asked for permission to deploy Jody and her team specifically for this search, and got the okay.

***

Jody stirred the bowl of tomato soup, swirling in a dollop of milk. She flipped up the golden-brown side of her grilled cheese sandwich, and thought about the day ahead. Working the late shift at the fire station meant her brain wouldn't calm down enough to sleep until 4:00 a.m., but staying asleep until noon was a feat she could never pull off. Daylight brought too many new adventures to keep her in bed. Her need to feel the thrill of danger had driven her to choose the firefighting profession. Rushing into burning buildings, saving lives, the burst of adrenaline when she joined fellow firefighters in rescuing victims. Knowing she could take care of herself no matter the physical challenge gave her the security she craved. So far, she'd found her firefighting job to be more tedium than excitement. Most days were spent walking neighborhoods in the annual round of inspections, advising residents about cutting weeds and removing hazardous conditions. She took her turns at the station cleaning and repacking fire equipment, and, most mind-numbing of all, learning to grocery-shop and cook meals for the crew.

She sighed deeply and invited Flag to her side, stroking the white ruff around the dog's neck. They were the perfect fit in both temperament and size. Her hand dropped to Flag's soft head where the dog leaned against her muscular thigh.

Jody thought about her last rock-climbing trip to Joshua Tree National Park, her knee only now finally healed from that accident. She remembered snowboarding at Mammoth, and that time she fell into a tree well while off the trail. Instead of being afraid to go on those adventures again, she only wanted more, a chance to do it better. Whether at Joshua Tree or Black Caverns, she always headed straight for the sheerest rock wall, the most challenging cave. Training for search and rescue with Flag brought her the same opportunity for excitement, and from the moment she learned they would be dropping from helicopters into remote wilderness areas, Jody was hooked.

For her part, Flag seemed enthusiastic for anything, as long as she could be with Jody. They'd been at it over four years, trained every week, and had been on more searches than Jody could remember. She loved it. Hiking through the forest with her dog, avoiding sheer cliffs, watching out for mountain lions, and finding lost people. Her only complaint about search work was there was never enough of it.

She sighed and tossed the nicely browned sandwich onto her plate. Today at work would probably be another boring day of paperwork, inspections, cleaning, and cooking. Scarfing her sandwich and soup, she donned her blue uniform, tucking the too-long shirt deep inside the narrow waist of the trousers. At five-six and a half, slightly above average for a woman, her outfit bagged in some places, and pulled too tight in others. The phone rang as she reached for the door.

Nine
Command Presence

After an initial sussing out of the situation, Sheriff's Deputy Brad Hogan strutted with the other county sheriff's deputy back to circling the abandoned sedan. CHP officers were still an hour out from the scene and this wet-behind-the-ears forest service yahoo—Greg Gardner his name badge read—clearly had no idea what to do. At least for the moment, Hogan and his partner were in charge. With suspicious scowls, they peered under the trees, speaking quietly to one another. Clearly the abductor had taken the abductee, a small child, from here out along that trail and into the backcountry beyond. CHP had jurisdiction as long as the vehicle identified in the Amber Alert traveled on California highways, and they maintained jurisdiction over the vehicle itself, but from the deputies' point of view, once the abductee had been removed from the vehicle and carried onto county property, the job of finding both the abductor and his victim became the responsibility of the county sheriff and his deputies.

Hogan's partner radioed in to make sure backup had been notified, while Hogan returned to his post at the trailhead, his thumbs hooked assertively under his belt. He considered his options. He could march in along the trail, find the little boy, and triumphantly carry him out. Hogan imagined the photos on the front pages of tomorrow's papers. That would impress his kids, for sure.

Then again, he had the abductor to think about. The abductor was alleged to be dangerous, which to Hogan meant armed with guns.

Hogan also could not claim familiarity with this part of the forest, especially since it fell under the law enforcement jurisdiction of the U.S. Forest Service. He rotated to look where Greg stood by his truck. The forest service guy had been having trouble with his radio, and appeared to have given that up in favor of his cell phone. He yakked excitedly to someone about having located the vehicle reported in the Amber Alert. Hard to tell if he was conducting official business, or just jawing with the wife. A minute later Greg and Hogan's partner rejoined him in looking again at the trail.

"Where does this trail go?" Hogan asked Greg.

Greg rubbed at an eyebrow, then gestured with one hand. "According to the map, it goes about a mile or so across this ridge top, winding around. Eventually it goes out to a pass between some rocks, then down to Turtle Creek."

The entire ridge top bordering Eagle Meadow on that north side was overgrown with Jeffrey and whitebark pines, with low-growing patches of the plant called mountain misery filling in wherever the sun had managed to penetrate through the trees. A thick duff of dead and fallen needles covered the forest floor. Walking anywhere except on the trail would be slow going. Hogan pushed out his lips and considered his next move.

"I made contact with the district ranger's office," Greg said. "Roxie said District Ranger Russell is requesting the assistance of canine search and rescue teams. You know, dogs. It'll take them a couple hours to get here."

"Great." Hogan said. "CHP will be here before that. And by the time those dog teams get mobilized, we'll have found that kid."

The sarcasm was lost on Greg. "Good!" he said. "That little guy must be getting pretty scared and hungry by now."

Hogan narrowed his eyes. This Greg guy really was a yahoo, he thought. Hogan looked out the trail again. "What's out there, features-wise?"

"Features-wise?" Greg said.

"Yeah, you know, like cabins to take cover in. Places to hide a kid. Bear, and all, you know, like that?"

"Oh. Well, as far as I know, this trail goes west to Lake Nell. Maybe six or eight miles. I don't think there are any cabins along the way there. Not until you get to the lake itself. The only cabins still standing are out at the lake, I think." Greg thought about it a while longer. "I don't know where you'd hide a kid. It'd be more like they've gotten lost. I think that's why District Ranger Russell wants to send in search and rescue teams."

Deputy Hogan nodded while the other deputy worked a toothpick in one cheek. Hogan tried to imagine a situation where he would provide an armed escort for a dog search team. He counted himself among those who had little faith in the ability of dogs to find lost kids. To be sure, he hadn't had a lot of experience working with dog search teams. Well, in fact, none. Still, it just seemed to him that by the time you got dozens of searchers wandering around an area, sooner or later that lost person would be found, whether a dog had been deployed or not. Giving dogs the credit for finding a missing person made for a nice news story. He just wasn't sure it was ever the real story.

In a situation like this, with a possibly armed suspect, sending dogs and their owners wandering loose out in the forest didn't seem like the brightest idea. Hogan could understand the need to recover the abductee as quickly as possible. The armed deputies should go in first, flush the perp, get shot at if anyone was going to get shot at, and take down the kidnapper. Hogan imagined the photo of himself receiving the commendation for capturing the armed and dangerous kidnapper. The wife and kids would have to show him some respect after that.

"Sounds like search and rescue would be a good idea," he said to Greg, "if the kid is still missing after we take out the kidnapper."

Greg nodded slowly, processing the plan Hogan outlined. Then he said, "And the thing is, there may be a fire out there."

"A fire?"

Greg waved vaguely off to the east. "Up the canyon a ways. Actually, that's the only reason I came out here. District ranger asked me to see if I could spot it from here. It can't be too big though, because there's no sign of it. It is kind of funny Roxie didn't mention it just now. I suppose it might've been a false report, or it's burned itself out. I guess everyone is thinking the kidnapper let his campfire get away from him, and now he's lost out there." Greg had heard about that old guy in the lookout tower. Might be the old smoke spotter had finally lost his marbles. The lookout tower would be decommissioned soon anyway, now that most smoke reports came in via cell phone from hikers.

"A forest fire, huh?"

"Possibly."

"Means we'd need to get in there quick and rescue that kid," said the other deputy.

"Yeah, sounds like," agreed Hogan.

They stood, still at the trailhead, listening to an evening grosbeak singing his trilled courting song hours ahead of schedule.

Ten
Deployed

The call from District Ranger Russell came in just as Jody and Flag were on their way out the door. He briefly outlined the situation and requested search and rescue assistance for a two-year old boy missing for at least three days. Jody noticed the ranger was short on details and said nothing about any potential danger. She decided probably no one knew much about the danger and she could find out more once she was at the trailhead. The important point was that, if she and her teams could get there fast enough, they would be among the first on the scene to look for the child.

Jody knew about the Amber Alert of course, and had seen the poster at the fire station. Everyone in the state had heard about the Amber Alert. Drivers everywhere searched the highways for the light blue BMW. No one expected it to turn up at a remote trailhead high in the Sierra. She took a few moments to look up the Amber Alert web page on her laptop and gather a few details.

A dimpled, curly-haired boy smiled back at her from the web page. If the boy, hardly more than a baby, had been lost on his own, the odds of finding him would be slim. But the district ranger had said the baby was with an adult, now reported to be the boy's father. This was one of those parental abduction cases.

Jody checked the weather service page, then began packing. The forest at that elevation would drop into the thirties overnight. The pair had already spent maybe three nights lost. By the time resources could be mobilized and on the scene, the two of them would likely be looking at a fourth night exposed to the elements.

Jody knew rushing to the scene early on a search meant there was always a chance the target would already have found their own way back by the time the dogs arrived on location, but the opportunity to have first crack at a freshly laid trail was too exciting to pass up.

Flag's tail wagged at the urgency in Jody's voice. The five-year-old border collie trotted to the closet where her harness and other search gear were stored and waited, trembling, beside the door.

While Jody threw last-minute supplies and fresh dog food into her go-bag, she wondered if her best search-buddy, Kris, might be available to deploy immediately. Jody left a message for Kris, then had the local sheriff's dispatcher relay the information to everyone else on the team for a stand-by alert. She dug through her file of old paper topographical maps, coming up with what looked like the correct quad map. As a backup, she downloaded the newer electronic version of the same quadrangle onto her iPad and tossed that into her bag.

She reported in to her shift supervisor at the fire station. Everything was quiet this afternoon, and an emergency search and rescue deployment took precedence over her firefighting duties anyway.

The shift supervisor gave her the release to take the search call and wished her luck. Perfect timing too, as this was an excellent day to be away from the station and from the personal entanglements brewing there. Sometimes the best relationships were ones separated by significant geographic distances, even if only for a few days now and then. Jody tweeted a quick message about being off on a search so no one could take her absence as a personal affront. She turned the ringer off on her cell to avoid distractions, got behind the wheel, and popped Aretha into the CD player.

"All set?" she asked Flag. The dog answered with a high-pitched whine. Flag always exhibited excitement when they hopped into the car for training searches, but even more so when they were headed on a real mission. Somehow, Flag knew the difference. Pulling on her neon orange baseball cap, Jody tugged her long dark ponytail through the opening in back. She and Flag were on the road twenty-three minutes after getting the call, a personal best for the pair. She'd stop in Stockton to gas up and program the on-board GPS. That should put her on site by two-thirty this afternoon. Plenty of time to find the lost pair.

By the time she arrived at the truck stop just north of Stockton, she'd made up her mind to add a tracking dog to the team for this mission. Air-scenting dogs like Flag and Kris's dog, Bullet, were always needed on search missions, but from what Russell said, the targets had walked out a trail from their car into a canyon. A good tracking dog should be able to nose out the path they'd taken. Lucky for everyone concerned, a great tracking bloodhound lived with her handler in the foothills just outside Angel's Camp. Jody contacted Andy, the handler, and he agreed to meet her at the trailhead and join the search as soon as he could get off work and pick up his bloodhound, Rose.

As she drove the winding narrow highway into the mountains, Jody wondered about the kidnapper and his victim. Every mission had a story behind it. Kids ran too far ahead and couldn't find their way back. Folks wandered into the forest for a moment of privacy and couldn't locate the trail again. Or an adult became injured and the companion, usually a dog or a small child, was incapable of going on their own to find help. Although this mission started as an Amber Alert, the pair now lost would have their story, too.

Eleven
Partners

Daddy stomped again when he came back from looking for the hiding place. His hands were hard when he lifted Jayden out of the tree, and that made Jayden scared.

"I'm never going to find any damn place for us, Jayden. How could there not be even one cabin down here in this dead-end canyon? Damn it, I'm ready to quit looking. It's been three days! I don't know what the hell we're going to do now."

Daddy spread the blanket on the ground under the tree and yanked off Jayden's wet overalls. There were no more clean pants, so Jayden stood there without pants. He wanted to cry more, but he didn't. Daddy did whatever he was going to do whether Jayden cried or not. Daddy rummaged around in the paper sack, brought out a can of tuna, and pulled it open. Hunger pangs knotted Jayden's tummy, but the smell of the tuna made him feel sick. He looked at Daddy, his knees buckled and he sank until his tiny bottom hit the weeds. His eyes filled with unshed tears.

"Momma?"

Daddy grumbled and dug in the bag again. This time he offered a spoonful of peanut butter. Jayden just looked at it, then back at Daddy.

"Momma?"

"Yeah, well, your momma's not here is she? Your momma's never here when you need her, is she? Your momma could be with you, but she leaves you with your grandmother while she goes off and does her own thing? Your mother and grandmother got the judge to steal you away from me and give you to her, then first thing she does is goes off and leaves you with Gamma. Well, your momma doesn't want you anyway.

She just doesn't want me to have you. Now she took herself right out of the picture, didn't she? Stupid woman. So that problem's taken care of. It's you and me now, Jay-bud, you and me. On our own. You're mine now and I'm keeping you."

This time, Jayden didn't make a sound when his tears began to fall. He could make no sense of Daddy's words, but he understood the anger. He scooted onto the blanket where the weeds didn't stick him and squatted, putting his hands over his ears to stop the yelling. Then he stuffed two fingers into his mouth, something he hadn't done in months. Immediately, he pulled them out again and stared at them in dismay. His lovely comforting fingers had betrayed him with their icky taste.

"Oh, hey now, Jay-bud." Daddy folded Jayden into his arms, pulling his fingers away. "It'll be okay little guy. I'll find us a cabin. You'll see. It'll be you and me, buddy. We'll be okay."

Daddy found another pull-up in the bag and tugged it over Jayden's feet. He dug more and found crackers and more juice boxes. As he pulled at the paper sealing the graham crackers, they both heard the arrival of the helicopter. Daddy grabbed the edge of the blanket and pulled it, along with all their food and Jayden on it, deeper under the trees. Daddy seemed frightened of the *whup-whupping* of the helicopter and that scared Jayden. He started to cry again in earnest. His wails were drowned out by the sound of the helicopter's rotors.

"Shit," Daddy muttered, "They're looking for us. They must've found the car already. I have to get back over there and pick up our stash. Then we have to get the heck out of here.

"Hey, Jay-bud, remember that old guy we saw up there? How about if I go run that old guy off and we take his shelter? At least we could have a fire in the fireplace there and warm ourselves up. How would that be, Jay-bud? A fireplace to sit next to sure would be nice, wouldn't it?" Daddy scratched at his chin. "I guess not, though," he said. "That place of his is too close to the trail and the road. We need another plan. Some place to stay. Just for another week or so. Just long enough to get this beard grown out." Daddy scratched again at the thick growth of dark brown stubble now covering his chin.

The helicopter made another turn in the canyon in front of their hiding place and Daddy sat back down. He wrapped Jayden in the blanket and held him close. Jayden pulled away, trying to avoid contact with Daddy's scratchy face and bad smell. Daddy pulled him tighter, held him harder, and Jayden stopped struggling. They stayed that way for a long time. Eventually, the sounds of the helicopter faded, and Jayden fell into a fitful sleep.

Twelve
A Girl and Her Dog

It took Jody half an hour longer than she'd anticipated to find the Eagle Meadow trailhead parking area. A dirt track just before the dam had a sign reading "Lake Nell" beside it, but District Ranger Russell had warned her not to take that road. Another dirt road appeared, this one unmarked, just past the dam. Not the correct turnoff either. She'd circled the obscure parking lot on her paper topo map, so even though she stopped twice to read it, she did eventually find the place. Vehicles already nearly filled the small lot. A dark green Forest Service pickup nosed up to a dusty light blue BMW, two county sheriff's SUVs with light racks, and two CHP sedans sat to the left and right of the BMW, and one mint green U. S. Forest Service crew transport truck filled the far right edge of the graveled clearing. The dog teams were usually called in late on a search mission, so Jody was used to seeing a collection of vehicles like this one. The staging areas were always crowded with law enforcement, emergency responders, volunteer searchers, media, and the family and friends of the lost.

A bunch of guys in various uniforms were milling around the front of the BMW. Jody eased her Forester over to the left of the other vehicles. The parking area had been carved out of a piece of Eagle Meadow, and the meadow continued for several yards beyond the gravel lot demarcated by logs. Jody pulled her car as close to the logs as she could, got out, and placed orange cones across the spaces behind. Her canine search and rescue teams could off-load their gear and dogs onto the meadow next to the lot and have a space where they'd be out of the law enforcement activity. She opened the rear hatch and began hauling exercise pens, water jugs, and a shade cover across the logs.

Once those were piled to the side, Jody got Flag out of the car on a leash and let her do her business. Still somewhat unclear as to the mission, she wandered over to where the men were standing at the trail sign. The group had moved a few feet down the trail toward the trees, but no one seemed much inclined to go beyond that point. One blowhard in a sheriff's uniform pointed and loudly proclaimed something about sending teams "out to the quadrants."

"Oh, great," he muttered when he caught sight of Jody. "A girl and her dog. Just what we need." He faced her, ignoring her orange search and rescue vest and hat. He'd resigned himself to following along with a search and rescue team, but not a girl. "Trail is closed, ma'am. No hiking today."

The hackles on both Flag and Jody's necks rose, but Jody quelled hers. She smiled and reached out her hand. "Jody Murphy, canine search and rescue team leader, and this is Flag."

Hogan ignored her hand. "Oh. Yeah, well, we're not ready to start the search yet. We'll let you know."

"Good," Jody said, continuing to smile. "Can you fill me in on the situation? I'd like to be up to speed when the rest of my team gets here."

"Yeah, sure. Why don't you go have a chat with Greg there, the Forest Service guy. He can give you the rundown." Having disposed of her annoying presence, the deputy turned back to the four CHP officers fidgeting with their bullet-resistant gear and peering off under the surrounding trees.

She walked toward the guy standing by the open door of his truck. He wore Forest Service khakis, but did not appear to be law enforcement. She read his name badge and introduced herself and her dog.

Greg pointed to the BMW and explained about the little boy being kidnapped. "There's no place else to go from this parking lot except down that trail, so they think the boy must be out there somewhere."

"The boy and the kidnapper?" Jody asked. "Or just the boy?"

Greg pursed his lips. "No way to know, I guess. But why would the boy be out there alone?"

"So ... both. Do we know if the kidnapper is armed?"

"Amber Alert said 'possibly armed and presumed dangerous,' so we don't know for sure if he has a weapon, but I'd say it's a good bet he does."

"Any chance you could radio around? You know, usually when we get to a search mission, law enforcement has mapped out the search area. Not very likely we'd take our dogs in after the boy if the kidnapper is armed. And these guys over here." She nodded in the direction of the law enforcement contingent. "They don't seem to know much about what's going on, but they look damn nervous to me. They must think there's some danger."

Greg jotted a note on the top page on his clipboard. "Is kidnapper for sure armed ... " he said as he wrote, then pushed the board onto the truck seat.

Jody studied the parking lot again. "So we've got search and rescue here to look for a little boy. Then we've got the sheriff and CHP here to track down the kidnapper ... "

"Well," Greg said, "I think CHP is just here to get the vehicle."

"Okay. And then we've got these forest service firefighters here ... " Jody and Greg watched the three seasonal firefighters hanging around their truck, engaging in horseplay while they waited for directions. "Why are those guys here?"

"Oh, I forgot. Our smoke spotter, up there in the lookout at Lake Nell? He reported a smoke out this way earlier today. You can't see anything from here, but they sent a helicopter to check it out."

"Might have been the target's campfire?"

Greg nodded. "Possibly."

"Did the helicopter report seeing anyone out there? They might have seen the folks we're supposed to find."

Greg slid his clipboard off the seat and made another note.

"How about you call in, see if you can get some answers? I'll be over there setting up."

"Yes, ma'am." Greg hopped onto his truck seat and grabbed his radio transmitter.

Jody rubbed her forehead as she walked back toward her car. This was a confusing situation. Probably one of the drawbacks to being called in early on a search. Anyway, she thought, this Greg seems like a nice enough guy. He just needs direction, someone to tell him what to do next. About then, Jody remembered to turn her cell phone back on. With the strong signal at the top of Eagle Ridge, it immediately dinged several times. Three texts and four phone calls, all but one from the same number. Sheesh, she thought, you go out with someone two or three times, and suddenly you're expected to keep in touch. She listened to the last message—Kris, the handler with the other air-scenting dog, reporting she'd be there soon. Jody returned the call and gave Kris specific directions for finding the trailhead. Andy had said he already knew how to get there because he'd hiked the area before. Jody put her phone on vibrate so she could monitor calls without being disturbed, and tucked it into her pocket.

Kris's RAV4 pulled into the lot a short time later. Carrying fifteen extra pounds, with graying blonde frizz and freckles, Kris was an unlikely-looking search and rescue volunteer. She had come to training meetings religiously for six months while she scoured shelters all over the central state, looking for the perfect canine partner. When she finally showed up one night with Bullet, no one seemed quite as convinced as Kris that he was the dog. Twelve- to fifteen-months old at the time, Bullet's indeterminate parentage left him resembling a coon hound shepherd cross. He responded to the name he had been given as a puppy, Bullet, but was otherwise completely undisciplined. After six months of obedience and another twelve months of search training, he was a different dog. His obedience was without question, and his loyalty to Kris intense. He was the most highly skilled air-scenting dog Jody had ever encountered, with the possible exception of her own Flag. Bullet had seen some tough times in his young life before Kris rescued him, so he knew the good life when he found it, and she was no less devoted to him. They both even learned to harness up and drop from a helicopter, although Kris lost all the color from her face on the way down and landed with her eyes squeezed tightly shut.

Kris got Bullet out of her car, and the handlers let the two best canine friends greet one another and romp around the empty edge of the meadow. The dogs were evenly matched in size and temperament, and they had a solid bond.

Thirteen
Hurry Up and Wait

Jody had just started to fill Kris in on the mission when Andy and his tracking bloodhound, Rose, pulled into the last spot behind Kris. Andy had wrangled an early day off from his job in the adjacent county sheriff's department. Rose wasn't big on romping, but she was happy to be out of the car and eager to get to work. Andy dropped his search gear bag on the ground and Rose immediately began nosing in it, coming up a minute later with her orange search and rescue harness.

Jody glanced over at Greg to see if he'd been able to get any answers yet. He still held the radio to his ear. She waved and he gave her a cheery thumbs up in return. "We need more information before we can lay out a search. Let's get started setting up our gear," she said to the others.

Jody, Andy, and Kris got the shade cover up in the meadow next to the cars. They arranged two wire exercise pens together to form an eight by eight foot square in the shade, plenty of room to accommodate three dogs. The walls of the exercise pen were only thirty inches high. Both Flag and Bullet could easily jump those, but they understood they were to stay inside. After trading beds and peering suspiciously at the treats the other dog had been given, each settled down to munch in contentment.

Jody flipped open the folding table that would serve as the center of their command post as Greg came up beside her, reading the notes he'd just made on his clipboard.

"Okay, so my dispatcher back at the supervisor's office called the Sacramento Police Department and spoke to the officer who responded to the scene of the kidnapping. The only witness to the actual kidnapping was the grandmother. She reported it was her son-in-law who took the baby."

"Yes, that's all on the Amber Alert," Jody said.

"Okay, and he used no gun or other weapon." Greg looked up and caught Jody's gaze. "Guy just grabbed the boy, threw him in the car, and took off." He looked down again. "Another individual present nearby at the time reported that the guy in the BMW almost ran him over. Dispatch thinks that's why the cops are calling the guy presumed dangerous, but no one seems to know for sure if he's armed. He didn't use a gun, and nobody saw one, but to be on the safe side, they're still saying 'possibly armed.'"

"'Presumed dangerous?'" Kris echoed. "That's ambiguous. Isn't this that Amber Alert? That sounds dangerous enough to me. And what about that woman who was found dead? Isn't there some connection there?"

"Yeah. That wasn't on the original Amber Alert, but the dispatch officer did mention that possibility. So far, though, no one knows for sure whether the father did that, or what exactly happened there. But the kidnapper, the guy who took the boy, he's the boy's father, according to the grandmother." Greg's tone was skeptical. "So, anyway, not a stranger ad ... abduc ... abduction." He looked down to read. "They're calling it a non-custodial parental abduction."

"Hard to know what to make of that." Jody felt a twinge of anxiety. The teams should get out there soon and find that baby. She didn't want to get shot, but every minute that passed meant one more minute of uncertainty about the baby's well-being. "The father might be dangerous, but more likely he's just lost out there with his baby." She checked her watch. "It's been maybe as long as seventy-two hours. He might be ready to be rescued by now." As the information settled in, the search team found their fear levels dropping, and their desire to get started on the mission growing. The guy might be a kidnapper, but he was also the baby's father. This situation might not be as dangerous as it first appeared. Possibly the father and baby were running away, hiding from the person who had killed the mother.

Greg wasn't finished relaying the news from the supervisor's office. "Okay, and also the crew in the reconnaissance helicopter did not see any sign of anyone on the trail or in the canyon. Of course they wouldn't be able to see down into any of the smaller side canyons, but along the creek, they didn't see any hikers."

Jody turned her back on the rest of her team and lowered her voice.

"And what about the fire?" she said to Greg. "Is that fire presenting any danger?"

"Uh ... other than saying it looked like an abandoned backpacker's campfire that got into that last canyon toward the falls, that's all. Oh, and Roxie—she's the administrative assistant at the district ranger station—she said District Ranger Russell sent the helicopter over to the lake to possibly get ready to do some water drops, but he's kind of waiting until the district fire management officer—that's my boss, Cullison—gets back from another fire. Russell's waiting to hear if we find the guy and the little boy before he starts dropping water. I guess they don't think the fire's going anywhere too fast."

"Thanks, Greg, that's good information."

Jody called to Andy, who was busily setting up gear. "Guess we'd better get this show on the road. They want us to find these people and get them out before anything else develops down there." She wasn't specific about defining what she meant by anything else.

She spread the map open on the card table and put a dot with a yellow highlighter on the inked circle that marked their location. She traced over the faint line of the trail from Eagle Meadow to the pass through Eagle Ridge with yellow marker. The trail went north across the top of the ridge, then dropped by switchbacks into the canyon formed by Turtle Creek. It ran along the edge of a cliff beside the creek for about a half mile, then doubled-back and dropped again and forded the creek.

That whole distance looked to be about three miles. North of the creek, several sharply rising ridges running along the western side of the Sierra closed off the canyon. A mile or so east of the ford, the trail ended at an escarpment topped by the flat granite backcountry. There were no other roads or trails between Eagle Meadow and Lake Nell, although a rough jeep track near the dam connected the five or so vacation cabins strung out along the lake shore.

She checked her watch, then looked past the brown trailhead sign and out along the narrow dirt trail. It was only 4:30 p.m. Still plenty of daylight left to conduct an initial search, at least up here on the ridge top. Andy unloaded and set up the radio transmitter while Kris poked poles into their bright red tents on the chance they'd be there overnight. Jody called them to the table and pointed out the features she'd marked on the pale green map.

"There's no apparent reason why our lost pair would have gone any direction other than out this trail and down and across the creek." Jody traced the yellow line into Turtle Creek. "Once on the other side of the creek, even if they've lost their way, they're kind of boxed in. The only open direction is west to the lake."

"What about these canyons here, and here?" Andy pointed.

"Look at those elevation lines," Jody said. "The walls of those canyons are really steep. And the boy can walk, but he's just a little guy. I don't see him climbing those walls. Even if the two of them make it to the top, then they're out on exposed granite. Not much place to shelter or hide up there."

"Lots of crevices to fall into, though," Kris said, "and not be seen. Remember that mission last summer when that hiker fell into a crevice in the granite and Bullet almost went in after him?

"Yeah," Andy said. "If that happened, no one's ever going to find that boy."

"The dogs would," Kris said, staring at Andy.

Jody summed up their thoughts. "Okay, we think the most likely possibility is that this pair is hiking this trail west to where it comes out at the lake. Possibly the dad thought leaving the car here instead of ditching it at the turn off closer to the lake would throw whoever he's hiding from off."

Kris's brow furrowed. "Wait a second. Is this guy lost? Or is he trying to hide? I mean, what are our chances of finding a guy who's putting some effort into staying hidden?"

"The way to think about it, I guess, is that the father came here to try to hide, and the little boy is lost," Jody said. "I'm betting though, that after three days and nights outside with only the supplies he could carry, I'm betting they're both feeling pretty lost."

She shifted her gaze, trying not to make direct eye contact with anyone. The truth was, this mission was shaping up to be more confusing than she'd thought when she accepted it. Search missions always held some degree of risk, but Jody didn't want to put any of her teams into a life-threatening situation. On the other hand, what a great chance this was to prove that dogs could be of real value in exactly these kinds of circumstances.

She knew that advance planning could significantly shorten the search, and probably lead to a more positive outcome. At the same time, she could feel her own adrenaline starting to pump, and she was anxious to get started.

Fourteen
FBI

"Anyway," Jody said, "my point is, if Eagle Meadow is one end of the trail, we can go in here, at this end. At the same time, we can try to get law enforcement to focus on the other end. See, down here by the lake? That's probably the father's intended destination, anyway. At least until he got lost."

Andy's brow furrowed. "How do we know they didn't already make it to those cabins and are holed up in one?"

"Good point," Jody said. "Law enforcement should check that out. And that dovetails nicely with my thoughts. If we can get those uniforms to go on down to the cabins, we can track from here with the dogs. Law enforcement can close off the other end of the trail, boxing in the kidnapper, and we'll search from here."

"And we won't have law enforcement trampling all over our track," Kris added.

"Sounds like a plan," Andy said. Kris bent over, studying the map, worry lines scrunched on her brow.

"Even if the kidnapper has taken that baby far up into one of these side canyons," Kris said, "those are areas where scent would collect and concentrate. If the dogs show interest in one of those areas, we can call law enforcement in at that point, right?"

"Absolutely," Jody agreed.

"Okay," Kris said. "Let's see if we can take this end and get those guys with the guns to the other end. At least that way, we won't be caught up in the middle of a gunfight if they decide to start shooting, right?"

"So how do we get law enforcement to go along with this idea?" Andy asked.

"Jody will be able to convince those guys, right Jody?" They all peered skeptically at the gaggle of uniformed officers. "If you can go and convince those law enforcement guys, I'll get Bullet and Flag ready, okay?" Kris said.

"Yeah," Andy agreed. "Yeah, you go convince them, Jody. You're the charming one." He raised his eyebrows and smiled encouragement at her.

"Right," she said. "Okay, I'll try. And Andy, let's start Rose tracking on the marked trail first. That's the obvious place to start, and we have the advantage this time that not too many other humans have been trampling the trail."

Andy started loading his fanny pack and untangling the twists and turns of Rose's search harness, almost ready to go. His bloodhound was trained to take the scent of a target from something like a piece of clothing or the target's sleeping bag and then track the target's path along the ground. As Andy learned when he first studied tracking, humans discard a stunning amount of organic matter every place they go, dead skin cells, hairs, sweat and other effluvia. All of that matter begins to grow bacteria the minute it hits the ground if conditions are right, and tracking dogs are trained to follow the scent of the bacteria. The dad and little boy should have left an easily trackable trail if they'd walked that way.

Jody rolled the map and tucked it under her arm. Convincing those law enforcement guys was likely going to be easier said than done. The map should help. Guys love maps, she thought. If she could get the attention of just two or three of them, and then get one of them to start acting like it was his idea, that's all she'd need. She took a deep breath, started over, and caught the attention of the deputy whose name badge read "Hogan." Sure enough, as soon as she spread the map across the hood of the nearest CHP vehicle, its driver and two others, including the deputy, ambled over and began poring over the page. They were joined a few seconds later by another of the deputies, who, Jody realized as she studied the face under the khaki cap, was a woman.

She'd just outlined her rationale for why law enforcement should take their vehicles and head downhill to the lake to close off that end of the trail, when a nondescript black sedan rolled into the last open spot next to a forest service truck. The sedan's door opened and a young woman, dressed mostly in black, stepped out and gazed in their direction. Didn't look like a wayward hiker hoping for the trailhead. Not in those shoes. She reached back into her vehicle and, extracting a shiny nylon jacket, pulled it on. She turned to close the door, flashing the large yellow letters FBI across her back.

Deputy Hogan bristled and the other deputies glared over their shoulders at the new arrival. The CHP officers were more discreet. "It is a kidnapping," one said to the other, loudly enough to be heard by most. "You had to expect the feds to show up sooner or later."

The FBI agent pulled out a phone and placed a call as she watched those gathered around the map. The merits of moving to the other end of the trail were being raised, but opinions were mixed.

Andy sidled up to Jody, with Rose on a short lead. The dog looked up at him, resplendent in her orange vest and harness, and wagged her tail, ready to go to work.

"Rose needs a scent article, Jody. Is there any way we can get into that car? There might be something in there she can use."

"I got a thing in here," one of the CHP officers said as he headed for the trunk of his car. He rummaged in a toolbox and came out with a flat steel lockout device. Andy cocked one eye at Jody. Neither of them would say anything, but they both knew that device would probably not unlock the door on a late model BMW. The CHP officer went to work on the passenger side window anyway. Greg had watched the exchange, then climbed back onto his driver's seat and picked up his cell phone. He tapped the screen for a moment, placing a call. A few moments later, he gestured at the FBI agent, summoning her to his truck, and handed her his phone. Jody caught his eye, and Greg gave her a thumbs-up. A minute later the BMW gave a "thunk" and the doors unlocked in response to a remote signal from the car company. Jody returned Greg's gesture.

Several uniforms rushed toward the car, then a commanding voice rang out. "Hold on there! FBI. No one touch that car." The agent moved immediately to the vehicle and flashed her badge to anyone kind enough to look. No one caught her name. "Everything in this car is evidence in a crime. I'll process the car, seal it, and CHP will have it towed to a secured facility. In a kidnapping, the FBI has jurisdiction working in conjunction with the local county sheriff." She sounded as though she'd memorized a book of regulations. She scowled at the uniforms, who backed off and clustered again around Jody and the map.

The FBI agent opened the passenger door, stuck her head inside, and took a deep whiff, collecting scent evidence. The smell of Jayden's dirty diaper on the floor in back wafted out and probably overwhelmed any other odor there might have been. The agent then gloved up and crawled onto the rear seat, photographing and bagging a few loose items. Andy crowded beside her, explaining his need for a scent object. After bagging and labelling the first of Jayden's socks, she photographed the second sock and put it into a bag also. She backed out and reluctantly handed Andy the bag with the second sock.

Andy held the bag open so Rose could get a good whiff. The dog's nostrils flared as she drew in scent, using shallow sniffs.

The idea to move to the lake end of the trail spread among the sheriff's deputies, and had gained in popularity with the arrival of the federal officer. A few voiced concerns that the canine search teams should have armed escorts, but Jody quietly put them off that idea. She wasn't afraid, and extra humans wandering around might compromise the dogs' abilities to scent. Kris and Andy might have preferred the company of guys with guns, but Jody made the decision for them.

Fifteen
Skeptics

The four sheriff's deputies were beginning to move toward their vehicles when Andy and Rose stepped onto the trail and walked out about fifteen or twenty feet. Andy had chosen to outfit his dog in the largest orange vest he could buy in hopes that hunters would be less likely to mistake his large brown dog for a deer. Andy also wore an orange vest and cap for the same reason. This was not hunting season, but no one could ever be sure. The law enforcement guys stopped and turned to watch Rose work.

Andy held open the baggie containing Jayden's discarded sock one more time, and Rose poked her snout inside. She took several short breaths with her nose in the bag, then pulled out, ready to go. Andy folded the bag, tucked it in his fanny pack, and said "Find that!"

Rose already had her nose lowered to the ground, whuffing gently. She turned her head back and forth, setting her long ears swinging, just barely touching the dirt. This action stirred up smells deposited on the ground and brought them up across her sensitive olfactory nerves. She searched for several minutes along the trail, but showed no interest in any scent she found there. Andy moved her a few inches to each side of the trail, then farther out. Even after ten minutes, with everyone watching, Rose gave no sign that she scented the baby on the trail. She looked up at Andy. He moved farther to the side and gave her another chance to smell the sock. She rolled her eyes up at him again and looked away. Her signal was clear; the baby had not passed here.

Shaking their heads and chuckling derisively, the sheriff's deputies ambled toward their vehicles. Jody swiveled, searching the lot. The CHP officers had stopped watching, and had their heads bent in discussion with the FBI agent. Jody eased close enough to listen. The officers would maintain possession of the BMW until the tow truck they'd already called could unload it in their locked lot in Jamestown. The FBI had responsibility for preserving the evidence contained within, some of which would remain inside the vehicle for the time being. One officer turned his back, providing a flat surface for the FBI agent to lean against and sign a release allowing the car to be towed.

The sheriff's vehicles had just gotten turned around when two white SUVs with red trim from the California Department of Forestry and Fire Protection pulled in and blocked the entrance to the parking lot and one lane of the highway outside. Fires inside national forests are within the jurisdiction of the U.S. Forest Service, but all agencies operate under mutual aid agreements, so the state firefighters were on scene to help. Unless the fire blew up in an emergency situation, Cal Fire would have to wait for direction from the district ranger before proceeding.

It took a good fifteen minutes of moving vehicles around to get the sheriff's cars on their way. Greg drove his truck at the head of the line, leading them to the entrance to the jeep track at the eastern corner of the dam.

"I'll be back after I get these guys situated," he called out his window. "I'm still supposed to try to get a look at that smoke." No one seemed to be listening except possibly Kris, who gave Greg a friendly wave good-bye.

After the deputies and Greg drove off, one of the CHP officers also left, and the other one settled in to wait for the tow truck. It would be hours before a truck could make the trip to retrieve the BMW.

The parking lot at Eagle Meadow became strangely quiet with the departure of nearly all of the intimidating law enforcement vehicles, and their equally daunting firepower. Jody gazed at the shadows along the edge of the meadow again. Now was the time to go, in spite of a possibly dangerous kidnapper. Jody felt keenly her desire to prove she and her teams could find and rescue that baby. At that moment, that desire overrode her concern about sending Kris and Andy, and their dogs, out there, seemingly defenseless.

In the now quiet meadow, Andy tried again to get Rose to track, this time closer to the BMW. Although Rose had given no indication that she smelled the baby on or near the hiking trail, at the car she did alert.

"*Woo-woo-woo,*" she barked, looking at Andy. "*Woo-woo-woo.*"

"Okay!" Andy said. Rose says he was here, right here by the car." Instead of simply assuming that Rose's lack of interest on the trail meant she wasn't doing her job, the handlers huddled to consider what her behavior might mean. They were joined by the FBI agent.

"I don't think I caught your name." Jody smiled, reaching to shake the agent's hand.

"Agent Cardona, FBI, evidence recovery technician from the Sacramento Field Office. And yours?" The agent pulled out a tablet, ready to enter names. They continued the introductions, taking longer than might be expected, since the dogs were included. Each dog was allowed to sniff the back of Agent Cardona's hand. That would help them in discriminating between the target's scent and Cardona's irrelevant one.

In the same way that humans can distinguish one face from another, the dogs knew the scents of the humans gathered in Eagle Meadow and could distinguish those from any potential targets. They wouldn't alert to the presence of a familiar human scent.

The agent seemed wary about holding her hand out for the dogs, masking her nervousness by explaining how the FBI was now using "vapor dogs" to identify people who either were carrying or had recently worked on explosive devices.

"The amazing thing about our vapor dogs is they can find a moving explosive scent, so like before a bomb is even planted, they can find the person carrying it. Isn't that incredible?" The canine handlers agreed. "The only problem is we don't have enough trained vapor dogs to deploy everywhere they're needed." Agent Cardona cautiously stroked Rose's head. "I've never really liked dogs that much," she added. And after a moment, "This one seems nice."

Rose gazed up at Cardona and let her mouth drop open in a wide grin, pressing the top of her head against the agent's hand.

"Okay, back to business," Andy said. "Why is there no scent of the baby beyond the car?"

Jody looked around. "What about the possibility the dad had someone meet him here in a second vehicle?" Joined by Cardona, they checked the compacted gravel at the rear of the BMW. Any evidence of a second vehicle, if there'd been one, had been obliterated by the arrival and departure of the other cars and trucks.

"No way to tell now," Cardona said, "but that is a possibility. From the information we've collected on the kidnapper, there's no indication this guy has any camping or backcountry experience. He could easily have had someone meet him here. Or at least we shouldn't jump to the conclusion that he's taken a live baby out into that canyon."

"We have to jump to that conclusion, ma'am." Jody lowered her brow. "That's the whole reason we're here, to search for a lost baby."

Kris voiced another obvious answer to Andy's question. "Possibly Rose isn't scenting on the trail because the baby never touched the ground, at least not on the first part of the trail, right? I mean, the dad might have been carrying him."

"Hmm ... possibly," Andy said. "But how could the dad carry the baby and a bunch of supplies and camping gear too?"

"We don't actually know the dad had any supplies," Jody reminded them. She gazed away for a minute, imagining a baby out along that trail somewhere, probably for longer than seventy-two hours, with no shelter, warm bedding, or food. A sense of increasing urgency charged the air. "We'd better find that little guy soon. He's in some real danger, but we can't just rush out there. C'mon, let's map out a quick search grid."

"Or possibly the danger is already over," Cardona said. The rest of them stopped and turned to her in confusion. "Well, possibly the baby wasn't walking because the baby had already, um ... well, you know, expired. Possibly the baby wasn't able to walk any longer, and the kidnapper came out to this remote location to dispose of the body. If that's the case, he might not be carrying any supplies at all, unless possibly a shovel."

Sixteen
New Arrivals

A long moment of silence followed this pronouncement. The search team had spent many hours training. Their rewards for this substantial investment were the happy endings when lost people were reunited with those who loved them. Not all missions have happy endings, but these searchers were not ready to give up hope on this one before even starting. However unrealistic, they had been thinking in terms of a dad and his son off on a hike, not a murderer attempting to conceal an already dead victim.

"Here's another answer to why Rose isn't showing interest on the trail," Andy said. "Look." Rose snuffled at something and tried to crawl under the CHP vehicle parked next to the BMW. "I think the little boy walked across this parking lot."

Jody watched Rose trying to push herself farther under the car. "I think you and Rose are right," Jody said. "Let's get this guy to move his car."

"No need," Andy said, walking his dog to the other side of the vehicle. Rose immediately picked the scent up there, and followed it the few feet to where it disappeared under Jody's Forester. Taking Rose to the other side of the Forester, Andy watched her catch the scent again and eagerly start across the meadow, her nose to the ground. "Okay," Andy said, triumphant. "We've got it now. The kid walked across this meadow and under those trees." He bent to his dog, ruffling her neck.

"Okay," Andy called again, "mark this as the 'last known position.'"

Jody wrote a tiny *lkp* on the map at the car's location. She drew an arrow next to that and noted *dot*, direction of travel.

She cut a look to Agent Cardona. "Assuming they traveled on foot from the car." Jody pointed at the map. "We're here, on this flat area, Eagle Meadow, near the top of this ridge. The trail goes to the other side of this flat area, about a mile away. Then, if you notice these elevation lines, you can see the trail goes through a narrow pass before dropping down the side of the ridge toward Turtle Creek. Andy, you and Rose could start tracking here, where Rose just picked up the baby's scent, and follow that to wherever it goes. Or you could go directly to the pass and see if Rose shows interest there.

"If Flag or Bullet don't show any interest up here in the meadow or along the ridge, the only way down is through that pass. No one but Rose can tell us if the target went that way. We need her at the pass."

Jody outlined the ridge top with a finger. "Kris, our teams will search here on top. We'll spread out and do area searches of the forest beyond the parking lot, and then north as far as where the ridge drops off. We want to be sure the baby is not here on the ridge top before we go over to the pass. You'll stay downwind from the trail, where Bullet will be most likely to pick up the scent of anyone who traveled nearby." Jody knew the real strength of a good air-scenting dog is that they can find the target's current location without following the exact route the target took to get there. If this target traveled along the ridge top, but then left the area, air-scenting dogs could determine that more quickly than a tracking dog.

"Flag and I will cover the ridge to the west, here." She drew a rough square with her finger on the other part of the search grid, farthest from their current location.

The way they had the grid laid out, they wouldn't miss anything, even if the source of the scent was moving. "After we've each covered our part of the grid, if we haven't found anyone we'll gather here at the pass." Jody tapped that spot on the map. "Figure out what we want to do next." Her finger kept tapping, telegraphing her anxiousness to get started.

"Yeah," Andy agreed. "I'd really like to get a look over the canyon from there at the pass. If Rose is on scent there, then tracking around up here on top is pretty much a waste of time."

Jody nodded. "That's what I was thinking. Well, whatever you think, and whatever Rose is telling you. Let's just agree that no one goes down into that canyon yet."

"You know," Andy said, "it's great if a dog finds a track, but not finding a track, well, that's good information, too. It's just up to us to figure out what it means."

"Hey, look at Flag and Bullet," Kris said pointing. The dogs had not been given the search command, but they had been released to explore the meadow. Both dogs were standing at the far edge of Eagle Meadow, peering under the trees, in obvious air-scenting interest postures. Bullet held the classic point position of a hunting dog, his snout pushed forward, one forepaw lifted, showing his pointer heritage. Flag held her tail at half-staff, waving gently. Jody noted her dog was not displaying her full, high and unfurled tail alert "flag" pose, but the dogs were sensing the presence of someone. Kris started out to corral them before they could egg each other into taking off on their own search.

"Wait, Kris!" Jody said in alarm. "Don't go. Better just call them back. We don't know what's out there." She gazed again at the shadows. "Or who." When it came to possibly perilous situations, Jody would rather tackle them herself than see a friend get in trouble.

Kris gave Jody a confused look. "No, we don't know who's there. That's why we're searching, right? Is there something you're not telling us?"

"Flag! Bullet! That'll do!" Jody called, ignoring Kris's question. The two dogs glanced at Jody, looked back under the trees, lowered their heads, and trotted to Kris, reluctance evident in every step. Kris gave them plenty of praise for their initiative.

Once she had the dogs back inside their pen, she studied under the trees for movement where they'd alerted. She couldn't see anything, but the dogs made it clear there was definitely something there to smell.

"That's exactly the direction Rose was tracking toward, right?" Kris said, glancing at Jody.

"Yes, well, maybe this will be a quick search." Jody wanted to keep positive thoughts for the mission. "Maybe they're having a picnic just over there."

Agent Cardona had returned to her inventory of the evidence inside the BMW. Having completed that, she'd come to stand beside the dog handlers. She gave a skeptical huff when she heard the picnic idea.

The gravel at the entrance to the parking lot crunched again. They looked up to see the new guy on the search team, Frank, pulling into the lot.

"Oh, yeah," Andy said, "I forgot to tell you, Frank called and said he wanted to join this mission." Frank had been attending their weekly search and rescue training sessions for almost a year, and bringing his half-grown border collie, MacDuff, along. The pair wouldn't be certified to participate in search missions for at least another six months, but for this mission, Frank could serve as a field assistant. He'd provide mission support, staff the radio, and relay messages. For MacDuff, the search provided a good chance to be onsite and get used to the atmosphere at the location of a real mission.

Frank appeared to have been leading a parade up the mountain. At least three media vans and a variety of other vehicles rolled into the lot and spilled out people. Orange-shirted community response volunteers streamed out of one van. Of more immediate interest was the small trailer riding along behind the van with a portable toilet perched on it. As soon as the van came to a stop and steps were placed leading to the trailer, a line began to form.

Bringing up the rear of the parade were two U.S. Forest Service SUVs, each bearing uniformed individuals. The first forest service uniform went immediately to the Cal Fire vehicles and began an animated discussion involving a good deal of arm waving and gestures. From what little the canine search team could hear, it sounded like a discussion about a reported forest fire.

Kris scowled and stepped to Jody's side. "Forest fire?" she said.

"Um, oh yeah, Greg said something about a fire reported in the canyon."

"And were you going to share that with the rest of us?"

Jody had almost forgotten about the reported smoke. From what she'd heard, it might be nothing more than an abandoned campfire, and probably already extinguished. The possibility that a small fire still burned in the canyon only added more excitement to the search. Kris apparently had a different opinion. "Sorry," Jody said. "I think they've already put it out. It just slipped my mind."

Kris gave Jody a doubt-filled look. "I just like to know what I'm walking into is all, you know?"

Jody apologized again. Tensions can run high on a search, and Jody had a bad habit of not remembering that situations she found optimally exciting were sometimes frightening for others.

The second forest service uniform, a tall woman, slid from her driver's seat. After close to thirty six unrelenting hours on the Buck's Lake fire, District Fire Management Officer Lynne Cullison had arrived at Eagle Meadow beyond exhausted.

She replaced her Smokey the Bear dress hat with a white helmet, and pulled on a heavy yellow jacket, freeing her long blonde braid with one hand. Within four minutes of her boots hitting the ground, Cullison had one of the seasonal firefighters suited up to accompany her, and they were on their way out the trail to get eyes on that smoke. From her actions it was apparent that the presence of a possibly armed and dangerous kidnapper did not concern Cullison. Her job was to manage fires in the forest, and she was busy getting that done. Striding out the trail, she moved too fast for anyone to warn her.

More forest service uniforms piled out of the second truck and began hauling equipment from the back, including a generator, a podium, and a large whiteboard. U.S. Forest Service Public Affairs had arrived.

Seventeen
Ready?

Matthew slipped his hand from under Jayden's sweaty head and stood. He crept to the edge of the trail, and settled in the shade, his back against a tree trunk. From there, he surveyed the steep bank of Turtle Creek, opposite. He could see most of the trail he'd hiked down a few days before. It disappeared behind boulders here and there, switching across the granite. In spite of the helicopter earlier, all seemed quiet now. He and Jayden might still be okay here for a few more days, although he wasn't sure how long he could stay hidden if they were after him for committing murder.

Movement to the right caught his attention. As he watched, glimpses of that old guy appeared between rocks. The guy climbed toward the creek, fifty yards or so west of the ford. If a trail passed there, Matthew couldn't see it through the brush. The only way across the creek Matthew knew about was the gravel ford, but the guy kept coming down on his own path. His scraggly head vanished again behind a tree. There might be at least one alternative way across the creek, Matthew thought. Something to check out.

He scanned east again along the top of the ridge, and watched as a tall woman wearing a yellow jacket and white helmet appeared at the pass. Matthew didn't know who she was, but she was dressed like someone official. The woman stood, looking upstream, but did not start down the trail. Matthew sat still, barely breathing, as she turned slowly, gazing into the canyon, along the creek, and at the trail. As long as he didn't move, he wouldn't be seen. What about Jayden, though? Any minute, Jayden would wake up, start crying, or even walk into view. Matthew had to find a way to secure Jayden so he wouldn't give Matthew's presence away.

***

In his role as field assistant at the search base camp, Frank called the canine searchers over and handed out waivers, releases, and emergency contact forms. Quiet prevailed while they filled in the necessary information and signed the forms. As usual, Jody hesitated over the line requesting the name and phone number of someone to call in case something happened to her. She was always tempted to write 911 on that line. Her parents lived in Illinois, a long ways to come rushing to her bedside, and anyway, they were too old to travel much. She had a brother living in Southern California, but he wasn't the type to come running in case of emergency. He'd probably tell anyone who contacted him to call 911. She glanced at the others, busily filling in names and numbers for husbands and wives. It might be time she tried to find herself another one of those. Just because it hadn't worked out the first time ... She'd have to get on that when she got home.

She glanced across the meadow while the others finished their forms. The folks in the orange shirts were from the local sheriff's community volunteer response unit. They looked to be getting ready to head out the trail without consulting the canine handlers.

In this county, the search unit included ground search teams, swift-water rescue teams, avalanche teams, and even a posse of equestrian search teams, but they had elected to not include any canine teams. When District Ranger Russell needed a canine search team, he had to call emergency services for permission to ask someone like Jody in from out of the area, as he had done that morning.

Jody had worked with this county's search coordinator on previous missions. She knew he did not hold the abilities of canine teams in high regard. She could have waved him over and explained about the dogs scenting at the edge of the meadow and not on the trail, but thought better of it. No need to invite traffic in the area the dogs would need to search. If he wanted to take his crews out to search, there wasn't much she could do about it.

Jody watched the new arrivals with increasing dismay as they began to mill around the edges of the meadow. Some of them wandered out along the trail behind Cullison. A couple of others were peering through the dusty windows of the BMW, prompting a startled yelp from Agent Cardona. Reporters looked up and moved toward them, possibly sensing a new angle on the kidnapping story.

Jody's left knee began to bounce. The scene was turning into a madhouse, swarming with way too many people. A few of the media were looking speculatively in her direction. The dogs had already identified the scent of a person in the forest to the west of the trail. It was time to get out there.

"We'd better get the dogs started. Any minute now some newscaster will be over here trying to interview us or wanting to pet the dogs. We aren't running a petting zoo here."

"Where's the grandmother?" Kris asked, looking around.

"What do you mean?" Andy said.

"The baby's grandmother. Why isn't she here? She must be frantic, right?" Kris and her husband Lowell didn't have any children, but she loved to play at being every child's favorite auntie, and was a whiz at calming frightened children.

"How do you know she's not over there?" Andy waved in the direction of the growing crowd.

"No, those are all volunteers. Where's the baby's grandmother?" This time she directed her question at Cardona. The agent looked at the crowd while she answered.

"If you recall from the Amber Alert, the mother is deceased. We have agents in Sacramento investigating the situation. I don't think we know what's going on with the grandmother yet."

Jody patted Kris on the shoulder, then tugged at her sleeve, but Kris wasn't moving.

"The mother was killed, the father ran away with the baby, and you don't know where the grandmother is? Did you hear this, Jody?" Kris's voice was reaching an anxious whine.

"She said they don't know the whole situation, Kris. The best thing we can do for the baby now is to find him, safe and sound, and quickly."

"Jody," Agent Cardona called her closer. They turned their backs while the agent asked a quiet question. "What exactly will your dogs be searching for? Can they locate evidence, bodies, or only live people?"

"Well, typically the dogs are trained to tell us when they smell a live human. They can smell evidence, of course, but they aren't trained to communicate to us when they've scented on evidence. You mean, like an item of discarded clothing or something?"

"Yes, something like that. Or even a gun or other weapon?"

"Hmm ... not very likely," Jody was forced to reply. "Human scent does transfer to various objects, but the dogs are trained to signal us when they find the source of the scent, not just when they detect a trace left by contact." She thought a moment. "We could get a firearms detection dog out here if you want. If you're only looking for one gun, though, that's a tall search order. Better off finding the guy with the gun than looking for just a gun."

"What about the possibility the only thing out there to find is a body? Will the dogs scent on a body or walk right past it?"

Jody's stomach turned over at the thought, then she switched back into professional mode. "Our dogs will scent on a body if it hasn't been dead more than a day or two. Bodies smell differently to dogs almost immediately after death, but enough residual scent remains for the dogs to alert even after a couple of days. If it's been longer than that, we'll have to bring in other dogs, dogs trained in human remains detection."

Cardona raised one eyebrow. No one wanted to need that.

Jody instructed Frank to do his best to keep the volunteer searchers in the parking lot until the dogs could search the ridge top. Cardona caught onto the goal and agreed to help with that, while sealing the BMW with tape and getting it ready to be towed. It was in her interest to keep folks from overrunning the area, too. This might be the scene of a crime.

The dog handlers quickly cinched on their waist packs, loaded with emergency gear. Everyone on the search mission pulled out their handheld radios, keyed in the correct frequencies, and checked the proper operation of each radio.

They clipped lightweight thirty-foot leads onto their belts. The dogs would stay on eight-foot leads at first, partly to keep them safe from a potentially dangerous human target. Mostly the shorter leads would allow the handlers to better read the cues being sent by their dogs' behaviors. Flag and Bullet would each exhibit subtly different behaviors depending on their proximity to the target, and, if the target was moving, the direction of travel. This would be in addition to all the subtle behaviors dogs normally exhibit that humans rarely even notice.

Kris picked up a fully charged taser, then put it down. "I'm not going to take this," she said. "My biggest fear is I'll accidentally taser myself while rummaging in the pack. I'm leaving it here."

Jody slipped her taser into an inconspicuous but readily accessible leather holster on her belt. She did not share Kris's reluctance to discharge the taser, although she didn't relish being in a situation that would require its use.

They buckled on the dogs' orange harnesses and search vests, and made sure their GPS tracking tags were securely attached. Dogs did go missing during searches, falling off cliffs, tumbling down hillsides, even slipping into swift water and floating long distances. The GPS tracking devices would help find a dog who'd gone missing, as long as she wasn't too far from the GPS base.

"All right," Andy said, "let's go find that boy."

"Baby," Kris corrected. "He's just a baby."

Not even two years old, Jody thought. Old enough to be scared. Not old enough to do anything about it. Jody knew that feeling all too well. She'd spent her life overcoming that scared but helpless feeling. An evil shadow lurking in the dark, her mother nowhere in sight. Jody rested a palm on the butt of the taser. No, she'd have no reluctance to use it. If the situation warranted, and the bad guy was close enough, she'd use it. Her only concern was that once she'd started firing, she wouldn't be able to stop.

Andy gave Rose another chance to sniff Jayden's discarded sock, then waved as he and Rose started off. Nose to the ground, Rose showed interest immediately, eagerly snuffling. A few moments later, Kris stood at the edge of the tree canopy, both fear and determination reflected in her expression. Bullet held his head high, ready to begin.

Jody walked with Flag to the edge of the meadow fifty feet from Kris, and took a deep breath. The start of another mission. Another opportunity to showcase the value and intelligence of dogs. A chance to help a lost baby.

***

"How can they just walk into the forest like that?" Cardona said, as she and Frank watched the dogs and their handlers disappear into the shadows. "I mean, there's not even a trail there."

"Well, they have to go there because that's where the search target went," Frank explained. "Yes, it would be easier to walk on the trail, but the target went that other way." He smiled and held out his hand. "Frank Morelos."

"Assistant Special Agent Cardona, FBI," she said. Then, blushing, she added, "Luisa Cardona."

"Oh, well, then, I am Francisco Santiago de Morelos." He grinned. In the warming afternoon air, he unzipped his jacket, causing the broad gold band on his left hand to flash in the sunlight.

Cardona shot a scowl off to the trees and muttered under her breath, "Sure, all the good ones are."

They turned to look at the forest again, but the searchers were no longer visible.

"I could follow them," Cardona said. "They might run across additional evidence." She glanced back to the parking lot. "Or I could stay closer to the kidnapper's car, maintaining the chain of evidence. Although that CHP officer appears to be covering that base."

They both gazed at the officer slumped low in his driver's seat, possibly asleep. The phone tucked in Cardona's pocket signaled an incoming call from the Sacramento office. She stepped away from Frank to answer it in private.

Frank keyed on the base radio and tried to raise the deputy sheriff. He got no answer, but a few seconds later Greg Gardner reported in. According to him, the four sheriff's deputies who had left the parking lot earlier were in position around the cabins. They had that far end of the trail sealed off. There seemed to be some problem with moving east from that direction, so it was unclear whether they would proceed or hold their position near the cabins.

Frank tried to follow along on the map as Greg explained the situation. Greg also relayed that more county deputies might be on their way to the trailhead at Eagle Meadow. They'd get those community response volunteers organized to look for the baby.

No sooner had Frank ended the transmission than another county sheriff's SUV rolled into the lot. One deputy climbed out and waved everyone in an orange shirt over to his vehicle. Frank heard him announcing that, given the potential danger posed by the kidnapper, no one would be permitted to go into the canyon until the kidnapper had been neutralized. Frank watched as various people wandered along the trail where Cullison had gone a half hour before. The deputy finally noticed and called everyone back into camp.

Cardona headed to her car and curled up in the driver's seat, the phone tucked at her ear. She disconnected, scanned her notes, and gazed out the windshield. After about ten minutes of that, she pulled two small evidence bags out of the kit on the backseat and set out along the trail, leaning over its edges. She seemed to be looking for something: broken branches, plastic wrappers from a food item, anything that might indicate the passage of the kidnapper or the child. It was her job to continue to look for, recover, and secure evidence, even while she waited. She went out the trail to where the parking lot and its numerous occupants began to disappear behind trees, then returned, her evidence bags still empty.

She moved closer to where the dogs had gone under the trees. The long shadows of early evening made seeing anything on the ground hard. Slowly, she stepped forward, scanning the ground carefully.

Eighteen
Cabin Hideout

Six miles to the west, two county sheriff's SUVs were deployed on the narrow dirt track leading to the few cabins along the east shore of Lake Nell. The ruts sculpted by spring run-off made driving next to impossible. Greg was giving the deputies whatever direction he could offer. He intended to head back to the trailhead where District Ranger Russell had asked him to be, as soon as he got these law enforcement guys oriented at this end of the trail. The officers gathered around him as he pointed ahead on the jeep track. He explained about the four or five cabins scattered along the barely passable road. The track itself petered out before reaching Turtle Creek where it fed into Lake Nell. The hiking trail on the north side of the creek also ended at the lake shore, but several hundred yards north and across the creek. Completely inaccessible to the SUVs.

Deputy Hogan squinted through the trees. "So, you're saying the trail the kidnapper will be on ends on the other side of the creek?"

"Yep."

"So, how, may I ask, do you suggest we get over there?"

Greg didn't have a good answer. "There's no bridge," he explained, "and this time of year with the creek running high, about the only way across is the ford five or six miles back. I guess possibly an agile person might be able to crawl over the rocks and jump across at a narrow place."

After some thought, he pointed out that the kidnapper would have the same problem if he wanted to bring the boy south across the creek and out to the highway. Climbing rocks and jumping across would be impossible while carrying a small child.

"We got a report the reconnaissance helicopter is parked near where the trail ends," Greg added. "Possibly you could get a message to them and they could keep an eye out for the kidnapper."

"Are they armed?" Hogan asked. "What are they going to do if an armed kidnapper shows up? Fly away?"

Greg could only shrug.

"Hey, Hogan," Deputy Tarrazo said. "What if we got that copter to carry us over the creek?"

Hogan screwed his face into a look of disgust and spit into the dirt. "Bright idea, Tarazzo. Then how do we get back with the abductor and the vic?"

Discreetly backing away, Greg waved and trotted to his truck, leaving the law enforcement officers to form their plan.

The four deputies stood in a loose circle, thumbs hooked in belt loops and chests puffed out, each doing their best to project the command presence they'd been taught at the academy. Hogan pointed toward the highway.

"Surveillance will need to be maintained at all points from the highway to the creek." He waved. "We're here to trap this kidnapper at this end of the trail. We can't let this guy slip past us. Got it?"

A long moment of silence followed. Hogan may have outranked a couple of the other deputies, but no one had put him in charge. Finally, Deputy Tarrazo grunted assent and the newest recruit chirped, "Yes, sir!"

Hogan waved at Tarrazo and the recruit. "Okay, then, you two stay here at the highway. Patrol this area. Make sure the abductor doesn't get past you." Gesturing to the fourth deputy, he said, "You're with me." The two of them loaded into their SUV and Hogan slipped it into gear. The vehicle crept ahead, dust billowing even in its slow wake.

They made it to the first cabin, pulled over and parked. Driving this road was slower than walking. At least they were now in sight of a couple of the cabins, and according to Greg's directions, the other cabins were no more than a half mile or so ahead. They stood near the porch of the first cabin.

"Okay!" Hogan said. "We're going to deploy around these two cabins. Search for signs of a break-in or another way to get inside. Make sure this kidnapper has not made entry. Meet me back here in fifteen!"

Heavy shoes clumped across wooden decks, door knobs were tried, window shutters rattled and pulled. Both cabins were locked securely, although without breaking in themselves, there was no way to tell if the kidnapper might be hiding inside. They left their vehicle and walked to the next set of cabins. All appeared secure there as well.

"Okay!" Hogan said. "No signs of a break-in here. Let's head out, see if we can get across that creek." They scanned the forest around them.

"If he's headed here, he could still slip in behind us," said Hogan's companion. "He could take up a position here in one of these cabins. Shouldn't someone stay here to prevent that?"

"Yeah, fine," Hogan said. "Good idea. You stay here, then. Wait for my call to come ahead." His tone dripped annoyance. "The fewer guns blazing when we locate the kidnapper, the better."

Hogan was trying for sarcasm, but the other deputy nodded solemnly. An argument could certainly be made that the fewer armed officers at a confrontation with a dangerous kidnapper, the better. Even now, the afternoon sun waned, and no one wanted to be in the middle of a shootout with multiple officers in the unfamiliar terrain of a forest after dark.

They hiked back to the SUV, and Hogan divided up snacks and water bottles from their emergency kits. He radioed the sheriff's dispatch office and explained the situation. He requested takeout dinners for the four deputies. This was beginning to look like it would be an all-night stakeout.

Nineteen
Hanging From a Tree

Kris and Bullet were making good progress in searching their section of the ridge top. Sunlight had already dimmed, so Andy decided to take Rose directly to the pass, hoping to pick up the baby's track there.

Flag pulled Jody forward as the handler's gaze darted ahead through the trees. She gave Flag's lead some slack and watched the dog's response. Keeping a dog on lead while at the same time letting the dog have the freedom to decide the direction of travel was a fine art. Jody began working her way back and forth under the overhanging branches, gently encouraging Flag to scent the air and explore a wider area. Flag pulled anxiously forward, excitement evident in her behavior. Clearly she smelled something or someone ahead. Jody considered again taking the dog off her lead and allowing her to go directly to the scent, but every mission was different. This one seemed a little too scary to chance that. She'd risk her own safety, but not Flag's.

Methodically, both air-scenting teams worked across their respective parts of the grid. Bullet stopped and pointed again, alerting Kris to the presence or recent passing of someone in their search section. Kris stopped her dog and conducted a long survey of the area visible around her, peering along tree trunks and even up into the foliage overhead. Her lips tightened, fear of confronting the kidnapper written on her face. Bullet continued to point, trembling now with excitement. The dog appeared to be convinced that at least one human still lingered somewhere on the ridge. Kris allowed her dog to creep slowly forward.

Flag alerted more and more strongly as she followed the scent into the forest, holding her tail high. Her throat quivered with a soft whine. She glanced back at Jody, and her tail began a slow swing. Jody wondered if Flag understood that her handler could not smell what she was scenting on. Or was air-scenting just a game to Flag, where her handler pretended not to be able to follow a scent?

It was approaching six when Flag yelped excitedly and began waving her tail, almost as though greeting a favorite friend. Jody found Flag's behavior baffling. She peered ahead, trying to see what the dog could so clearly scent. A few more crunching steps across the forest floor, another pause to scan forward, and she saw it. A dark object. Might even be a body, hung sideways in the branches of a large cedar about thirty feet ahead. Hanging eight or so feet off the ground, the object swayed slightly, but the shadows were too deep for much light to catch it. Jody stopped, watching. Flag only wagged harder, dancing at the end of her lead.

Cadaver dogs search for dead bodies and even long-dead human remains, but Flag wasn't one of those. She would not be alerting to a body, especially not with a wagging tail. Looking at the object, Jody was inclined to be afraid, and she pulled out her radio, intending to call for back-up. Flag's behavior stopped her. The dog exhibited no concern. Her ears were dropped and when she turned, she showed Jody a big grin. Her whole body trembled with happy excitement. Jody trusted her dog's behavior and signals more than her own instincts. She moved closer until they were almost under the object. From there she could see the rope looped over the branch and wrapped around the trunk of the tree, securing the dark canvas bag in position. No stray body parts were hanging out of the bundle, and it wasn't dripping blood.

Flag scratched at the base of the tree. Jody moved the duff there around with her boot and uncovered the empty wrappers of several Slim Jims and string cheese. No wonder Flag had alerted.

She loosened the dog's lead and pulled out her radio. She got a message through to Kris to come back her way, then keyed in the frequency for the base radio and asked Frank to send out Cardona. Flag may have been alerting only to the scent of cured meat, but if the bag had some relationship to the kidnapping, Flag had successfully, if accidentally, located what might be important evidence.

***

Agent Cardona had grown tired of searching the ground fruitlessly for evidence, and her Ferragamo flats were not up to the task of tramping through the forest. Already, there looked to be a scuff mark on one. She returned to the command base where she found Frank fiddling with the connections on the radio. The update she'd received from her colleagues in Sacramento revealed disturbing new information, and she wanted to relay that to the searchers as soon as possible.

"Frank, can you get your team leader on the radio? I've got an update on that kidnapper, and some other information. You might even want to pull them in. This guy is more dangerous than we thought."

"Sure," he said. He began turning dials and flipping switches, but even after several minutes, wasn't having much luck.

"Oh, hang on," Cardona said. "I've got a good cell signal here. What's her number? I'll just call her myself."

Frank pulled out Jody's incomplete emergency contact form and recited her phone number. Cardona listened to Jody's phone ring four times, then the call went to voice mail. "Well, shoot. She must have it switched off. Go ahead and get her on the radio."

Just then, the radio fired up and Jody's call came through. She explained about the bag hanging in the tree, giving Flag credit for the find. The canine search teams were out to find the lost target, not process evidence in the kidnapping. Jody wanted the FBI to handle that part. Cardona agreed. She returned to the trunk of her car, where she exchanged her flats for studier oxfords, and retrieved the black bag containing her evidence kit. She walked to where Jody had disappeared under the trees, and stopped.

She turned to look back at Frank. "There's no trail here," she called. "Where do I go?"

As Frank came up beside her, a sharp whistle sounded in the distance. "Hear that?" Frank said. "That's your locator. Follow the sound of that whistle." Looking doubtful, Cardona stepped warily forward and was soon lost to sight among the trees.

Twenty
Evidence

Within twenty minutes, orienting by the short blasts Jody blew on a whistle, Agent Cardona and Kris had joined her. The three women and two drooling dogs gazed at the swinging duffel bag. Cardona snapped a series of photographs, including several focused on the well-executed clove hitch knot looped around the trunk of the tree that secured the bag in position.

"You know," she said, "if this bag does belong to the kidnapper, and he hung it himself, he may have more outdoor skills than we know about."

Embarrassed to admit her dog had been drawn by the scent of food, Jody pointed out the wrappers at the base of the tree. "We found these right here. The kidnapper may have stayed here, at least for a while. Or else someone other than the kidnapper got into the bag and helped themselves. If that happened, that knot that's there now wouldn't have been tied by the kidnapper."

"True. Prints on those wrappers could help us determine if someone else got into the bag, or the kidnapper just had a snack before hanging it."

Cardona went to the base of the tree and snapped more photos, walking slowly around the trunk, then stopped. From behind the tree she said, "Hello. There's something else here." Stuffed into a branch fork at about eye level was the plastic wad of a used diaper. "Guy must have stayed here a while."

Kris lifted her eyebrows. "If this kidnapper left a trail of used diapers, he might be easier to track than your usual target, right?"

Cardona spread a plastic garbage bag on the ground beneath the duffel and tore open another bag containing latex gloves. She tugged them on and scraped sections of the rope with a multi-purpose knife, letting the loosened threads fall into the evidence bags. Only after she had collected every kind of evidence imaginable did she begin to loosen the rope and allow the canvas duffel to drop to the ground. Flag stared happily at it, waiting for Jody to give permission to explore inside. Gingerly, Cardona undid the clasps and folded open the bag, trying her best not to lean over and deposit trace evidence of her own inside. In a neat package at the top of the duffel sat several plastic bags of string cheese, which had probably been unrefrigerated for at least several hours, and more Slim Jims. Even to Jody's inferior scenting ability, the odor was intense. Flag had definitely alerted to the food smell and not a human target.

The duffel also contained a jar of peanut butter, a sealed box of protein bars, bags of nuts and dried fruit, and an economy-sized bag of toddler diapers. Little shirts, pants, socks, and a jacket filled the remainder of the space in the duffel. These had to be the kidnapper's supplies. The only perishable item in the bag was the string cheese.

They stepped back and discussed the ethics of removing what were clearly supplies for the kidnapper and his victim.

"We should leave the stuff here," Kris said, "and let the kidnapper come to us when he returns for his stuff, right?"

"That is a plan," Jody agreed, "but if he wants his supplies, he's going to come whether they're here or not. He's not going to know we found them and removed them. This bag is evidence, plus it's distracting to the dogs."

"Look, no offense," Cardona said, "but you folks are not trained in law enforcement or investigation. You're in over your heads here. I'm taking this bag back to base, and I want you to come with me. I'm requesting an FBI SWAT team. They can get here overnight, be ready to go at dawn." She pulled the large plastic garbage bag around the duffel and tied it off, pointedly ignoring Jody's scowl.

Jody tried to decide if an FBI evidence recovery technician outranked a senior canine handler in the matter of a search. Flag's successful location of food wrappers only intensified Jody's desire to find the kidnap victim and prove that she and her dog could provide critically important skills in a search of this nature. If they could find the child before the FBI arrived, before they trampled the track to oblivion, that would be the best outcome.

Kris's thoughts were off in a different direction. "Yes, but that's all stuff the guy's going to need to take care of the baby, isn't it? Should you really take it?"

Kris had a point. No one wanted the baby to suffer. The duffel might be evidence in a kidnapping, but more important to Kris, it also contained items the father would need to take care of his baby. Cardona came up with an argument that placated her. "If I take the supplies now, when we find the baby we'll have what we need to make him comfortable until we can get him back to civilization."

Jody could hear the skepticism in Cardona's voice, and knew the agent had doubts the kidnapped baby would be in need of anything by the time the searchers found him. She also appreciated the agent not mentioning her doubts to those who were so selflessly searching.

Jody had another thought. "At the very least," she said, "this bag is evidence that the kidnapper came out this way. I mean, it's evidence he didn't have someone pick him up and drive away."

"Also," Kris added, "this bag being here is probably why Rose couldn't track the baby or the kidnapper on the trail, you know? They didn't walk on the trail. They came under these trees, possibly stayed here a while, and stashed the supplies out of sight of the parking lot and trail, right?"

"Are your dogs scenting the kidnapper near this bag?" Cardona asked, scrutinizing the spaces between the tree trunks around them.

Jody wasn't sure how to answer. Flag had definitely alerted, but her alert to food overwhelmed any signs she might also be scenting the presence of the target or other humans. "Not sure," she said. "This bag distracted her." She made eye contact with Cardona. "We're going to keep searching."

Cardona nodded, but furrows creased her brow and she didn't move. "Listen," she said, "I think you should pull out and let law enforcement handle this kidnapping situation."

Kris scowled. "Why should we quit? We'll probably find the baby before the FBI even gets here, and with all the law enforcement guys at the other end of the trail, no one will get shot accidentally in the process, right Jody?"

Cardona sighed, then extracted a slip of paper from a jacket pocket. "Okay. You know the guy we're looking for is Matthew Tolliver. Thirty-four years old, no record, no arrests. Wife's name was Cecily. She was the baby's mother. Found dead in a storage garage the same day the baby was kidnapped." Cardona gave them a stern look and continued. "Matthew is the baby's biological father. The baby's name is Jayden, aged twenty-three months. Cecily and Matthew were recently divorced, final decree granted last September. Court initially awarded joint custody of Jayden to both parents. Then last month the mother got full custody after filing a petition for enforcement."

"What does that mean?" Kris asked.

"I'm not sure," Cardona said. She turned the paper over, squinting in the dim light under the trees to make out the tiny pencilled writing. "I think it might have something to do with Matthew not bringing Jayden home on time after several visits. Here's the rest of what I know." She read again. "Tolliver is an assistant accounting clerk with a state agency. Owing to his not having any record or arrests, we don't know much about him. Born and raised in Sacramento. One thing we do know ... " Here she looked up and made eye contact with each of them. "Tolliver owns a handgun. A nine-millimeter semiautomatic Ruger. Our agents have searched his apartment, and the gun is not there. Until that gun is found somewhere else, we are going to have to assume Tolliver has the gun with him."

"A handgun," Kris said. She surveyed the surrounding forest. "How much of a range does a handgun have?"

"Oh," Cardona said, "it has range. Plenty of range."

Kris nodded solemnly but didn't say anything.

"Also, and I don't think I need to repeat this, the baby's mother was found dead in her car. She'd been bound and gagged with duct tape. This Tolliver guy may have no criminal record, but clearly he's gone over the edge. He may even have had a psychotic break. You really want to be out here in the forest with him? And with night coming on?"

From the looks on their faces, everything Cardona said only strengthened Jody and Kris's resolve to find the baby. If Tolliver had become a killer, the baby wasn't safe with him either. They had to rescue Jayden, or at least narrow down his location.

Cardona could see that arguing was likely a lost cause, but she couldn't give up yet. "So anyway, that's why it would be best if you people and your dogs pull out. At least wait until the SWAT team can get here and do a sweep of this area. Come on back to camp until this kidnapping situation has been resolved. You've found evidence the kidnapper is almost certainly out here, so that is extremely helpful. But the SWAT team, they're specialists in kidnapper apprehension and victim recovery. Those guys are trained to find and neutralize bad guys. Once they get the kidnapper, if the baby is still missing, well, then by all means we can get you and your dogs back out to find him."

At her mention of the dogs, Jody and Kris each began absent-mindedly ruffling the fur on the animals' necks. Concern for the life of the lost baby overshadowed any anxiety the handlers felt for their own safety, but neither was willing to endanger her dog.

"Where is Jayden's grandmother?" Kris asked. "Is she at the command post yet?"

Cardona pursed her lips. "Not yet. There's no family there."

"I just don't understand why that baby's grandmother isn't here," Kris said. "This guy, the father, kidnaps Jayden from her, kills the baby's mother, and the grandmother's not even here? It doesn't make any sense. Doesn't anybody but us care about this baby?" Kris shook her head. "Okay, well, I guess we'd better get busy and find him then, right?"

She looked at Jody. "If there was a guy with a gun up here on the ridge, one of us would have gotten an alert from the dogs by now, right? I mean, Bullet is alerting to some scent, but we've covered our whole area and no one is present now. And there's not a lot of daylight left anyway, so probably we should finish the search up here, okay?" She turned to Cardona. "Thanks for the information. Why don't you give us a few minutes to talk about this situation? And we'll see you back in camp one way or another, okay?"

The FBI agent shrugged. "I can't force you to leave. I am strongly advising that you come back to camp now." She hoisted the bag over her shoulder.

Jody could see that, bagged in plastic, the duffel was heavy and slippery. "You need some help with that?" she offered. She would be the last one to give up the search early, but had misgivings about asking Kris and Bullet to join her in what might prove to be a life-threatening situation. She could send them back with the excuse of helping Cardona, although the agent looked like she was doing okay with the heavy bag.

"Nope, I got it," Cardona said, marching off between trees. Kris and Jody watched her go.

"I hope she knows where she's going," Jody said, thinking about all those search missions where the target had been sure they knew exactly where they were going.

"Did she leave a trail of breadcrumbs?" Kris said in a weak attempt to lighten the mood.

Jody watched where Cardona passed from sight. "I sure hope we don't end up having to mount a search for her in a couple of hours."

Twenty One
Hidden

All day, the fire had been creeping along the floor of the small canyon. A gentle wind had pulled it up the eastern flank, but the sheer granite and lack of fuel there impeded its growth. Just before the breeze began to die down in the late afternoon, the fire caught a shift in wind direction. It crawled through the top layer of forest duff and ignited a few fallen pine needles draped over a twelve-inch high bed of mountain misery. The resin-rich plant exploded into brilliant white flames, sending dark clouds of smoke into the branches of the pines above. The patch of vegetation was small, and the fire's burst short-lived. It dropped down into the duff again and resumed its slow crawl toward something else to burn.

***

From his perch at the edge of the creek, Ted watched the smoke. Rocket-propelled grenades made that kind of thin stream of smoke when they landed on a fuel-rich target. Ted pulled his body behind a rock, keeping his eyes on the spot where the grenade had landed, watching for figures in camouflage to come crawling out of the devastation.

***

Flag gazed at the duffel bag filled with treats as it disappeared through the trees on Cardona's back. Jody filled Flag's folding bowl with kibble and put it a few feet away. Kris did the same for Bullet and the dogs tucked into a noisy crunching. The women watched the dogs eating, and Jody felt her own hunger pangs. She wondered, not for the first time, why Purina didn't make human chow. Kris rummaged in her pack and broke out a selection of protein bars.

Jody rolled out the map and they squatted on the ground to plan the next phase of their effort. Cardona's words of warning had heightened their anxiety, and Jody had every intention of finding a good reason for Kris and Bullet to leave the ridge and go back to camp. She hadn't counted on Kris's resolve to find the baby.

"Bullet's been scenting toward the ridge line along here, you know?" Kris pointed. "We can go back where we were when you radioed. My guess, though, is whatever scent Bullet is onto is pooling on top of the ridge from down in the canyon around Turtle Creek, or else blowing directly across the canyon, you know? Another half hour or so, when the sun gets lower and the air cools, that scent is going to drop back into the canyon and we'll lose it. My best guess? That baby is somewhere down in that canyon." She tapped the map. "At least, that's what I think."

Jody was all for continuing the search. She would keep going in any case, but she had misgivings about encouraging Kris to persist in a search that might turn dangerous.

"So, what do you want to do?"

"Well, Bullet and I could continue to the pass, over here?" Kris pointed at the map again. "We'll meet Andy and Rose there. If there's enough light left, and the dogs are still telling us the baby passed through there, we can follow the trail down to the creek." They bent close to see the elevation lines crowded closely together, indicating a steep drop off to the creek below.

"The slope along that side of the ridge is treacherous," Jody said, "and the trail makes several switchbacks. It'll be dark, or close to it, by the time you get to the bottom."

"Probably. You want to follow us in? Or what are you thinking?"

"I'm just wondering if we shouldn't finish the search up here, establish a clear target location, you know, someplace where the dogs agree they've got the boy's scent, then use that as a starting place in the morning." Jody sat back. If it wasn't for the kidnapper, they would keep going on this mission until they found the baby, but she couldn't see dragging her team members into harm's way after dark. Not to mention, there still might be a fire somewhere out in the canyon.

Kris interrupted her thoughts. "If the dogs get on scent, you know they're going to want to go all night until they find him."

"I know, but I'm thinking about the guy who did the kidnapping. How dangerous is he? The agent said he might even have a gun." As she spoke, Jody felt her determination to continue the search increase, even in face of the risks.

"You think he's going to be less dangerous in the morning?" Kris's words were uncharacteristically brave. Sounded like her concern for the baby was beginning to overrule her naturally cautious nature.

"He might be. You know, another night out here with a hungry baby, and he might be ready to be found by then. He might even bring us the baby." Jody couldn't process any scenario where a father would intentionally allow his own child to go hungry.

Kris rolled onto her butt and they both considered the problem. The dogs had finished eating and were using the break to take a nap. Then Flag poked his nose into Bullet's face. Bullet rolled over and flopped a leg over Flag's shoulder, giving Flag a chance to gnaw gently on Bullet's paw, which set off a flurry of rolling in the duff, jaws agape, tails waving. Jody sprung up, trying to avoid the cloud of dust. Kris only laughed. The same two highly trained search dogs who had been working hard to find a lost child only a short time ago had turned into goofy puppy friends.

The handlers went back to discussing their options. "We can't let our search protocol be determined by our guesses about that guy's frame of mind, right, Jody? We've got a lost baby out here. We have to find him. I think we should go ahead, don't you?"

Jody nodded slowly. She thought she should go ahead. She wasn't so sure about the others.

Flag abruptly broke off her romp, rolled upright, and cocked one ear. She'd heard something. Jody listened, and she could hear it too. Someone creeping across the forest floor just out of sight behind the trees. One step, a snapping twig, another step.

Kris, busy stuffing food wrappers into her pack, did not notice the sounds. Jody wrapped her hand gently around Flag's muzzle before the dog could let loose with a volley of barking. She tried to get eyes on whoever was moving out there. She didn't want to alarm Kris. At the same time, they were on a search. They were supposed to be trying to find someone, but this someone was clearly not interested in being found.

"Uh, sure, we should go ahead. That's a good idea for you to meet Andy at the pass. Do you have what you need to be out all night, if it comes to that?" The sounds of movement had grown fainter, and Jody remembered to breathe again.

Still peering into her pack, Kris said, "I've got a space blanket, food, lights, all the usual stuff, but I'm not really thinking we'd be out there all night. How about this? Bullet and I will go to the pass and meet Andy. We'll go down as far as the ford at the creek. If we haven't gone on scent by then, we'll come right back up and head for camp."

Jody nodded. If the kidnapper was up here on the ridge and not anywhere near the pass, that would be the safest plan for her companions. And if Kris and Andy should run into anyone on the trail, two humans and two dogs sounded like enough of a crowd to be intimidating. Unless whoever they ran into started shooting. "What about the gun?" she asked.

Silence. "Well," Kris finally said, "that's something to think about. Honestly though, I'm more concerned about the baby. Anyway, didn't you say earlier you thought the kidnapper would head toward those cabins? Isn't that why the sheriff's deputies went over there?"

"Yes, that's true." Jody still struggled with feeling responsible for pulling others into what was turning out to be a dangerous mission. "Okay. I want Flag to give me a good read up here, to finish on this ridge, undistracted by food scents."

Jody squinted in the direction of the earlier sounds, and elected not to mention anything to Kris. Whoever or whatever had been moving over there, it wasn't their search target. Flag stood and gave a good shake, as she always did when readying herself to get serious about working. Jody stroked the dog's head, and Flag leaned against Jody's leg.

"Anyway," she reasoned, "someone left the bag of supplies, and it's not impossible they're still up here on the ridge. I want to check. When we're done here, we'll meet you at the pass, or on your way back up."

"And even if we get on scent at the creek," Kris said, "we'll return to camp tonight. That'll give us a place to start in the morning, right?"

"Right."

"Okay. I'll radio you if there's any change, okay?"

"Roger that," Jody said. Kris smiled at the small joke. Jody and Kris had picked up the expression from a favorite television crime drama.

Jody watched Kris and Bullet skirt a copse of thin tree trunks as they trudged away. The hair on the back of Jody's neck prickled and she could swear someone lurked behind her. She would rather the search teams stayed closer together on this mission, but she trusted Kris's instincts. When it came to finding a lost toddler in the woods, Kris and Bullet were the best team in the business, and the one Jody would want searching if she had a child who'd gotten lost.

She caught the pungent woodsy fragrance of mountain misery as Kris tromped through an unavoidable patch, following right behind Bullet. Mountain misery got its name from the way it entangled passing hikers, snarling in pants and socks. Except for taking high prancing steps, Bullet didn't seem to notice the plant.

Jody stood, rotating slowly, taking in the trees surrounding her on the forested ridge. Long and narrow, the ridge ran at least from Eagle Meadow almost all the way to the cabins at the lake's edge, a distance of several miles. A rock wall bordered its northern boundary, cut through in places to the steep canyon below. Kris was headed to one of those passes where the trail led between rocks.

As far as Jody could tell from the maps, the only ways off the ridge were back out to the meadow and parking lot, now filled with emergency responders, west to the cabins where the sheriff's deputies waited, or through that pass. Already, shadows grew longer as the sun dropped. Goosebumps rose on Jody's arms. She told herself it was the evening chill, and tugged a sweatshirt on before clicking the waist belt on her pack. She stood still, listening for any sounds of movement, even someone else breathing nearby in the rapidly darkening forest.

Twenty Two
Sunset

The approach of crunching footsteps startled Jayden awake. His first thought was a hope to see his mother peering over the rail of his crib. But it was Daddy who came into view. The boy shivered in the deep shade. Birds sang in the trees overhead. The loud sounds of the helicopter were gone. His pants drooped, wet again, and the red welts of his mosquito bites itched. He climbed to his feet and tried to follow Daddy to where he stood in the sun nearby.

"Oh, hey, little buddy." Daddy tousled Jayden's soft blond curls, but didn't pick him up. Jayden tried a whine and Daddy reached down to hoist the boy in his arms. Halfway up, Daddy changed his mind, and put him down.

"Geez, Jayden, you wet your pants again. I thought those pull-up things were supposed to last all day."

Jayden had no answer and didn't even understand Daddy's words. He whimpered.

"Look here, little buddy." Daddy took Jayden's hand and led him to the base of a prickly tree, turned him to face the tree and tugged off his soaking pants. "Can you pee here, Jayden?"

Jayden looked up, confused.

"See, here? Make your pee go right here on this tree. We'll make this our pee tree, okay?" Comprehension still eluded Jayden. He understood what it meant to pee, but had never considered the possibility he could exercise any kind of control over that. The pee came when it came.

"Look, Jayden. I'll show you." Daddy unzipped and let loose with an impressive torrent, splattering the base of the tree. Then it stopped. Jayden stared in amazement. "Now you do it."

Jayden looked at Daddy's wet spot and then at himself. Nothing happened. It was as if Daddy had made magic. But Daddy had made it. Jayden wanted to make magic happen too, only he didn't know how to make it start.

"All right, Jayden, maybe next time. I'll get you some dry pants. You stay right there." Daddy went over and rummaged in bags on the blanket, coming up with fresh pull-ups and stinky but dry pants from yesterday. He was halfway back when Jayden felt a strange tingling and a tiny arc of pee launched from him to the ground. Jayden was astonished, and for the first time, he focused on the physical sensation of peeing.

When the arc stopped, Daddy rushed at him and swung him high, laughing. "Way to go, Jayden! That's my boy!" Jayden found being thrown into the air frightening, but Daddy seemed to like it. Even though he rarely understood the connections between his own actions and Daddy's responses, he loved to make Daddy laugh. He might even try to pee on a tree again someday.

It wasn't until Daddy had removed Jayden's shoes that he noticed the baby's bleeding heels and the angry red rash around his legs. Two of the mosquito bites on his arm were broken open from frantic scratching, and blood oozed from those wounds, too. Daddy rocked back on his heels and looked at his son.

"Oh, Jay-bud, I'm not taking too good care of you, am I? I bet you're hungry, too. You're my boy now, and I've really got to step it up. I need to get you a place to stay and some real food."

Daddy finished putting on the dry clothes and led Jayden back to the blanket, where they indulged in a feast of graham crackers, peanut butter, the last handful of big purple grapes, and more juice boxes.

"That's it, Jayden. I need to go get our supplies and find us a sheltered place to sleep. This camping-in-the-woods thing isn't working out the way it did when I was a boy." He stood and looked up across the canyon to where the switchbacks ended and the trail cut through a pass. “Possibly we should even try to get back to the car and drive the heck out of here.” He shook his head. “I don’t know what we’d do after that, though. The cops are after that car.” He pulled out his wallet and ran a finger across the few hundred in cash tucked there. “I know we can’t use credit cards. I tossed my phone right after I heard that radio broadcast about your mother, so they can’t track us with that. You’re my boy now, though, and you belong to me. I went through a lot to get you, Jay-bud, and I’m not giving you back. Not to anyone.”

He re-packed the paper sack, folded the blanket, lifted Jayden into his arms and looked around. After a short search, he found a better oak tree nest than the one in the other canyon. This one had two branches forming a sort of platform about five feet off the ground. It wasn’t high enough, but anything higher and he’d have trouble getting Jayden into it. He put Jayden down, made a bed on the platform with the blanket, and stuffed the paper bag into a nearby fork of branches.

“Jay-bud, you’re going to wait for me again up here in this cool pirate ship tree.”

Jayden looked anxiously up at the blanket stuck in the tree. He didn’t want to go up there, and he didn’t want Daddy to go away. “No, Daddy,” he whimpered.

“Hey, Jay-bud! That’s the first thing you’re going to say to me is ‘No, Daddy’? It’ll be fun, Jayden. You’ll see. You need to wait quietly for Daddy. I’m going to go get our supplies, fresh diapers, clean clothes, and more food. You just wait here quietly, and be my good boy.”

One thing Jayden knew was that big people might ask him what he wanted, but they never listened. Things just happened to him, like peeing. Daddy lifted him high up, put him on the blanket, made him sit all the way down, and warned him what would happen if he moved. Jayden peered at the hard ground far below. Too scared to even wiggle, he stayed where he’d been put.

***

Behind the glass walls of the fire lookout, Charlie peered through binoculars at the place where he'd seen the smoke earlier in the day. The sun still threw shadows through the forest, but they were long and dimming as the rays dropped toward the western horizon. Even with a few of the windows opened, the air inside the glass-walled cab stayed calm. Outside and down, the flag on its pole fluffed out slightly toward the west. No longer warmed by the overhead sun, the air would move into the canyons and settle over the lake, taking any signs of smoke from a small fire with it to the ground. Charlie didn't see any smoke at all. That might mean the fire had gone out, if they were lucky.

Stepping closer to the glass, Charlie could also see the red and white helicopter parked at the edge of the lake. Earlier, two crew members had bustled about the machine, checking one thing and another. They had unpacked the heavy canvas Bambi bucket and left it nestled up to the copter. As far as Charlie knew, the helicopter had not dipped the bucket or carried any water to the fire. The crew appeared to be waiting for something.

A couple of hours before, a dust cloud had arisen along the jeep trail behind the cabins on the east shore of Lake Nell. Must've been several vehicles to stir up that much dust. Some big deal for the seldom-visited lake. Since then, he'd not seen any movement, and when he went down the stairs to his living quarters to make a turkey sandwich, he didn't see anything on the local news about any fire near here. It wasn't his job to police activity at those cabins. He hoped he wouldn't have to call it in if a bunch of rowdies had moved in for a party.

The setting sun sent a blaze of light across his forest from under an approaching thundercloud, and lit up the granite escarpment to the east. Charlie used the illumination to search the skies again for any signs of rising smoke. And again, he saw none. In the past, Charlie had seen the horrific consequences of a fire on the forest and on the animals who lived there. Even though this was likely to be the last smoke Charlie would ever have the opportunity to report, no one would be happier than he if this one burned itself out.

***

In the canyons, the sun had already set and darkness had settled. Farther up, on the granite of the high backcountry, the rays of late afternoon sun threw long shadows, highlighting crevices and irregularities in the rock face. The district's backcountry ranger laid the pieces of his radio around him and began to assemble the device. He laid the antenna wire across the rock, cranked the battery, and fiddled with a dial. Static, then a tone. Roxie had gone home for the day, so his report went directly to dispatch in the forest supervisor's office. Squinting into the setting sun, the ranger reported no sign of smoke in the previous location, or anywhere else in his field of view. He'd encountered four hikers in the area that day, all headed north on the Pacific Crest Trail and all carrying the required permits. He'd left two full bags of collected litter and garbage at the horse campsite on the western ridge. A rider from Aspen Meadows pack station would pick those up in the morning. No sign of a guy with a baby today. Tomorrow, he reported, he would head for the eastern flank of his territory and hoped to meet up with another ranger from the adjacent district. That was it. Nothing more to report. Over and out.

Twenty Three
Woo-woo-woo

Crashing across the last batch of mountain misery, Kris came within sight of the pass through the granite. Andy already waited there, lying on his back against a warm rock. Rose came partway toward them, wagging her tail. Then she demonstrated that she'd located the scent of the little boy by touching her nose to the ground, then lifting her snout. *Woo-woo-woo!*

She focused on one spot. Possibly, Kris thought, Rose had only found the baby's scent on that one place. She never veered far from the pass in any direction. Kris, Andy, and Bullet watched Rose stop and look at them, then call again. *Woo-woo-woo!*

"So the baby was here?" Kris said.

"Yeah, well, here, but only here. Rose can't catch the scent any place else."

"Not even over here," Kris pointed, "off the trail, along the ridge top? Flag found a bag of the kidnapper's supplies and Jody thinks they were off the trail."

"Makes sense," Andy said. "Either that, or the guy carried the baby most of the time, and put him down right here." He pointed at a wad wrapped in plastic stuffed between two rocks. "Put him down and changed a diaper."

"Oh, ick, not another one. Where do these people think a dirty diaper is going to go when they leave it? Do they think it just disappears or something?"

"Keep in mind, this guy is a kidnapper," Andy said. "The ecological issues surrounding the proper disposal of diapers are probably not uppermost in his mind."

Kris went to stand at the pass, looking out over the canyon. Bullet leaned against her knee, his nose lifted to the chilling evening air. Although the falls were out of sight, the sun blazed against the granite where Turtle Creek fell into the canyon. The creek tumbled below them, eventually disappearing to the west on its way to Lake Nell, running fast and icy with snow-melt. A faint haze floated in the air to the east, but Kris could see no plume of smoke or anything that might suggest a fire. If Bullet could smell it, he gave no indication.

"So, you think the guy picked the baby up again and went on down the trail here?"

"If he's not up here on the ridge, and he's not back at the trailhead, that's what he had to do. If Flag or Bullet didn't get a scent on the ridge top, he must be down there somewhere. At least with finding this diaper here, we know he didn't have someone else pick him up in another car."

"Also," Kris said, "we know the baby was alive at this point."

"Yeah, that, too."

Andy joined her and they both looked silently at the canyon. "And," Andy pointed out, "if he went down to the creek, there's no way to stay on this side because the slope is too steep. You don't need a dog to tell you that. He had to have crossed the creek there at the ford." From where they stood, a shallow stretch was visible where the creek spilled over a patch of gravel. "And here's what I don't get."

"What's that?" Kris asked.

"We're supposed to be searching for a guy who got lost, but how could anyone get lost on this trail? Even when you're down there along the creek, it's perfectly obvious how to get back to where you started. Are we looking for a lost person, or who exactly is this guy?"

"Jody says we're looking for the baby. He's lost. The kidnapper is the sheriff's problem, right?"

"Even though the two of them are presumed to be traveling together?"

"We don't know for sure they are still together. From here, you think the baby went down this trail to the creek, right? So then where?"

Andy held Kris's gaze for a moment too long, uncertainty clouding both their faces. They turned and looked at the trail again.

"Yeah, that's the question," Andy said. "Once they got to the creek, where did they go from there? That's where you need a trailing dog. That's where Rose and I start in the morning."

"So you're not going down there now?"

"It's going to be completely dark in another hour, Kris. I know ordinarily we'd go ahead with the search after dark. I mean, the boy is still out there, but so is the kidnapper. And there's this dangerous trail to contend with, too."

"Oh, forgot to tell you. Cardona found out the guy owns a gun. Doesn't mean he has it with him, but the FBI didn't find it in his apartment, so she said it's prudent to assume he does have the gun with him."

"A father kidnaps his own baby at gunpoint?" Andy said. "What's next?"

They looked into the canyon again.

"So, what else?" Kris asked. "Other than the diaper, did you learn anything else, or find anything?"

Andy pointed to an empty plastic water bottle zipped into a clear bag. "Found this discarded at the side of the trail. I even took a few pictures of it, and I used my pocketknife to pick it up so I wouldn't disturb any fingerprints." They were all learning more about crime investigation than they'd ever hoped to need to know. "Other than that, nope," said Andy. And then he added, "Well, except that fire manager woman. A tall blonde? She was here when I got here, looking for that fire someone reported."

"Did she see anything?"

"No, she said she couldn't see any smoke. Said she'd gone halfway down to the creek and still couldn't see anything. She did say she'd be back at dawn to check again. Possibly even hike down there in the morning. She headed back just after Rose and I got here."

Kris glanced at Bullet, who pulled gently on the lead, clearly scenting the passage of a human on the trail. He may have caught the scent of the fire manager's earlier passage, or possibly smelled someone else not far away.

"So, are you going back now?" Kris asked Andy.

"Yeah, I think so. Like you said, seems like law enforcement should be out ahead of us on this one. It's obvious the kidnapper came through here, and the baby, too, so from here to the creek, Rose would track, but it'd be dark by the time we got to the creek and we're not crossing that in the dark." The hair on Kris's neck prickled as Andy's gaze shot around them. Andy wasn't known for his willingness to tackle dangerous situations. In this case, his reaction seemed appropriate. Kris nodded. Bullet pulled ahead more insistently.

"I think Bullet and I will go on down as far as the creek. Bullet is telling me there's someone ahead on the trail, and I want to give it all the daylight we can. We've got enough light to make it down and headlamps and light sticks for the hike up and into camp on this flat part of the trail. The kidnapper might even have fallen or left the baby on this side of the creek, and we could find him before it gets dark, right?" Bullet chose that moment to lift his front paw, pushing his snout into the air. "See?" Kris said, "Bullet is scenting something not too far away. Anyway, like you said, if we don't find anything, we'll know exactly where to start in the morning."

"Are you sure? I don't like the idea of you being out there by yourself."

Kris smiled. "I'm never by myself, Andy. I've got Bullet." She hitched her pack higher, and pulled out her radio. She connected with Frank and in a couple of sentences, outlined her plan. She also asked Frank to relay a message to her husband, Lowell, that she and Bullet were onsite, fine, and hopeful for a happy outcome. With the daylight fading fast, she wanted to avoid getting caught up in a lengthy conversation.

She dug Bullet's long lead out and traded it for the short one, gathering up the slack in one hand. The two of them started down the crumbling granite on the steep slope.

"All right. You want me to wait here for you?"

"No, no. We'll go down and come right back up, you know? Anyway, Jody's right behind me."

"All right, but if you guys don't get into camp an hour after I do, we're coming back out for you."

***

The helicopter crew sat on rocks along the sandy shore of Lake Nell, dining with little enthusiasm on pre-packaged rations and crackers, the beauty of their surroundings largely lost on them.

The water in the lake, framed by thick forests of dark pines, shifted to a deep indigo as the sun drew closer to the horizon. Silhouetted in black, three loons flew low over the water. Miniature waves set off by an almost imperceptible breeze across the lake's surface lapped gently onto the decomposed granite beach.

The setting sun dropped below a high and threatening cloud deck. Sunlight warmed the faces of the crew, and glinted on the granite outcroppings at the north end of the lake. Those clouds would settle lower along with the falling air pressure during the night, and a westerly wind might begin to blow. The clouds could bring rain, but they could also bring lightning strikes and new fires. And the wind might blow life into the abandoned campfire.

Although they had all the necessary equipment on board, the crew hadn't planned on spending the night on the beach. District Ranger Russell had other ideas. Concerned that the small fire back in the canyon might blow up at or near dawn, he wanted the helicopter with its water bucket nearby. Water drops wouldn't be made after dark, but in the early morning the sun-warmed air moving upward through the canyons might ignite even the smallest lingering embers into flames.

Still over an hour before complete darkness descended over the lake, the crew extracted tarps and sleeping bags from the cargo hold and spread them near the struts on the leeward side of the copter. Each pulled out a cell phone and discovered they had several bars. Their cell signals were pinging off of the fire lookout tower across the lake. They settled in to entertain themselves reading email and playing internet games.

Twenty Four
Lying in Wait

The pain had been radiating along Charlie's left side and up into his arm for most of the afternoon. It felt like when he was a kid and his dad would grip his arm so hard the blood would stop flowing. His hand would tingle when he was finally released. In fact, he realized, he felt a kind of tingle in his hand at that moment. After his late lunch, the thought of making the return climb to the cab had filled him with dread. He didn't want to be halfway up when his heart finally gave out. If that happened he would fall to the ground and spend his last few moments lying among the rocks and dirt. His body might not be found until the critters had ravaged and scattered his bones.

He'd made himself a second hearty turkey sandwich on crunchy whole grain bread. And not those wimpy slices of turkey in plastic packages from the supermarket either. He liked the big hunks he got at the deli counter in the market in Groveland. And this time, he'd added a thick slice of jellied cranberry sauce, like they did at the restaurant in town. The sandwich would be his dinner, if he decided to spend the night at the top of the lookout tower. He took the climb very slowly, stopping to rest every few steps. At one point, the thought of eating that thick turkey sandwich was all that kept him going.

Only the faintest rays of light remained by the time he dropped into his comfortable chair in the glass-walled cab. His binoculars rested on a small table alongside a glass containing two fingers of Jack Daniels. He set the waxed-paper-wrapped sandwich on the edge of the table, and cradled the glass with one hand, sipping. Tucking the plaid wool throw around his lap, he remembered how his wife bought the blanket for him as a birthday present when they made that trip to Maine one year.

Keeping it hidden was challenging as they packed and unpacked the rental car at every overnight stop. And, truth be told, he had spotted it once, but he kept her secret until he unwrapped the blanket at his birthday dinner a few months later, and he managed to be surprised and happy all over again.

He took another sip of the bourbon, a big bite of sandwich, and sighed. This was the life. When he bit the dust, this was the way he'd like to be found. Nothing could be better. Wait, he remembered ... didn't he have ... ? He set the glass down and struggled out of the chair. Rummaging through several drawers in cabinets lining the wall, he found it. A fat Havana cigar. Stashed in that drawer for so long, it was probably too stale to smoke. He sat, pulled the throw over his lap again, lit the cigar, and took a long drag. Only slightly stale. He took another sip of bourbon, another bite of sandwich, and, after he'd chewed and swallowed, another drag on the cigar. He sighed and looked out over the austere green and gray landscape of his domain. Might be, he'd take a short nap. He silenced the ringer on his phone. Wouldn't hurt to have it off for a few minutes. Yes, this was definitely the life.

***

Less than a mile south along the lakeshore and on the other side of Turtle Creek, the sheriff's deputies searching the cabins had decided to split up. There was no direct line of sight among the cabins, and although none of them showed any signs of having been broken into, the kidnapper could still show up at any moment and take a stand in one of them. Or possibly, he was hiding in the surrounding forest, or out on the trail, still trying to get across the creek to the highway.

Hogan hitched up his pants and gave an exasperated sigh. He had imagined himself the hero, but standing around the cabins in the dark was neither getting the kidnapper caught, nor saving the victim. And while they all cooled their heels, someone else might find the lost kid.

Like the other officers gathered there, he knew kidnappings were the jurisdiction of the FBI. And like everyone else, he expected to see an FBI Special Weapons and Tactics team appear at any moment to take over the search. But under mutual assistance protocols, the county sheriff's deputies were in charge until the SWAT team arrived on scene. Hogan wasn't the only deputy hoping they would find the abductor and rescue his victim before that happened.

Although Hogan did not outrank the others, he told himself his natural leadership ability would compel them to follow his direction. When it came time to decide who would maintain a lookout on the jeep track and who would move to a forward position and presumably be the first to engage the kidnapper, Hogan made sure he was the one at the forefront.

He and his partner would move ahead to the creek. Each of them took large Mag flashlights from the SUVs. Deputy Tarrazo and his partner stayed with the vehicle parked at the highway. If backup arrived, they could watch the cabins. No one had adequately prepared for an overnight stakeout in the forest. Darkness began to envelop the shadows under the trees and around the cabins.

Hogan put off his departure as long as he dared, still hoping the dinner he'd requested from dispatch would arrive. Meanwhile, the sun kept dropping. Finally they could wait no longer. Hogan and his partner started out bushwhacking through the underbrush toward Turtle Creek. It quickly became apparent that veering to the lakeshore, and then making their way along the decomposed granite of the beach might be a faster way to go. That increased the possibility the kidnapper could circle around behind them, but he might slip past in the dark anyway, so they took the chance.

Twenty minutes later, they found themselves at the wide delta where the creek fed Lake Nell. The water rushing into the lake, cold and deep, made any crossing on foot impossible. Even if they could swim across, their thick leather black oxfords, which were not made for hiking in the woods or swimming across lakes, would be destroyed and the heavy equipment on their belts would be immersed as well. The creek water had been icy snow only hours before, and the broken rock of the shore would cut tender bare feet to hamburger in only a short hike, even if they could wade through that flow. Clearly they were not getting across Turtle Creek there.

Hogan's companion grunted. "That kidnapper's got plenty of room to circle around behind us now. He's probably already escaped." They both peered into the darkness.

"The other deputies would have radioed if they'd seen him," Hogan argued.

"Well, I guess we should stay here on this side of the creek then, and watch for the guy to try to cross."

Hogan remained convinced the kidnapper had not gotten behind them, nor was he interested in any approach that involved waiting. They agreed to separate, each keeping watch over as long a section of the creek as could be managed.

"I'm hiking along this south side of the creek, heading east," Hogan told his companion. "I'll look for a way to cross the creek and radio if I find one."

Taking comfort in the heavy duty flashlight at his side, the loaded gun resting in its holster, and his fully charged taser, Hogan moved inland over boulders along the bank until he could no longer see the signal from the other deputy's flashlight. He hunkered among the roots at the base of a large tree and scanned his territory, noting potential places a kidnapper might be hiding under the rapidly lowering shadows. Sure, the kidnapper was also the baby's father, but in Hogan's view, anyone who would steal a baby would be ruthless. And besides, the kidnapper had also probably been the one who'd murdered the mother. That guy might leap out at any moment, guns blazing. Hogan caressed his own firearm, and unsnapped the retention strap, ready for action.

***

A lone sheriff's department sedan cruised Highway N301, searching for the correct turnoff at the Lake Nell dam. A pile of fragrant takeout burgers, fries, and onion rings rested on the passenger seat in foam boxes and plastic bags. They had cooled and congealed to the point where the scent no longer enticed, and still the deputy could not find the turnoff. He'd taken one dirt road where a small sign pointed to "Lake Nell" and driven a couple of miles out that way. The road passed the dam on the right and then headed up a steep grade. He'd concluded that was the access road to the lookout tower on the west side of the lake, and not where he needed to be.

With some difficulty, he got turned around and drove back down to the highway. As the last of the sun's light faded, he pulled over just across the bridge where the highway dropped into the canyon below the spillway and consulted his map again. Concluding he must have missed the turnoff, he rolled onto the highway and headed back the way he had come.

Twenty Five
"Find!"

Jody dumped the last of the water from Flag's folding dish, dusted off the dog's search vest, and watched as Flag engaged in a long shake, preparing to work. As the sounds of Kris and Bullet crashing through the underbrush faded, Jody listened for other movement nearby. All she heard was silence. In a forest alive with dozens of small creatures, silence could only mean one thing. A dangerous predator lurked too close.

"Find," Jody said softly, urging her dog in the direction where she had earlier heard the sounds of footsteps. Flag might have been confused by unfamiliar smells drifting around the ridge top, but Jody still had more faith in her dog's ability to smell the presence of a possibly dangerous intruder than in her own ability to hear one. They went back to work. She directed Flag outward in quarter-circles of increasing distance west from their location.

They had gone on in this way no more than fifteen minutes when Flag's tail went from down to half staff, giving a faint sign that she smelled someone unfamiliar. Jody stopped and looked in the direction Flag moved her head slowly back and forth, sniffing for the strongest direction of scent. Jody saw nothing, but also still heard nothing. She stopped all movement and listened. Again, nothing. They moved forward, Jody giving Flag more lead.

Intently focused, Jody took her gaze off the dog and peered between tree trunks, looking and listening for movement. Flag's sudden furious barking startled Jody and set her heart pounding. That was not an alert to scent. It was an alarm of danger. The dog jerked hard on the long leash, pulling Jody.

Quietly, she corrected Flag, but no amount of training could have eliminated Flag's panicked response.

Even above the sound of barking, Jody heard clearly the thudding and snapping of twigs made by footsteps running away. Someone had been there, watching them. Jody quickly rummaged in her pack, located the flashlight and aimed it toward the fading footfalls. Whoever had been there was out of sight.

Flag stopped barking, but stood still, at full alert. Caught in the flashlight beam was the corner of a stone hearth. Both Jody and Flag trembled with anxiety and fear. Flag came to lean against Jody's knee, and together they crept toward the structure. It was a fireplace with a lean-to of branches piled against it. The cabin that had once surrounded the fireplace was long disintegrated. Flag kept the feathers of her tail held high, and her snout pushed forward.

They stopped twenty feet from the hearth and waited, watching for movement. Flag's alert indicated a strong scent, but Jody couldn't see anyone hiding inside. If the person who had run away had been the object of Flag's alert, that person was already gone. The possibility remained that someone else might still be hiding nearby. Flag was not air-scenting for a particular individual, but for anyone nearby.

Jody watched to see which direction Flag's head would turn. Just like two ears provide the information needed to triangulate and determine the direction from which a sound comes, two nostrils help a dog locate the source of a scent.

After two full minutes of tense waiting, no sign from her dog, and seeing no movement at the hearth, Jody slid the taser from its pouch and put Flag in a down-stay. The dog had done her job, locating the unfamiliar human scent. Flag was not a police dog and not an attack dog. She stayed behind while her handler crept forward, a flashlight in one hand and the taser in the other.

Jody eased closer to the structure. Still not seeing anyone, she leaned over and peered behind the branches, into the recesses of the fireplace. Someone was definitely using this place to hole up. A ratty sleeping bag lay crumpled on a bed of drying weeds in the fireplace itself. A can of beans, its pull-top lid open, was half-hidden at the base of the hearth. An old plastic soda bottle held cloudy water. The bottle looked as though it had been used and reused for a long time.

Silently, Jody edged across the front of the structure, trying to see into every spot small enough to conceal a toddler, or detect any signs a baby was being kept there. Nothing indicated a baby had ever been there. Rose would be able to tell them, but Rose was off searching elsewhere. After pointing her flashlight into every dark corner, Jody satisfied herself that the makeshift home did not currently hide an occupant.

Between the sounds of movement she'd heard earlier and Flag's alert, it was clear someone had been there only a short time before, but they had gone. It could have been the kidnapper, but whoever it was, they were not behaving like a lost person.

Jody moved back to Flag and pulled out the topographical map, intending to mark the location of the hearth so it could be found in the future. The oncoming dusk and the shadows under the trees obscured the map. She pointed the flashlight and turned it on again.

Not six inches from her ear, Flag let loose with a loud bark, staring intently behind Jody. She whirled, pointing the light, and flushing in panic. A twig snapped somewhere just out of sight and Flag barked again, twice. The dog used her deep, threatening voice.

"Hello!" Jody called, trying her best to imitate Flag's intimidating tone. The light illuminated nothing, and only served to identify Jody's location to anyone watching. She flipped it off. No reply answered her call. The sound of her own heart hammered in Jody's ears. She needed to get out of there. Confronting a dangerous person was not part of her job, or Flag's job either. Rationalizing that the baby did not appear to be present, and they weren't interested in finding anyone else,

Jody stuffed the map into her pack, gathered Flag's leash, and strode away, heading east toward the pass. She willed herself not to run.

Imagining eyes staring at her from behind, she walked deliberately forward, giving no outward sign of the fear that gripped her. She refused to exhibit any weakness. Flag seemed as happy as Jody to get away, and she trotted ahead. The dog's calming demeanor gave Jody confidence. They headed toward the planned rendezvous with the other search teams. Each mission had its exciting moments, but not all of them kept this much adrenaline pumping for this long.

Flag held her tail at half-staff all the way, indicating she still had a scent on someone. Jody kept a suspicious eye out, but had no way of knowing if Flag's body language signaled the earlier presence of a kidnapper and baby, the recent passage of Kris and Bullet through this part of the forest, or the scent of someone unknown.

***

Even though he was a relative newcomer to the forest, not much happened close to Ted's stone home that he did not know about. He'd spotted that thing hanging in the tree the same morning that guy with the baby left the ridge top. Probably was a trap. Most likely the guy was a sentry, doing reconnaissance and setting traps. Ted wasn't going to fall for that.

He'd been concerned at first about the excitement in the parking lot and all the vehicles coming and going. Looked like a whole battalion of enemy soldiers preparing to settle in for a long encampment. When a couple of patrolling soldiers came closer to his home, he picked up the heavy stick he kept for self-defense. Running silently, he took off west along Eagle Ridge, away from the trail and the approaching patrol. They had dogs with them. Ted liked dogs and wished he'd had the opportunity to meet those dogs. He wouldn't mind having a dog himself. Someone for company, and also to help him sense and avoid the approach of the enemy. A dog might even help him hunt and catch a squirrel now and then. Ted wasn't sure how it might be accomplished, but he'd like to see if he could get one of those dogs to stay with him.

The enemy soldiers kept coming along the ridge top, so he headed down to the creek on a trail used only by himself and a few deer. He jumped and dragged himself over boulders to cross the swiftly moving stream at a narrow place where the beavers had dropped a tree between the rocks. He squatted on the deer grass behind two boulders to let his feet dry. He'd encountered no other enemy soldiers on this trip. He felt certain the dogs would not be able to follow his smell across the creek, and he was hidden from intruding enemy eyes by the granite rocks. He cradled his big stick close to his chest.

Twenty Six
A Thin Wail

Jayden awoke, still curled uncomfortably in the crook of the tree on his blanket-nest. He shifted position and pulled his arm out from under his body. He didn't have the energy to lift his head. His mosquito bites still itched, his face and neck were hot and achy with sunburn, and his pants were wet again. The rash started up a fiery stinging whenever he shifted, so he tried not to move much.

He thought about crying. Daddy had left again. Who would hear if he cried? He felt a lonely hole of emptiness when he thought about Momma and Gamma. Where were they? Why didn't they come get him? A fat round tear slid down his smudged cheek, followed by another and another.

He lifted his hand, thinking about putting those two fingers in his mouth for the comfort they always gave. He looked at the dirt collecting in the folds of skin and something gooey stuck on the end of one finger. That would not taste good. He put his hand down.

Struggling to a painful seated position, he pushed his feet out in front of him and regarded the drop from his nest to the hard earth below. He could see no way to get down except to turn backward, slide, and fall. The fall would be a long one. Fear stopped him.

Jayden had exhausted all his options. He felt sick and sleepy. He began a thin wailing, a faint signal sent out to an empty and unresponsive universe of big people.

***

From the start, Bullet showed interest in a scent as he and Kris began their descent into the canyon. Kris kept the dog on a long lead, and tried to keep it loose. Being more sure-footed on the crumbling slope and in the dusk than his handler, Bullet pulled Kris gently toward the creek-side of the trail. She had to correct him several times in order to avoid being pulled off the edge. The slide down to the creek would be a treacherous one. Bullet's signals, head held high, pulling downhill, kept Kris moving. Bullet stopped at one point and leveled his head, searching the forest on the other side of the creek with his eyes. His ears stood erect and pointed forward, gathering sound. His nostrils flared and then closed, processing the smells of the forest and its inhabitants. Even with the rush of water rumbling over rocks and across the gravel bed, Bullet's sensitive ears had picked up a sound.

About halfway down, on the third switchback, Kris climbed atop a few small boulders on the downhill side of the trail to have a look for herself. The dog's hearing was far more acute than her own, and if Bullet thought he heard something, she trusted him. She pulled binoculars from her pack and tried to steady herself on top of the boulders. It was a risky move with Bullet below her, pulling downhill on the lead. Kris called him into a sit-stay and set the binoculars to her eyes. The last faint rays of light were not enough to let her see much, and the moon had not yet crested the horizon. Although the creek below still splashed, with the sound of her own footsteps on the gravel now quiet, she focused her attention across the canyon. She thought she heard something, too. A keening wail, like a small lonely child might make.

The sound bounced among the rocks, impossible to locate with the creek making so much noise. She focused first up and down along the creek itself, seeing only shadows. She checked Bullet's signals. He maintained his sit-stay, but still pointed across the creek and downstream. Raising her binoculars again, Kris searched the nearly impenetrable darkness under the trees.

If time had slowed down, she might have had a chance to react to the sudden crunching sound behind her, and might have even seen the object swinging toward her skull. As it was, she only experienced the lightning flash of her head exploding as she pirouetted off the rocks, spinning silently through the air and crashing head-first onto the loose granite gravel of the slope. Her unconscious body slid toward the icy waters of the creek.

Bullet watched his handler's unexpected behavior without comprehension, as was so often the case. As she slid past, he could only grab at her, slamming into rocks himself. One back leg lodged hard into a crack. Locking his jaw, he held onto the shoulder of Kris's jacket. The momentum of the fall dragged her into the water. The tendons and ligaments anchoring Bullet's leg to his body pulled inexorably across his hip and threatened to tear away from their bone attachments. Still, he held on. The air-rending scream that would have accompanied the wrenching and tearing in his hip silenced as his teeth sank tighter into Kris's jacket and the raging water tugged at her body.

The heavy jacket gave way first. Bullet was left with a mouthful of rip-stop nylon and insulation as Kris's body floated swiftly downstream. One arm appeared to flail in the air, or only flopped as her body rolled over in the water. Bullet watched as Kris's purple jacket was swept away, vanishing around a rock. Focused on her disappearance, the dog never noticed her assailant disappearing silently into the forest at the top of the ridge.

This was not the first time in his short life that Bullet had dealt with difficult circumstances. His first year of life had been tough, but his tenacious nature allowed him to survive. The same strong-willed instincts served him there on the banks of the creek. He spit out some of the fabric and tried to pull his back leg from between the rocks. It was jammed tightly, and the dislocated hip would not respond to his efforts. He backed one step away and leaned, first to one side, then the other. Still jammed. He used his forelegs to push backwards, and the weight of his body finally wrenched the unresponsive leg from between the rocks. He tried to stand, and moved as though to leap into the creek and follow his handler downstream. The injured hip would bear no weight and he slipped on the uneven and shifting rocks. He sighed and looked around. About six feet upstream a muddy area of deer grass and sedges sat at the edge of the creek. Using his three good legs and dragging the injured one, Bullet slowly crept to the flattish area, turned so he could watch the creek for Kris's return, and laid down. He put his head on his forelegs and waited.

Twenty Seven
Reporters

Andy and Rose trudged back into camp, following the enticing aroma of Frank's marinara with meatballs sauce simmering on the camp stove. Meals on a search mission were often grab-and-go affairs, so Frank had brought along a large pot of his homemade sauce and was prepared to boil up as little as a single serving of pasta at a time as each searcher returned to camp. He pulled open a salad kit bag, complete with a tiny foil packet of dressing, and dumped a pile onto each of three paper plates. They had time to eat and no idea what surprises the evening would bring, so they'd take advantage of the moment. Frank waved Agent Cardona over and invited her to join them. She sat, but cocked one eyebrow skeptically.

Of course Cardona had eaten food outdoors before, but not often. Sometimes a backyard barbecue with grilled burgers, and once her large extended family had opted for a birthday picnic in a park. Even so, green salad and spaghetti with sauce on paper plates under the trees seemed outlandish. Wouldn't bugs get into the bubbling sauce, sitting as it did on a camp stove under pine trees? She glanced up at the overhanging tree. Surely some kind of tree parts would fall on their plates.

Her doubts were overcome by the fragrance of the marinara and her own hunger pangs. She contributed a handful of chocolate brownie energy bars for dessert. Andy filled Rose's supper dish and moved his folding camp chair close. They munched on the salad while their pasta boiled.

Frank had just gotten up to serve the meal's second course when, from inside the exercise pen, Rose started a low growl and Frank's puppy, MacDuff, yipped several times. Both dogs gazed at something in the shadows under the trees. Assuming a woodland creature crept there, checking out their unexpected presence in the meadow, Frank hushed the dogs and went back to draining the pasta. As they ate and talked, each kept one eye out and watched the shadows for the returning search teams.

"They won't search all night then?" Cardona asked.

Andy answered. "They would if they were on scent, or had some reasonable expectation of finding the target before dawn. It's harder to read the dogs in the dark though, and easier to miss something important."

Cardona watched MacDuff, as he tried to distract the other dog from finishing her last bite. Rose glanced at the puppy, looked at her last three kibbles, and walked away from the dish. MacDuff bounced forward and vacuumed up the last of the food while the older dog watched over her shoulder.

"How come MacDuff can't search?" Cardona asked. "Are you still training him to smell humans?" Rose glanced at the FBI agent, and almost rolled her eyes. Frank laughed, too.

"Oh, he can smell humans," Frank said. "There's no need to train a dog to smell, or even to smell certain scents. They all do that. The trick is to teach them to communicate with us."

"And for us to learn to understand their communication," Andy added. "That's the hard part."

A reporter from a television station in Sacramento wandered over and parked his hip on the fender of Jody's Forester. Not much had happened on this assignment and he needed something, anything, to fill in his evening report. Hoping to shake loose some news from them, he offered what information he had, reading the screen on his phone.

"Amber Alert says the kidnapper is a Matthew Tolliver from Sacramento. The baby's father. He's a clerk with some state agency. The baby's name is Jayden."

Andy nodded. The reporter was only repeating what they already knew. Frank had jotted both names on a pad next to his radio. Knowing what name to call out might be helpful in this search. Cardona continued to chew her salad. Her FBI jacket was draped over the back of her chair in such a way that the large yellow letters were not visible.

The reporter looked expectant. "You guys learn anything new?"

The others looked at Andy, the only one who'd been out on the search. "Um ... " he said, "we did find evidence that Jayden was taken at least as far as a couple of miles out this trail, out to the pass."

The reporter's look became quizzical. "By evidence, you mean your dog did something that made you think the baby had been at the pass?" His tone dripped obvious skepticism.

"Yeah," Andy said. "She clearly indicated that."

The reporter looked away, disbelief and frustration reflected in his expression. He started to get up and put away his phone.

"So I stopped there and looked carefully around the area," Andy said. "Found a discarded diaper, so Rose was on target. And I would not have found that without her signal."

Cardona perked up. "Did you bag it and bring it back for evidence?"

"Um ... " he said. "I did bring it back. I'll get it for you in a minute." He ducked his head, looking embarrassed, but said no more. In fact, he had left the diaper in the garbage bag with the other trash he'd collected, and couldn't immediately recall what he'd done with that when he'd returned to camp. Retrieving it now would mean doing so in front of an audience. He and Rose were trained to search for lost people, not to collect evidence of a crime. "I did find a plastic bottle too, and I photographed and bagged that. Thought there might be fingerprints on it. I didn't think about fingerprints on the diaper. I picked up a fair amount of trash."

In a whisper, Cardona said, "That's all evidence, Andy. I'm going to need to bag all of that."

"If you found evidence of the baby being definitely at the pass, what's happening now?" The reporter persisted.

"Yeah, well," Andy said. He pointed off toward the ridge line. "One team is searching up here on the ridge, and another team went on down the trail as far as the creek. We needed an air-scenting dog on that part of the search. In the morning we'll cross the creek and use my tracking dog to pick up the baby's trail there."

"You've got searchers out there tonight? All night?"

Andy started to explain about both Jody and Kris coming back soon, but the reporter interrupted him, again reading from his cell phone. "This Matthew Tolliver ... reports are he owns a gun. A registered handgun. Law enforcement searched his apartment and couldn't find it. He must have it with him. Aren't your searchers in danger?"

Either a breath of the cooler evening breeze drifted through the group at just that moment, or the question generated its own chill among those gathered there.

"The whereabouts of the gun are undetermined," Cardona said.

"I think that's what I just said," the reporter said in a dismissive tone. The phone in his hand pinged, and he went back to looking at the screen. "Anyway, I'm just saying, the guy still has his gun. Could be dangerous." No one disagreed with him. The reporter slid his phone into a pocket and wandered off in search of something more newsworthy than a used diaper.

Frank keyed on the radio and tried to reach Jody or Kris. Darkness had fallen, and he felt increasing concern about the search teams.

Cardona gathered the paper plates and prepared to stow them in the garbage bag. Andy stopped her. Self-consciously he rummaged through the trash and extracted the bag he'd brought in from the trail, the plastic wad of diaper inside. Cardona stared at the offensive object.

"Let me get an evidence bag," she finally said, and moved off.

Frank joined them as Cardona held the evidence bag open and Andy dropped the diaper inside.

"We're going to have to hang this garbage in a tree," Andy said.

Cardona looked confused. "Hang it in a tree? Why would you hang garbage in a tree?"

"Have to keep it away from bears," Frank said.

"Bears?" Cardona had never been a camper, and never spent a night in the woods. She gazed around the lot full of vehicles. "Why can't we just lock it in one of the cars?"

Frank smiled and shook his head. "Haven't you ever seen pictures of what a bear can do to a car?"

"Yeah," Andy added. "Peel it open like a tin can just to get a dried-up french fry you dropped between the seats months ago."

If night had not already fallen, the guys might have seen the color drain from Cardona's face. An outdoorsy girl she was not.

They returned to their chairs and finished the remainder of the meal in silence, each lost in their own thoughts.

"I'm going to check in with Sacramento again," Cardona said. "See if they've found that gun yet, or anything new."

She locked herself in her car, then scanned the crowded parking lot. She'd been planning to sleep in her car, since no more suitable accommodations were available. Now she wasn't so sure. Possibly she could leave the scene. Try to find a motel in one of the tiny towns she'd passed on the way here. The prospect of a two-star motel in an unfamiliar town had even less appeal than the rear seat of her car. Possibly the guys were pulling her leg about bears? And anyway, look how many cars a bear would have to go through before reaching hers. That was the clincher. It would be a major headache to get all these vehicles moved so she could get her car out.

She noticed a small knot of community volunteers getting ready to bed down in flimsy tents. Any hungry bear would eat them first before coming to get her, locked safely inside. She made up her mind. She would stay put, stay on the scene, and sleep in the car, as planned. The rear seat would do nicely. She dialed the Sacramento office of the FBI.

Twenty Eight
Lost and Alone

Off duty for the day and finally at home, District Ranger Russell popped the top on a can of his favorite brew and fussed around with the remote to get a local news channel. Still a few minutes until the broadcast began, but he liked to be ready. Just enough time to check dispatch for the latest reports, if any, about that smoke. Russell would like to pull those fire crews back to the ranger station if possible. No sense in them spending the night out there if the fire had become a non-factor. He yanked his boots off while he chatted with the dispatcher. He asked about Cullison and was informed that she had checked in at Eagle Meadow. Must have driven straight through from that other incident without stopping at the ranger station. Well, good. Cullison could check out that smoke and take charge out there. Reports were the smoke had disappeared on its own anyway. He hung up and settled into his recliner.

***

No one waited at the rendezvous point at the pass when Jody and Flag arrived. No surprise, as Jody had gotten Frank's radioed message that Andy would head back to base while Kris would go as far as the creek. Jody wasn't happy about Kris's decision to go down alone, especially after the scare she'd had at the site of the abandoned cabin. She felt responsible for calling her teammate onto this search, and worried that something might happen to Kris or Bullet.

Jody tried both her radio, and then her cell phone, but Kris did not respond to either. She yelled Kris's name, then listened, hearing only the rushing of the water below.

She tugged her headlamp over her forehead, flipped it on, and scanned the loose rock of the steep slope. She could see only parts of the trail in the narrow beam of her headlamp. Those were barely distinguishable by a slight leveling and faintly paler line among the rocks. Even that disappeared thirty feet out, where it dropped between boulders.

She pulled her flashlight out and searched the rock slope under the more powerful light, still seeing nothing but rocks. Kris may have had enough light to start down this trail, but Jody looked into darkness. Starting down after dark was more than dangerous; it would be just plain stupid. On the other hand, Kris had to be on her way back up. Why didn't she respond to her radio? Jody had no choice. She had to start down in search of Kris.

She changed out Flag's short leash for a longer line. Neither of them would be sure-footed on this trail, and the longer lead would prevent one who might slip from dragging the other one down. She tightened her headlamp, her hand hesitating over the switch. With it on, her head made a bright target. The flashlight made an even bigger target, visible for hundreds of feet, but she couldn't go forward without light. Flag's night vision was significantly better than any human's, so the dog should be able to see where she placed her paws. Jody needed the light.

She turned off the flashlight and stowed it, but left the headlamp on. They started down, taking each step carefully. "Here I am," she muttered to herself, hoping a kidnapper with a gun did not lie in wait, watching her. Jody intended to go only as far as the first switchback. She would stop there to see if she could spot lights indicating Kris and Bullet's return from the creek.

Surprised to get past the first switchback with no sign of her friends, Jody tried again to raise Kris on the radio. Still no response. She did manage to connect with Frank back at base. His efforts to make a connection with Kris had also been unsuccessful. They decided the surrounding granite canyon might be interfering with radio signals deeper into the canyon, making communication with Kris difficult.

"Oh, and a couple of other things." He hesitated. "Andy made it back to camp."

"Yes, good. What else?"

"What?"

"You said a couple of things. What else?"

"Oh, the kidnapper, Matthew ... you know he might have a gun?"

"He is armed? Cardona said only that they hadn't located the gun."

"Yes. Well, yes, he might be armed. He does own a gun. It's just ... Jody?"

"Yes?"

"Be careful, that's all."

"Roger that."

She gave the rocks around her one more good look. She and Flag continued beyond the next switchback. Jody found a rhythm, planting one boot in the loose gravel, swinging the headlamp to look for Kris, then planting the other boot. No sooner had the rhythm established itself, than the ground crumbled beneath her and she went down. Her boots straight out in front to form a plow, she slid on her palms and rear, struggling to at least stay on the trail. One boot jammed up against a rock, and she yelped as sharp pain shot through that ankle. Grinding to a halt, she stayed where she'd stopped and caught her breath. Chunks of decomposed granite stung where they embedded in her palms. Pinpricks of blood appeared through the raw and dusty skin. She pulled out what rock she could, and fished tissues from a pocket. Wrapping those around both hands, she held them tight to stop the bleeding. Hiking this trail after dark was a treacherous risk. She felt sick, thinking about Kris and Bullet out here, possibly lost, or worse.

"Kris!" she yelled from her seated position. She got no answer. Carefully, she stood, planted the uninjured foot, and took a tentative step on the other. Pain radiated up her leg. She could bear the weight, but walking would hurt. She kept going. She would wrap that ankle when she found a good stopping place.

Flag pulled at the end of her lead. The dog glanced back at her slowly moving human companion, who took careful steps behind.

At the third and last switchback, just before another set of boulders, Flag stepped off the trail to the downhill side and gave a long whine. Jody could see nothing beyond the glare of her headlamp, but Flag was behaving as though she could see, pointing her nose into the night, and turning her head. More likely, though, she scented someone. Flag searched the slope below, ears pricked, and nostrils flaring. She whined again. Jody stopped for another long look, glancing back and forth between Flag's signals and what little she could see. The dog's behavior did not really indicate a search alert. Instead, her behavior demonstrated awareness of a friend nearby. Had to be Bullet and Kris, but Jody couldn't see anything. She hauled out the big flashlight and pointed its beam down the slope, revealing nothing.

"Kris!" she called.

Flag looked at her and whined again. The dog turned to the slope and the creek at the bottom. She barked once, a welcoming friendly bark, Jody thought, possibly tinged with a bit of anxiety. Jody tried to look where Flag pointed, but could see only the whiteness of water tumbling in the creek highlighted against the dark night. Tufts of deer grass and sprouts of willows grew at a spot just upstream that popped into view when she pointed the light that way. Jody scoured the slope between the trail and the creek. Still nothing.

She squatted, easing the weight off the injured ankle, and considered her options. Continuing forward in the dark was proving even more dangerous than she'd feared. Climbing back up would be equally dangerous. Kris and Bullet had to be out here somewhere, but where? She made one more long, slow sweep with the flashlight. As her head turned, something glinted in the light. She looked again. A black object rested fifteen or twenty feet down the slope, not much bigger than a fist. The beam from the flashlight reflected a glimmer on its edge.

"Stay," she said to Flag, not wanting the dog to interpret her downhill progress as a sign to follow. Crouching, Jody eased first one foot, then the other down the slope, sucking air through her teeth when her weight came down on that ankle. She kept going until she could see the object clearly. A pair of binoculars, abandoned among the rocks.

Flag, still up on the trail, barked and whined again, this time looking anxiously at Jody. Jody stayed planted and scanned the rocks around her. She couldn't tell if the binoculars belonged to Kris. They weren't dusty or weathered and so did not appear to have been sitting where they were for long. Sweeping her light from above, Jody picked out a faint disturbance in the rocks. Something heavy might have gone sliding from the location of the binoculars down toward the creek. She considered following the faint trail to look for more signs of someone sliding, but getting back up would not be easy.

Flag gave a third bark, definitely a happy welcoming tone this time, and her tail began to wag. Jody tried to follow Flag's gaze with her own eyes to the small patch of willow sprouts. From her new position, she thought she saw movement there, and when she turned the brighter light in that direction, two glowing red eyes flashed in the beam. Dark fur, a brown snout and pink tongue. Had to be Bullet. The dog sat still, not moving forward, but Jody thought she could make out the dog's orange search vest. Still clutching Flag's lead, Jody watched in distress as Flag broke her stay command and began to half-walk, half-slide toward the other dog. All three of them would soon be at the edge of the creek with no way to get back up to the trail. Only three of them. What had happened to Kris?

Jody marked the location of the binoculars with a small cairn made of rocks she could reach without moving her feet, and stuffed the binoculars into her pack. She continued her duck-walk downslope, trying not to disturb what might or might not be the trail of a sliding body. The stubby plants along the way showed no signs of having been grabbed at or disturbed in any way. Whatever, or whoever, slid down had not been trying to hold on. When Jody reached the creek, she could see a chunk of the edge crumbling into the water. A heavy weight might have plummeted from there into the icy stream. Possibly that was what happened to Kris. Jody aimed the flashlight and scanned the rushing water and the creek banks for any signs of her friend. Just there, almost under her boot, she found a small swatch of torn purple rip-stop. A weight descended on her chest. Kris's jacket was made from purple rip-stop. If something had happened to her sweet friend, Jody would never forgive herself. She tucked the swatch into a pocket.

Having made it down the slope to where Bullet sat, Flag stood beside her friend. They licked one another's faces in greeting. Not their usual enthusiastic romp. With one last look downstream, Jody crabbed her way toward the dogs. She hoped Kris waited there too.

Twenty Nine
Desperation

Bullet did not stand, even when Jody came up beside him. He barely looked at her, staring instead downstream. A soft whine trembled in his throat. Speaking softly, and running her hand over the soft fur on his head, Jody turned to scan that way. Not even moonlight illuminated the creek, and the faint beam of the headlamp still offered no sign of Kris.

Jody turned her attention back, only then noticing Bullet's right rear leg laid out at an unnatural angle. Hard to tell if a bone might be broken, and Jody knew better than to touch the bones and ligaments at the hip joint. Even a well-trained dog will bite when a painful injury is touched.

"Hey, guy," she murmured. "You okay? What's going on here?" Gently running her hand over Bullet's back, she noted no blood on his body. For the leg to be bent at that angle, most likely the hip joint had been dislocated. That could be fixed, and Bullet would recover from the physical injury. The loss of his human companion was a far more serious matter.

"Let's get you some help, Bullet. Flag and I will find Kris, we promise. Right, Flag?" Jody placed the flashlight on a rock to illuminate the scene, and pulled her radio out. She searched the banks of the creek again, waiting to make radio contact.

From her standing position, Jody caught sight of a bit of white fluff under Bullet's chin. She pulled it out. A shred of the insulation from Kris's jacket. Clearly, Bullet had tried to keep his friend from being carried away, and failed. No wonder he acted so distressed.

She tried to reach Kris's radio first, and again, got no reply. She tried three times to raise Frank at their base camp, and finally made the connection. The radio waves were encountering too much rock and no direct line of transmission from this position at the bottom of the canyon. It didn't help that her search team couldn't afford the best equipment. Between crackling static and the roar of the creek, she struggled to explain the situation to Frank. The small group gathered around the base radio joined in the conversation, asking questions, and adding to the confusion.

"Bullet's injured. He can't walk. We've got to get him to a doctor, now!"

"We'll come out with a sling and carry him," Andy suggested.

"That would take too long. It's too far. He'd be in pain with all the bouncing around. And Kris is missing! Bullet won't leave here without ... " A squawk of static interrupted the transmission.

"Did you say Kris is missing?" came the reply.

"Yes! Kris is missing! We need a helicopter out here to evacuate Bullet!" Jody voice grew louder as she began to panic about being heard over the increasing static.

With more loud buzzing, the radio cut in and out, then disconnected entirely. After several tries, Jody got through again, just long enough to yell, "Send a helicopter! And I need help down here to look for Kris!"

"We're coming now," Andy yelled in reply, not sure if his message got through.

***

Ted tried to stay low and invisible from the trail, just in case any more enemy soldiers might invade his canyon. Only a few moments after he'd made the crossing, that guy called Daddy crept out of the mouth of a canyon, across the boulders, and found Ted's secret beaver-tree bridge. No sign of the little boy. The guy climbed up the slope and disappeared into the trees at the top. Ted waited, but saw no more movement.

He gathered armfuls of sticky bedstraw to sleep on, creeping through narrow passages between the larger rocks. With all of this activity in the canyon, it would not be possible to return to his snug bed in the stone hearth tonight. So many enemy soldiers and their dogs poked their noses in everywhere. He would stay hidden. He finished laying one thick layer of bedstraw over the damp earth under an overhanging rock and stood to see where he might find softer deer grasses for the top layer of his mattress. Upstream ten feet or so he saw a flat area overgrown with a nice patch of healthy deer grass. Leaning on his big stick, he made his way there, but before he could begin gathering grass, something caught his attention.

So many strange sights had accosted him the past few days that he almost didn't take note of the purple bundle bouncing in the water at the edge of the creek. He couldn't see well in the dark, but the bundle twirled as though caught in an eddy. As he stared, the purple resolved itself into a head with straggling hair and a puffy jacket. He cut over to the edge of the creek, and recognized a potential enemy. A woman soldier, and she appeared to be asleep, floating, face up. That didn't make any sense to Ted. He squatted, reached out and stopped the motion of the body with his stick. He studied her for a time. After a while, she groaned. So she wasn't dead, but she soon would be if she stayed in that icy creek. She might have supplies with her that Ted could use, and she didn't look dangerous. Not at all like an enemy. Ted grabbed her shoulders and dragged her partially onto the bank, where her body rolled toward him and her head flopped over.

He did a cursory visual inspection for explosives. She still did not awaken. Ted could see the oozing wound and matted hair at the back of her head. A vein in her neck still throbbed. Still alive, but she'd been hit. Ted pulled the rest of her all the way out of the water and laid her body in a shallow sandy area between two rocks. Gently rolling her from side to side, he relieved her of her pack. Might be something good in there. He scanned the water uneasily, looking to see if she was accompanied by a dog, or perhaps other soldiers. Hauling this lady out of the water had just about exhausted Ted's resourcefulness. He gathered handfuls of grass and tucked them over and around the purple lady to keep her warm. Sooner or later, the medics would find her. He took her pack and left her, creeping back to his own hiding place. Later, nearly asleep, he heard more than saw the Daddy guy slide down the slope and crash across the creek. Ted held perfectly still so he wouldn't be seen in his nest of weeds.

***

"Jayden. Jayden, wake up!" Daddy shook Jayden. The little boy opened his eyes, but he wasn't much interested in moving. He could see the top of Daddy's white face in what little of the rising moonlight winked through breaks among the tree branches. The bottom half of Daddy's face, covered with a grizzle of beard, disappeared in the dark.

"Jay-bud! Come on, boy." Daddy dragged Jayden from his pirate-nest and propped him against the trunk of the tree. Jayden's body hurt, his mind was foggy. He felt feverish, his tongue glued to the top of his dry mouth. When he moved, the rash on his bottom burst into fiery pain. Daddy tried to make him take a sip of juice from a box, but the straw slipped to the side of Jayden's face. He didn't want any juice.

"Come on, son. We gotta get closer to those cabins. Daddy gathered what was left of their supplies, folded Jayden's limp body into the blanket and carried him for a distance. They walked into another side canyon, this one deeper, wider, and darker than the others. They both settled in the shadows under the low-growing branches of a trio of cedars.

"Okay, bud, new plan," Daddy said, breathing hard. "Those bad guys got all our food. I checked. They found our stash and took it. Or that old guy might have taken it. All we've got left is what's in the bag here." He pulled the paper sack down and rummaged through it, coming up with one box half-filled with crackers and the peanut butter. "If we finish off this peanut butter, I can go down to the creek and get us some water. I been drinking right out of the creek, but you probably need water, huh, bud?" He squatted beside Jayden and extracted a sticky plastic knife from the bag. He picked off a couple pieces of forest detritus, and loaded the knife with a scoop of peanut butter and offered it to his little boy. Jayden's mouth was slack and he made no effort to eat. He didn't want the peanut butter. Daddy tried to push the peanut butter into Jayden's mouth. Jayden looked at his father, his eyes glazed and unfocused.

"Okay, okay, buddy. I get it. You don't feel so good. We're going to take care of that though. You and me, we're a team now. You're mine and you got me, so we're going to take care of each other."

Daddy dropped his head between his knees and made a loud sigh. "Only thing is, I'm not sure how, exactly. I thought we were only going to have some fun for a couple of days. Now ... we need a new plan. They got our car, too. There's a bunch of people up there. And dogs. Looks like they're going to be there all night. I thought we'd have some fun camping. Now ... anyway, now, I don't feel so good. I think I might be sick, too." Daddy stopped talking and looked to the top of the ridge on the other side of the creek, scratching at the stubble on his face.

"Okay Jayden, new plan. We're going to Mexico. What do you think, bud? C'mon, wake up." The baby opened his eyes, listening but not moving. "I'm hitchhiking into town. I'll buy us a new car and get some real food. You hide here until I come back." Jayden closed his eyes, then startled awake again at the sound of Daddy's voice. "Here, Jayden, eat these." Daddy tried to push more of the tiny white candies into Jayden's mouth. They stuck on the boy's dry lips. Jayden pushed them off with his tongue.

"Well, shit, Jayden. You have to help out a little, you know? I can't let you go wandering off into the forest, and you can't stay up in a tree if you won't take these." Daddy stopped talking while he tied one strap of Jayden's overalls to a nearby sapling. "There," he said. "That should keep you here until I get back. Don't worry, buddy, I'll come back and get you."

Daddy scratched the new growth on his chin again. "Wish I had more of a beard, but this'll have to do. Our days of fun are over. Time to move on. You just need to hang in with me, Jayden. Okay, bud? I went through a lot to get you and now ... now you're all mine. I'm not sending you back to that witch of a grandmother, that's for damn sure." Jayden lifted his hand and rubbed his hot cheek with two fingers, but made no other response while Daddy rambled on without meaning.

***

Buried deep under the duff at the far eastern end of the canyon, the fire still breathed life, although just barely. It sent thin tendrils of smoke into the cool evening air, invisible to any human eyes. Creeping ever closer to dry fuel, it sought, as does everything in nature, to gain strength and grow. A slight breeze pulled what life remained in the fire ever farther west, until it reached the dry grasses at the mouth of the next small canyon. There, every once in a while, a hot red pine needle or tiny dead twig flared, each time brighter than the last as the light faded and darkness fell.

A doe and her fawn, bedded in soft grasses and curled up for the night at the foot of a small dead pine, startled at the crackles made by the burning of a twig. The doe's nostrils flared, catching the scent of smoke. She stirred, then rose, nudging her fawn. The two of them left their nest and trotted closer to the creek, away from the fire.

Thirty
Searchlight

On the ridge top, Frank fussed with the radio, trying to find the correct frequency to get a message through to the helicopter crew sitting at the edge of the lake. Rescuing injured dogs probably did not feature in their job description, but they were reasonably close, night had fallen, and Frank felt desperate. He had to settle for leaving an urgent message at the helitack base at Bald Mountain. His message said the searchers needed help in rescuing an injured member of their team.

The only person staffing the base phone that evening was not authorized to dispatch a helicopter himself. He had to check with his off-duty supervisor, who then had to track down District Ranger Russell's home phone and rouse him out of a fitful sleep.

The cobwebs took a while to clear for Russell, who initially thought the searchers wanted his copter to find the kidnapper. That kind of a search would be up to the county sheriff, not him, and certainly was not coming out of his budget. Once he realized a member of the search and rescue team needed help, he readily gave the approval. That message traveled back down the line, eventually getting to the night dispatcher who then tried to raise the helicopter crew still parked at the edge of Lake Nell.

Engrossed in their cell phones, they almost didn't hear the radio in the copter's cockpit crackle to life. The pilot sprinted to grab the handset and settled into her seat. The co-pilot sauntered over to the other side of the cockpit and listened in. Dispatch gave the crew Frank's radio frequency so they could check with him about the exact nature of the request for interagency help.

Frank gave the crew Jody's probable location, and asked them to cruise the length of the creek looking for any signs of Kris. He didn't mention the dog, figuring that by the time they got the copter over Jody, she would be able to talk them into picking up Bullet. The crew quickly folded and packed the Bambi bucket into its storage compartment. They ran through a speedy pre-flight, including a check of the searchlight mounted on the underside of the copter. What with the relaying of messages, the helicopter lifted off some thirty-five minutes after Jody's initial connection with Frank.

***

Time passed slowly for Jody, Flag, and especially for Bullet. Jody's hands stopped bleeding and she'd broken into her first aid supplies for a roll of vet wrap and some pain meds to treat her ankle. She swallowed the pills, but decided not to remove her boot and wrap the ankle just yet. There wasn't anything she could do for Bullet's injury. She continued to murmur words of comfort and reassurance, stroking the dog's shoulder. Except for licking her face a couple of times, he never gave up gazing downstream.

By the time they heard the distant whap-whapping of the copter heading their way, full darkness had settled around the three of them. Jody ignited the two light sticks in Flag's harness, flipped her own headlamp on, and turned on her flashlight. She waved the light over her head, hoping its beam would be enough to attract the helicopter to her improbable location at the bottom of the canyon.

The copter came slowly, low over the creek, its brilliant searchlight sweeping back and forth among the rocks and brush along the banks. At one point, maybe a quarter mile before reaching Jody, the copter stopped and swung around. Its light turned to shine into a side canyon. Then it pulled out and continued coming. The dazzling intensity of the search beam flooded Jody's feeble flashlight as the copter drew directly overhead and hovered.

Although the canine search teams practiced helicopter drops and rescues during training, they'd never tried it at night under the glare of a searchlight. And the helicopter crew had only practiced rescuing injured firefighters. Making the assumption that even though she could not hear or see the helicopter crew, they could at least see her, she signaled for them to drop their rope ladder or a tow line and harness. Normally, both the dog and handler would be harnessed to the tow line, and both would be hauled into the body of the helicopter. Doing that now would leave Flag alone. That would never happen. Flag already cowered under the gale of wind and uproar caused by the helicopter suspended above. Jody needed the co-pilot to drop so the two of them could harness up Bullet without touching his injured hip. Then the co-pilot could carry Bullet up in his arms. Who knew if this helicopter crew had any experience with rescuing injured dogs?

Her signals finally communicated what she needed. The rope ladder dropped, and the co-pilot swung out and started down. He got close enough that he could hear Jody over the racket the rotors were making, then crawled back up the ladder and tossed down the tow rope and harness. Slowly, careful not to cause Bullet any more pain than necessary, Jody slipped the straps of the harness around Bullet's mid-section and across his chest, attaching the device to the harness he already wore. The co-pilot got himself into a seated position and between the two of them, they gently lifted a whimpering Bullet onto the co-pilot's lap.

"Get this dog up to base camp at the trailhead in Eagle Meadow," Jody yelled, as Bullet looked warily at the co-pilot. "On top of the ridge." She pointed, not sure if the co-pilot understood.

"We're here to rescue a search team member, not airlift an injured dog. You're coming up after I get him into the copter, right?"

Jody felt the blood rush to her face. Over the sound of the copter, she yelled, "Bullet is a search team member!" She shook her head, then had to grab her baseball cap, nearly blown off by the wind from the rotors. "No, I'm not coming up. My dog and I have to find the handler. You take the injured dog up to our base camp." She pointed again. "I'll stay here. After you drop him off, you need to help me search along the creek for the handler."

"Oh, yeah, we did see an old guy downstream, about a quarter mile." The co-pilot pointed. "Long hair, barefoot, ragged pants? He freaked and ran away from the creek under some trees, though, so probably not your missing handler?"

"No. The handler's a woman. You didn't see her? Purple jacket? Orange vest over that? Did you even look?"

"Hey! Our mission was to rescue an injured search team member. This dog, I guess. So, no, we didn't spot anyone except that old guy. Watched him run. It's dark, you know. Sorry, we didn't see anybody else."

"Okay, yeah, thanks. That guy doesn't sound like anybody we want to find." To herself she thought, he doesn't sound like the kidnapper either, although he might have been the guy who hurt Kris, assuming Kris didn't just slip and fall.

The possible danger she was in began to dawn on Jody. More than one potential attacker apparently roamed this canyon. She didn't say it, but she'd reached a point where she regretted continuing this search. But it was too late to go back. She had to go on, at least long enough to find Kris.

"Please, after you drop the dog off, can you come back? Turn on that light and search the creek banks? She's probably injured and we need to find her soon. Whatever you can do to help. And when you get Bullet to the top of Eagle Ridge? Tell Frank to call Lowell. Very important. Call Lowell and tell him what's going on. Got it?"

"Yeah, yeah, I got it. Call Lowell. Very important."

Jody waved her hand in a circle, signaling the pilot to haul in the tow rope. The co-pilot and Bullet rose upward and disappeared into the body of the copter. A few seconds later, the wind and noise subsided as the copter lifted and crested the ridge.

In the resulting silence, Jody sank to sit on her knees in the soft sand. Kris's precious dog was on his way to safety and care. But where was Kris? Jody swept the flashlight up and down both banks slowly, and called Kris's name. She didn't want to waste energy and scare herself by wondering how Kris had ended up in the creek. The only part of the puzzle over which Jody had any control was looking for and finding her friend. She couldn't allow herself to think about Kris being injured, possibly in the creek itself, underwater. No, she wouldn't think about that. She'd only think about how to find her friend.

"Okay, Flag," she ruffled the fur on the dog's neck. "Where do we go now? What's our plan? We promised Bullet we'd find Kris, so we'd better get started." Despite her words, Jody found it hard to stand. Adrenaline had powered her through Bullet's rescue. Now she was drained, and that ankle throbbed with every movement.

The darkness felt ominous. Jody stirred, motivated by the fear that she might be being watched. The others would be coming in an hour. If she could get herself upstream the twenty yards or so to the ford where the trail intersected with Turtle Creek, she could wait for them there. She yelped whenever weight was put on that ankle. She needed to get that wrapped soon, before it swelled any more. The headlamp reflecting off the rock slope gave Jody enough light to hobble her way to the gravel ford, Flag lagging behind, still at the end of her long lead. Jody found a spot a few feet up the bank where the mist from the tumbling water didn't reach, and not too close to larger rocks where snakes might be snuggled against the still-warm granite. She located the first aid kit and vet wrap again, tugged off her boot and sock, and wrapped her injured ankle tightly.

Once she'd done that, she flipped off her headlamp and sat quietly for a few moments, watching the whitecaps made by the foaming water dancing through the dark. The night was too deep to see if anyone crept nearby, and the creek made too much noise to hear approaching footsteps. She pulled Flag close and the two leaned against one another. She was completely dependent on her dog to know if danger approached. They watched, then napped, then watched again, waiting for bobbing lights coming down the trail that would signal the arrival of Andy and Rose.

***

The sound of the helicopter coming closer had awakened Ted and sent him into a post-war stress panic. He crouched in the shadow of the nearest large boulder, listening to the copter drawing near. In the barren desert of Ted's war, helicopters were usually friendly troops. It'd been a long time since Ted had seen any friendly soldiers, and he wasn't taking any chances. The rocks around him blazed into brilliance, then blackness again as the searchlight strobed back and forth. The copter was definitely looking for someone to kill, and in Ted's mind, that could be only him.

Suddenly directly overhead, the searchlight threw everything into deep black shadow and dazzling white light. Ted scuttled from between the rocks and ran for his life toward the trees along the western flank of the nearest canyon, expecting at any moment to see the ground around him explode with the sound of automatic gunfire. The searchlight pursued his jagged path across the rugged terrain. He kept going even after he reached the relative safety of shadows under the trees, and made a sharp right turn in an evasive move, heading deeper into the canyon. If they continued to fire after losing him in the shadows, they'd hit nothing but dirt. Lost in his own psychotic landscape, the roar of the helicopter's rotors became the sound of detonating shells and exploding artillery fire. In the darkness, Ted's arm grazed the rough bark of a tree in passing. He stopped, grabbed an overhead branch, swung himself against the trunk, and began climbing, not stopping until he was twenty feet off the ground. He crouched there in silence, still absorbed in the hell of his own mind.

Thirty One
Man Down

Deputy Hogan nearly slid into the creek when the helicopter roared to life. It then abruptly appeared about fifty feet over his head. It sped off down the canyon, its searchlight sweeping the banks of the creek. Something had definitely broken loose down there, and Hogan was going to miss all the action. He steadied himself against a nearby tree and unholstered his radio. Making the connection with the other deputies, he radioed that he was going in.

"'In' where?" came the reply.

"In! Into the action! They've spotted the abductor! The copter went in to provide support but the people down there don't have guns. I'm getting across this creek and taking care of this situation myself!" Then, as an afterthought, he added, "Back me up!"

The near-darkness and shortage of flashlights made for a confusing response among the remaining deputies. The two left at the rearward position guarding the entrance to the highway agreed at least one of them should move forward.

Deputy Tarrazo grabbed the large flashlight from the vehicle and took off trotting along the dusty jeep trail. After a hundred yards, he ducked behind the roadside underbrush, hidden from view of the first cabin. He became entangled there, so advanced farther into the forest, still paralleling the road, he hoped. Twenty minutes of that, and he stopped, convinced he was circling in the wrong direction. The flashlight made the forest leap about in crazy patterns that left him feeling confused. He took aim on a tall pine to his right and headed that way, thinking he would eventually cross the road, or at least run into the lakeshore. The ground dropped away as he moved forward, indicating that he was headed downhill. At first that seemed right, then as the ground got steeper, it didn't feel so right. Rocks rolled under his shoes, he tripped, first over a small log, then over more rocks, and then he fell. The flashlight went flying. With no way to determine the how far he might fall, his shoulder hit the ground first. The momentum snapped his neck back, cracking his head on granite. His body rolled to a stop against an ancient stump.

His partner, left behind at the highway, switched on the swiveling red and blue lamps of the SUV's roof light rack. She turned the ignition switch one stop, adding the amber and white lamps to the display lighting up the area in front of the vehicle. The surrounding forest burst into the colorful but eerie atmosphere of a crowded nightclub complete with strobe lights and a disco ball. Trees and bushes danced silently in the flickering red and blue shadows. The deputy un-racked her Remington 700 and took up a position in front of the vehicle, rifle at the ready. Essentially a sitting duck there in the light, she knew having those lights on was correct protocol and anyway, it was still unclear if the guy they were waiting for was even armed. Somehow, in all the confusion, the information about the kidnapper's gun ownership had not been relayed to the sheriff's deputies.

Without waiting for confirmation, Hogan scrambled over the boulders bordering the creek at his position. His leather oxfords were no match for the slippery wet granite, even with their synthetic-rubber soles. His progress halted at the creek's edge. Shining his flashlight across, the foaming water rushing through the rock channel intimidated him. The water flowed deep and fast, and icy cold. He continued his rock scramble another dozen feet to the east and took one more look. Still scary. Here, two rocks leaned close together, almost spanning the torrent, although both rocks shone wet in his flashlight beam. If he could creep out far enough onto the one, then leap and somehow grab onto something when he landed on the other side, a crack in the rock, a bush, anything, he might make it. He inspected the boulder on the other side. There didn't appear to be anything to secure his position once he'd committed to that leap.

Hogan rolled onto his haunches, not an easy task with all the equipment hanging from his belt. What if he went back to the cabins and tried to locate a watercraft of some sort? Surely the owners of those lakefront cabins would have the odd canoe or kayak stashed somewhere. With a boat, he could paddle through the lake around the creek to the other side.

Alternatively, once back at the cabins, he could simply round up everyone else and they could head back to the trailhead at Eagle Meadow and go in from that direction. Thinking about it now, he couldn't remember why he and his fellow deputies had not just marched in on that trail anyway. Damn that stupid search and rescue broad for getting him into this mess. She probably sent his guys away on purpose so she could have all the glory. In the darkness, with no one to see, Hogan's face turned a deep shade of purple as his anger simmered. No wonder his wife and kids made fun of him and called him a loser.

The more he thought about it, the angrier he got. Taking a shaky breath, he resolved to show everyone. He would make that damn leap and go get that abductor, and the abductee too. Hogan crept out as far as he dared onto the leaning rock, stood up and took a long slow breath, readying his legs and his will for the jump that would either end his life or bring him unbounded glory.

***

Frank borrowed all the flashlights and camp lanterns he could find and set up a circle of lights in the flat area adjacent to the search base. He'd never done this before, and only hoped the helicopter pilot would be able to see and maneuver into that landing spot. He locked MacDuff inside his car, lowered the shade cover to the ground, and tried to secure anything else that might go flying. A crowd gathered to watch the copter land. Two community response volunteers offered to take

Bullet down the mountain to the emergency veterinarian who'd already been alerted to expect the dog's arrival. The helicopter came in low over the camp, blowing gear in all directions. Frank and a volunteer carefully ferried Bullet to the backseat of the waiting car. Seconds later, it left on its mission.

The media, hoping to cover the rescue of a kidnapped baby, got several emotion-laden images of Bullet being carried. A local news stream went live with an image of Frank anxiously stroking Bullet's head as the dog was settled into the car. Videos of the helicopter crew being slapped on their backs for coming to the rescue were readied for the eleven o'clock news slot, just in case nothing more dramatic happened before then. Those images would satisfy the audience for a short time, but the programs would lose their viewers if they didn't come up with some more news soon. They'd already missed the prime-time slot. It would be perfect if the baby could be rescued in time to make the late-night broadcast.

Concern about the missing searcher was slow to build. Frank downplayed reporters' questions, explaining that Kris would be returning with Jody. Andy and Rose had managed to slip away shortly after the radio call and were already well on their way to Jody's position.

The helicopter co-pilot pulled Frank aside. "Got a message for you," he said. "Call Lowell. Jody said to tell you to call Lowell right away. You know what that means?"

"Yeah, yeah. That's the handler's husband."

"The handler who's missing? Jody wants us to go back and look for the missing handler, but we can't do much in the dark. Chances of a collision, getting disoriented, anything could happen in the dark. We can come back in the morning."

Frank looked up and noticed a couple of reporters drifting closer. He tried to keep is voice low. "What if that kidnapper took her? Hit the dog and took her?" Frank's voice rose. "Wouldn't you keep searching then?" He thought about Kris lost and alone, or possibly held by a dangerous kidnapper.

"Kidnapper?" The co-pilot sounded confused. Then he had more bad news. "We did see a raggedy old guy beside the creek. Jody said he wasn't your handler. So don't know who that might've been. He ran under the trees, which is sort of my point. We really can't see much in the dark."

The reporters showed increasing interest, one of them waving her photographer over. Frank looked around, his lips forming a tight line. The co-pilot stepped close, almost whispering, "Look, your best bet is to get law enforcement in here. We came out to check on a runaway campfire. If you've got a bad guy out there ... or more than one ... hurting people, you need to get law enforcement on this."

"Yeah, sorry. I'll call right now. And thanks for bringing that dog up."

"No problem. Happy to help. Oh, and call Lowell."

Frank waved as he moved to his radio.

Thirty Two
The Darkness Deepens

Eagle Meadow swarmed with activity. An hour or so earlier, Greg had the misfortune to be found lounging in the cab of his truck when his boss, District Fire Management Officer Cullison marched back from her trip to get eyes on the smoke. She had not seen any smoke. After so many hours chasing fires around the forest, she had to take a break, find a shower, a bed, and get some sleep. At the same time, she wasn't inclined to take chances. She put Greg in charge. She instructed him to organize the parking situation in case a fire camp needed to be set up, and told him to hike out every couple of hours and check that canyon for smoke or fire. The guy in the lookout tower wasn't making any more reports, but a fire would have to be sizable and active to be seen after dark from that far away.

***

Once the helicopter had departed, the community response volunteers busied themselves setting up their base camp in the flat area. Tents and tables and strings of bright lights went up in a flurry. Generators hummed. Someone had moved the logs demarcating the parking area, and vehicles of every description were being moved from their haphazard parking positions into more organized lines. At about eleven o'clock, a catering van from the nearest Indian-owned casino arrived and opened its doors, serving coffee and hot pre-packaged meals. The kitchen crew back at the casino was already at work preparing breakfasts to be delivered beginning at dawn.

Under pressure from the media to provide at least a summary of what was known so far about the kidnapping, or some kind of footage to use on news broadcasts, the U. S.

Forest Service Public Affairs Officer readied his equipment to give a short, multiple-agency press briefing. He surveyed the crowd for someone from the sheriff's department to explain the situation, but spotted no one. A lone CHP officer, still waiting for the tow truck, volunteered to say a few words and answer questions. Agent Cardona shrugged into her FBI windbreaker and the public affairs officer hustled her in front of the cameras.

***

Frank looked up Lowell's number on his phone. It was still displayed on the list of recent calls from when he'd spoken to Lowell close to dinnertime. He dialed the number again, controlling the concern in his voice. As a city police officer in his day job, Frank had sometimes been required to inform the next of kin, never an easy task. He tried to take a hopeful tone with Lowell, whom he'd awakened from a deep sleep. Lowell said he'd get on the road immediately, and stop on the way at the emergency veterinary hospital to check on Bullet. Frank promised to call Lowell's cell phone the minute the search team found Kris, or he would have Kris make the call herself, when she returned. If she returned.

Frank disconnected. Jody had reported only that Kris was missing. Frank didn't want to overreact, but after he saw her injured dog, and then the co-pilot reported the vagrant, he had to do something more. The press briefing looked to be wrapping up, and Agent Cardona was drifting his way. He waved, got her attention, then drew her aside where they wouldn't be overheard.

***

The bark on the tree Ted perched in poked painfully into his bare feet. He'd been frozen in that crook between the trunk and two branches for hours, and had even fallen asleep there for a while. The sound of something large moving across the forest floor awakened him. His eyes were well-accustomed to the dim light thrown by millions of stars in the clear night sky. He couldn't see everything, but he could see enough.

An enemy soldier crept below, coming out of the night, moving toward the creek and the trail running alongside it. It was the man called Daddy. The guy moved stealthily enough, but seemed concerned only with remaining concealed from anyone out on that trail. He showed no signs of being aware of Ted's presence. Daddy appeared ill-equipped for any mission. He carried no backpack of supplies and wore no helmet. He only clutched a weapon in one hand. Ted could see now the weapon was as long as an M16 rifle, but not shaped like one. More like a club.

Ted held his position and slowed his breathing to avoid detection. The soldier reached the moonlit trail and dashed across, disappearing into the boulders and low growth bordering the creek. Probably headed for Ted's secret creek crossing, hidden between the rocks. Or possibly he wanted to steal Ted's purloined pack of supplies.

For a long time after the soldier passed, Ted considered what to do. His stomach rumbled even after the snack of protein bars he'd liberated from the woman's pack. He was thirsty, and his tongue felt dry. His legs cramped underneath him, and he'd have to reposition soon. If the soldier had left supplies at a bivouac deeper in this canyon, Ted might be able to locate those and help himself. On the other hand, if the soldier had left supplies there, he would no doubt be coming back for them, meaning he might be returning at any moment. Possibly Ted should try to make his way back to his own recently acquired supplies. With the helicopter gone, the night felt quieter, safer.

Driven by hunger and discomfort, Ted resolved to return to his bed among the boulders, using the cover of darkness to make the trip. He stretched his legs out and slid stiffly to the ground. He stopped to listen. The helicopter had been gone for hours, but that's not to say it wouldn't return at any moment. He spent a long time looking toward the trail, searching for any sign of the enemy soldier.

In nearly complete silence, Ted slipped toward the mouth of the small canyon. As he edged forward, he looked for a big stick to replace the one he'd left on his bed between the rocks. If the enemy soldier returned and confronted him, Ted would need a weapon. Light from the rising moon helped, but the sticks he found were too small or too rotten to use.

He hesitated at the edge of the trail, moonlight shining from the east. He would be exposed there in the brightness, like a target. He looked west, in the direction the soldier had disappeared, but saw no one. Looking east again, he was startled by several small lights bobbing less than a quarter mile away. More enemy soldiers. Could be a whole squad, which would be nine armed men. Ted could bolt the remaining distance to the cover of the boulders shouldering the creek, but he would be visible the whole way, and within easy rifle-range. Once at the creek, he'd be trapped there, between the trail and the creek.

He pulled back into the darkness and relative safety of the side canyon, where he crept deeper into the shadows. He quickly made himself a small nest in the pine needles at the base of a large tree, and curled up. It was more comfortable than the crook of branches, but only marginally. If the squad of soldiers came this direction, he could watch them pass the mouth of the canyon from this position. If he didn't see them pass, he would check again in a while, and decide if it was safe to cross the trail and head home. If the soldiers found him at the end of this canyon, he'd have to formulate a new plan.

Thirty Three
Moonlight

Andy and Rose made it to the pass overlooking the canyon in record time, trotting almost the entire distance, lighting their way with headlamps, light sticks, and flashlights. As they left camp, Greg had joined them, saying this seemed like as good a time as any to check for signs of that fire. Together, they stood at the pass scoping out the trail ahead. Loose granite shimmered in the glare of their flashlights and the trail switched back and forth as it descended. They hesitated a moment. Jody and Flag had made it to the ford, but Kris had disappeared somewhere along the way. At the time Kris started down there had been some light left in the sky. Darkness enveloped Andy and Greg now. Not even the glow of the moon lit the way. But they had to go down. They had no options. Jody and Flag were waiting at the bottom. Andy and Rose were needed to help find Kris. Andy radioed Frank that they'd reached the pass, and were ready to head down.

Greg scanned east. No glow of fire was visible from the pass lookout. No sign of fire at all. He could have gone safely back to camp. Instead, he started down with Andy. He could help with the search, and possibly hike out to where that fire had started, make sure it was really out. Treading carefully, planting each footstep deliberately, Andy and Greg, with Rose ambling behind, made it creekside in just over an hour.

Jody had spotted their lights only moments before, feeling a sudden release of tension as help arrived. A tear even made its way down her cheek. She swiped at it. Flag gave a soft bark in greeting.

"Thank heavens you're here," Jody said. "I don't know what we can do in the dark, but we have to look for her. Let's go!"

"Hold your horses," Andy said. "First thing is to get across the creek here, and we can hardly see. The light from our headlamps will just bounce off the water and we won't be able to tell where we're putting our feet."

"I know, but we have to get over there. We can't search on this side of the creek. The slope is too steep."

"Look behind you, Jody. The moon is rising, and it's going to be almost full tonight. Give it another few minutes and we'll hardly need our lights. Here, Frank sent you a meatball sandwich." He handed her the grease-spotted paper-wrapped bundle.

Anxiety had taken Jody's appetite, but the aroma of the sandwich brought it back, and she'd need to keep up her strength for what might be a long night of searching ahead. She unwrapped the sandwich and sank her teeth into a huge bite. She chewed, watching as the moon slowly illuminated the water gushing over the gravel. She broke off a small piece of meatball and shared it with Flag.

Fifteen minutes later, the moon threw enough light to attempt the crossing. Although along the rest of its journey to the lake, the creek roared and twisted between banks of boulders, at this ford, the water rushed about a foot deep over gravel and small rocks. This was the only visible place to cross. Filled with spring runoff, the creek appeared to be at least twenty feet wide, and moving swiftly. Deep and fast enough to pull humans off their feet in the loose gravel if they weren't careful, and too deep for Flag to cross on her own.

Jody offered Flag the last piece of her meatball, crumpled the sandwich paper and wiped greasy fingers on her jeans. "Let's go!"

With one end of a long lead tied securely to his belt, Greg, the heaviest of the three, stepped into the water and kept going. Andy played out the slack on the other end of the lead. It wasn't ideal, but should give them at least a chance to hang onto Greg if he stumbled or the current proved too strong. After slipping once and almost falling, he waded safely out on the other side and pulled the lead taut. Jody clipped one lead to her belt and handed the other end to Andy. That would get Rose across when it was her turn. Then Jody looped the lead now stretching across the creek through her elbow and scooped up her forty-pound border collie. She'd secured Flag's harness to her own belt in case the dog struggled to get free, and spoke in soothing tones as the two of them crossed. She did not mention the throbbing pain in her ankle to anyone. She hoped the icy creek would numb the injury.

Andy lined up, the last to cross. At close to ninety pounds, Rose couldn't be carried. Andy clipped his dog's harness to the second long lead and pushed her ahead into the creek. She hesitated when the cold water hit her belly, but like dogs everywhere, she trusted her human not to take her into a dangerous situation. With Jody pulling on the other end of the lead, Rose struggled across, reached the bank, and shook herself, splattering everyone.

Following right behind her came Andy. In the middle of his crossing, he went down with a slippery misstep, soaking himself to mid-thighs. Gasping, he sprang up and pranced the last few steps, escaping from the freezing water.

They all sat down to dump water out of their boots and change into dry socks. The waterproofing on everyone's boots had been sorely tested, and even laced tightly, water had over-topped them.

"How are we going to get Kris across that if she's injured?" Andy asked, his gaze locked on the roiling creek.

"Too late to think about that," Jody said. "We have to find her first, and worry about how to get back later."

"Probably the helicopter would come back for her, don't you think?" Greg said. No one had an answer.

Pointing to the steepness of the south bank they had just come from, now bathed in moonlight, Jody explained her rationale for thinking Kris might be somewhere along this north bank of the creek. She told them about the signs that Kris may have slid or fallen into the creek.

"And Bullet tried to grab her," she said. "He got a grip on her jacket, but it tore and he lost her. I think that's how he got hurt."

Andy reassured Jody that Bullet was being well taken care of, probably already at the veterinary hospital.

"Yes," she said, "and now we have to find Kris. If we get lucky, she'll be somewhere stream-side." Holding her voice steady, emotionless, she went on. "She might be snagged on something in the creek itself." They had all just walked through that icy water. If Kris had fallen into that hours before, and still floated there, she would not be found alive.

They had to look until they found her. And in the deep shadows thrown by the luminous moonlight, they might look right past Kris's body caught up on a rock or lying at the creek's edge.

The dogs' talents would compensate for human sensory failings. Using their superior night vision and sense of smell, the dogs could find Kris and even the lost baby no matter how dark the shadows. Tempted to let the dogs off leash, the handlers elected instead to put them on long leads. Although the dogs would be in charge on this mission, one injured search dog was more than enough.

The temperature dropped and the rocks grew cold in the darkness. Jody knew it might get as cold as 30 degrees by dawn. They would need to keep moving just to keep warm. The moon climbed along a path that would take it directly overhead, and the rocks and trees were already splashed with bright light. The search conditions were as good as they were going to get that night. Jody was ready to go. She grabbed a stick and drew a rough map in the dirt of the trail. "Andy, I want you and Rose to see if you can pick up Jayden's scent over here." She drew an arrow on her dirt map pointing toward the right side of the trail and short side canyons there. "Rose might also let you know if she scents Kris, so you can be looking for both. If Kris pulled herself out of the creek, she might be in one of those smaller canyons, and that would be the best use of

Rose's tracking skills. Flag and I will stay as close to the creek as we can, along here, air-scenting." Jody considered the rocky bank. More than enough opportunity to make a wrong step and add injuries to her already painful ankle, but she was responsible for Kris's being lost, and she had to find her. Andy stood, and Rose shook herself, getting ready to work.

Greg looked east where the smoke was seen earlier in the day. He'd heard no more reports of smoke since about mid-day, and couldn't see any himself, even from this new vantage point. All the same, Greg was a fire prevention technician, and here he stood with his shovel and official forest service helmet with the headlamp on it. He should go see what he could see up that way.

"Think I'll hike east," he said, pointing. "I want to check out that situation with the possible fire."

"Good idea," Jody said. "And I want you to keep your eyes out for our search target, and even Kris, too. Head back here as quickly as you can." Jody felt responsible for everyone in the canyon, and a little reluctant to see Greg go off alone.

Thirty Four
Snakes

Greg pulled his helmet lamp down to better light the trail ahead. "I can probably catch up with you. You guys are going to be moving slowly, searching for your friend, aren't you?"

"Right," Jody agreed.

Greg took a few steps east on the trail. All of them were absorbed in their chosen tasks, and no one said anything about a kidnapper with a gun.

Rose showed interest in a scent almost immediately, her head held close to the ground, her ears swinging. As she and Andy moved away from the rushing water, her snuffles grew louder. She pulled up the slack in her lead, heading to the east, following Greg. Everyone stopped. Rose was doing her job, searching for the scent she'd been given of the little boy. She was responding to the presence of the baby on the north side of the creek. He may have even walked on this trail. He had to be nearby, possibly somewhere in one of these small canyons. He and his father might be hiding behind a rock or up in a tree. Andy praised his dog and gave her a few treats. He looked at Jody.

"What should we do now? Rose still wants to find the baby, and she's tracking him this way." They stared at each other, thinking.

Jody's priority had become finding Kris, and quickly. The baby might still be east near the falls, although they'd all made the assumption the baby and his father had gone west toward the cabins. But now the search mission to find the baby had taken a backseat to finding Kris, at least from Jody's point of view.

"How about this," Greg said. "I'm going east to check out that fire. I'll look for the baby this direction," he waved, "and you guys go that way with your dogs. So we'll cover all the bases."

"Good thinking, Greg." Jody wasn't convinced Greg would find anything without a dog to help, but any plan that got them back to looking for Kris worked for her. She flipped open her taser holster, drew out the device, and handed it to Greg. He held it in his palm, looking dubious.

"Do you know how to use that thing?" Andy asked, and Greg shook his head. Andy stepped close and provided a fifteen-second tutorial. Greg tucked the taser into a front pocket and flashed Jody a thumbs up as he turned to go.

"Okay," Andy said, "So now how do we get Rose to change gears?"

"Wait," Jody said. "I have an idea." She pulled her pocket open and pointed her headlamp at the shred of purple ripstop Bullet had torn from Kris's jacket. "Let's try this. It's not the best scent article, I know, but it was Kris's."

Careful not to transfer the scent of her meatball sandwich to the scrap, she let Andy use a clean poop bag to pull the piece of jacket out and offer it to Rose. It was impossible to know what Rose made of this new scent. For her, Kris's scent had already been established as an irrelevant one, so it was anyone's guess whether she would now pick it up and track the lost woman.

Jody pointed and Andy offered the scent article to Flag also. The border collie sniffed, looked up at Jody, and sniffed again. "Find that," Jody said, hoping her dog understood that the familiar scent of Kris was the one to seek. Kris often volunteered to be the hidden victim on training searches, so Flag did have experience scenting for her friend.

Andy gave Rose another sniff at the fabric, and they started out again. Andy walked Rose about thirty feet to the west before saying "Find." Immediately she went right back on scent, this time heading west. This might indicate Kris had dragged herself from the creek and walked down this trail, or, more likely, the little boy had passed both east and west. Air-scenting dogs follow their noses to the current position of the target, but tracking dogs follow the route taken by the target. Even where the trail fell into deep blackness under the trees, Rose tracked, her nose to the ground, her ears swinging.

While Rose snuffled along the right edge of the trail, Andy close behind, Jody moved Flag closer to the creek, some forty feet away. That far away, Jody and Andy could not see each other, hidden as they were by rocks and brush.

"You ready to go to work?" Jody said to Flag. The dog gave a shake and a happy wiggle, then looked up at Jody. She was ready. "Find," Jody said.

Clambering over boulders and between willow saplings, Flag repeatedly got her long lead caught up and had to be disentangled. Half the time, Jody couldn't even see her dog, and followed blindly where the lead went. Flag did appear to be scenting someone, but there was no telling who it might be.

Jody called her dog back, and scratched behind Flag's ears. "Hey, girl," she whispered. "Let's find Kris, okay? Kris." Again, Jody wondered if Flag understood to search for the familiar scent of a friend. Had Flag caught Kris's scent? Or might the dog be ignoring Kris's scent and pursuing someone else? Would Jody climb over the next rock and find herself face to face with a crazed kidnapper?

Flag leapt onto a boulder and then disappeared again in the shadows ahead. Her lead went slack. The darkness between the rocks hid the dog, and the creek masked any sound. Had something happened to Flag? After studying the route ahead with her headlamp, Jody pointed the light at the lead and followed it around the next boulder. Flag's fluorescent neoprene lead had become pinched under another rock, with Flag pulling hard at the other end. In spite of the danger, Jody had to let Flag off-leash. Her heart stuck in her throat when she did it, but finding Kris, and soon, took precedence over caution.

"Go, girl. Find Kris." Once off lead, Flag disappeared over the top of the next boulder. Any sounds she might be making were rendered inaudible by the rumble of rushing water. Several long scary minutes later, she reappeared, running up to Jody. Then she took off again, her white patches flashing in the moonlight. Roughly five minutes later, she appeared again. This checking back with the handler every few minutes was normal behavior for a herding dog out on a leisurely hike.

Her behavior could also be interpreted as a signal that she had located the target. The air-scenting dog runs from the target to the handler, and then back to the target, much in the same way that Lassie used to cajole Timmy to accompany her back to the old mine. Jody had to scramble to keep up with Flag.

"Flag!" Jody called. She felt panicky at being left behind, in the night, trying to climb over rocks. She placed the foot with the injured ankle on the top of one slippery boulder and, grimacing in pain, tried to pull herself up. The foot slid, and the boot jammed in the darkness between rocks. Her injured ankle was trapped, stabbing pain shooting up her leg. She leaned her head into the darkness and blindly clawed at the laces securing her boot until they loosened. Stifling her groans by clenching her teeth, she extracted her foot, leaving the jammed boot behind. She took the injured ankle out of the action by crouching on the knee, and prepared to kick with the other foot at where the stuck boot was lost in the shadow between rocks.

The rattling was almost inaudible at first, growing stronger as Jody froze. With one heartbeat, she knew exactly what that sound represented. In the crevices between these rocks, a rattlesnake, possibly several, had burrowed to hibernate last winter. With the coming of spring and the warmth of sunlight on the rocks, the snakes were awakening. Her boot slipping between rocks had disturbed and alarmed at least one snake.

Every instinct told her to run, but without that boot to support it, the injured ankle would bear no weight. If she didn't move, and soon, the snake would strike, or Flag would check back in, prancing around between the rocks, and be bitten herself.

Flag had been snake-proofed using aversion training, and would immediately back-off in the presence of anything resembling a snake. She'd even been known to recoil from a twisty piece of manzanita branch. But this snake was invisible, hidden between rocks. If her paw slid into the snake's hiding pace, she would be bitten, and a rattlesnake bite in this remote location would be fatal to a dog.

Jody couldn't call Andy for help for the same reason. Doing so would only bring others into danger near the now very audible but still invisible snake. She had to get that boot out and get far away, fast.

The air was cold, possibly already into the 30s. This meant that, although alarmed and able to strike, the snake would be lethargic and slow to move. Jody's only choice was to kick at the jammed boot until it loosened, then reach into the darkness and pull it out.

It took two kicks before the boot moved. The rattling had increased, so possibly more than one snake waited there, maybe a whole nest full. Bites from rattlesnake young deliver more venom than bites from older snakes, and the young tend to be incautious and bite instead of moving away from a threat. It was time to reach into the darkness with one hand and grab the collar of the boot. Jody was paralyzed with fear.

The sound of Flag clambering toward her broke the spell. She would be more likely to survive a rattlesnake bite than would Flag. She pulled the sleeve of her jacket as far over her hand as she could and made a quick reaching jab, hoping she'd be a split second faster than the snake. Her fingers closed around the collar, and she used the power of panic to jerk the boot free. Something did brush against her sleeve, but whether it was the rock or a striking snake, she did not slow down long enough to investigate. She crawled backwards fast, dragging the boot with her and calling Flag.

Waves of pain washed over her as she stuffed the injured ankle back into the boot, and tied the laces. She was too shaky to stand as tears of relief streamed down her face. Flag's warm tongue swiped at her cheek. "Hey, girl." Jody ruffled the dog's neck and winced. She dug out the first aid kit and dry swallowed two more pain killers.

"Let's go find Kris!" Flag started away again, but more slowly. Jody scrambled after the dog as best she could, allowing herself a low moan with every step. This close to the creek, no one would hear her, and expressing the agony seemed to help. She couldn't afford to let herself be distracted by her own pain. As she traveled, she continually aimed her headlamp along both banks of the creek, and also between rocks before planting her boots. She saw no signs of Kris.

She was going to have to search smarter, and not rely as much as she usually did on getting her own eyes on every square foot. The deep shadows, her own inability to climb every rock, and the need to find Kris fast, combined to force her to have even more faith in her dog's natural talents and extensive training than usual.

Letting Flag go on ahead, Jody stopped, scanned the rocks, bright in the moonlight now shining from directly overhead. Could a violent kidnapper be watching her even now? If he'd selected Jody as his next victim, she had no way to escape. She could hardly walk.

She moved closer to the bank, where Flag seemed to prefer searching. She wouldn't be any safer there, and the traveling was no easier, but she was trusting her dog.

If Kris had been conscious when she hit the water, she would have pulled herself out at the earliest opportunity. Although deep and running fast, the creek was narrow, with boulders and small trees reaching nearly across in places. Kris might have been able to get out on her own. Flag was following someone's scent there along the edge.

The swiftly moving water also created places where a body, even a conscious body, could be pulled between rocks and under. And upstream only a few miles, this creek had been snow and ice. Even a few minutes submerged could result in a bitter hypothermic death. Jody couldn't be sure what Flag would do if she scented Kris's body in the creek. She called Flag back to her, and tried to keep the eager dog in sight.

Jody's ankle numbed and she became bolder as she bushwhacked through brush and low branches nearer the creek. Andy and Rose persisted in their search, tracking on the north side of the trail and at the mouths of the smaller canyons. The moon continued its journey across the night sky, throwing trees and boulders into shifting shadows as the night wore on.

Thirty Five
Buried Embers

Greg marched, making as much sound as he could. The light from his headlamp swept the trees and made their shadows dance. He carried his sharp firefighting shovel high and visible against his shoulder, taking comfort in its heft. Reassuring to have it along, just in case. In case of what, he tried not to dwell on. The roaring creek to his right and moonlight falling in front kept him mostly on the trail in spite of the darkness. In less than an hour, he had drawn close to the falls. Faint light illuminated the flat area near the creek frequented by backpackers. By aiming his headlamp, he was able to locate where the campfire had burned beyond its original bed, through the dry grasses, and into the side canyon. Greg switched off his headlamp. If there was any active fire remaining, it would give itself away with an orange glow in the night. Greg held his breath and peered into the side canyon. Nothing. He turned his headlamp back on and swung its beam slowly, about a foot off the ground, looking for reflections in eyes staring back at him, worried he might be sharing the night with an unexpected companion. Still nothing.

He followed the blackened grasses farther into the side canyon and came to where a couple of young trees had burned. California's long drought had weakened trees of all ages, and made them susceptible to infestations of the mountain bark beetle, now decimating forests throughout the Sierra. It was impossible to tell if these skeletal trees had already been dead when the fire reached them. The eerie ash-gray stubs of branches seemed to reach toward him in the bouncing light of his headlamp. He backed away, and looked around again. He still could not see even one glowing ember remaining from the earlier blaze.

A black shadow lying on the ground caught in the beam of his headlamp. Cautiously, he approached, not sure what it might be. Upon closer inspection, it proved to be only a fallen trunk. Probably had lain there for many seasons before the fire consumed its flanks. Greg pushed with his boot and succeeded in rolling the log over slightly. A few points of dying fire flickered out when the fuel was disturbed. To be on the safe side, Greg pounded the points of light to oblivion with his shovel, threw dirt on top of what was left, and scraped twigs and dead leaves away from the perimeter of the log.

That appeared to be the end of the fire, and he had seen no evidence that a baby or a kidnapper still resided there. He walked out to the mouth of the side canyon, looked around one last time, and started his hike to catch up with Andy and Jody.

***

In the darkness, Greg nearly stepped on a buried rivulet of fire eating its way deep under the forest duff toward the next side canyon. The fire sent up no light, and no scent, but quietly crawled along first one pine needle, then a blade of dead grass. Biding its time, waiting until it could reach a more viable source of energy, or for that cat's paw of air that might breathe life into it again.

***

Deputy Hogan hunkered uncomfortably on the same rock he'd been on for what felt like hours, still on the south side of the creek. He had inspected his proposed landing point across the raging water until the battery in his flashlight threatened to fail. He felt confident he would have been able to make the jump safely, if he had been properly equipped for such a feat. In light hiking boots, carrying no equipment, and in broad daylight, the leap would be no problem. With moonlight the only illumination, and dressed in his uniform and heavy oxfords, carrying fifteen pounds of tactical gear and the flashlight, his confidence failed him.

The consequences of attempting the jump and not making it were hard to predict, aside from likely drowning. If he personally survived, his gear might not. His oxfords could get dunked and be ruined. He'd probably land on his sidearm and damage some vital internal organ. And what about that memo they'd gotten recently about being careful to wear a raincoat over the taser while directing traffic at the scene of an incident in wet weather? Apparently tasers had been known to fire spontaneously after getting wet, injuring and burning officers.

These thoughts and other equally discouraging ones had immobilized him for hours. After one last long look at the gap he would need to clear and the rock that would have to hold him once he landed, he gave up the idea. Glory or not, it wasn't worth the risk.

His legs and knees were stiff in the cool night air after so long without movement. He slid to the back of his rock, and slowly scrambled farther upstream, looking, without much hope, for another possible crossing. Finding a comfortable spot on a boulder, he pulled out his radio and tried to contact the other deputies scattered through the forest.

"SD-two-sixer. Come in anyone. What's your status?"

The first response came from his partner, also stationed along the creek watching for the abductor to attempt a crossing, "SD-thirty-four here. Still waiting. Any signs of that guy?"

Hogan's teeth began to grind. Close to retirement, the older deputy looked forward to a comfortable pension and more time with his grandkids in a few weeks. Hogan knew the guy wouldn't risk his life on some foolhardy glory-seeking rescue. For a brief second, Hogan wondered about his own motivations.

"SD-thirty-four here," the deputy called again. "Do you copy? I'm waiting for dawn, then heading back. Damn hungry here. SD-two-six, do you copy?"

"Yeah, yeah, I hear you. Are you sure you didn't fall asleep and miss the guy?"

"SD-thirty-four here. Heck Hogan, I don't even sleep at home in my own bed. Sure not going to drift off out here on a rock. SD-thirty-four out."

Hogan tried again. "SD-two-sixer, Anyone else out there? Come in, please."

Only one deputy was left watching the entry to the highway from the jeep track. She stood at the rear of her vehicle when the call came in and had to jump to grab her radio on the front seat.

"SD-eight-nine here. What's up, SD-two-six? Over."

"Any signs of the abductor there? Over."

"SD-eight-nine here. No, sir, nothing here. Got a call from dispatch. Tried to raise you. Dispatch says the kidnapper has taken a second victim. One of those searchers. Over."

Hogan held off his response while he cursed into the night for several seconds. Then he depressed the push-to-talk button and, in barely controlled fury said, "Where the blazes are those other deputies? I thought they were coming to help. Everyone fall asleep or what?" There was a pause, then, "Over."

"SD-eight-nine here. Deputy Tarrazo headed in to assist you a long time ago. Right after you called." After hours waiting in the silent darkness, the red and blue lights on top of her vehicle flashing hypnotically, the deputy had given up actively standing guard. Desperate for something to keep her awake, she'd undertaken an inventory of the gear packed tightly into the cargo hold in the SUV. She'd found a stash of out-of-date energy bars and half a flat of bottled water. The energy bars were a welcome find initially, but after two chocolate-flavored ones and a blueberry-muffin bar, they'd lost their appeal. There had not been any sign of the eagerly awaited takeout dinners.

"SD-eight-nine here. Be on the lookout for Tarrazo. All's quiet, here. Over and out."

The fourth deputy, Tarrazo, the one who'd hiked away from the vehicle at the highway, did not answer his radio at all. No one had seen or heard from him since he left his vehicle in response to Deputy Hogan's earlier request for assistance. It was a big forest, it was dark, and no one knew what might have happened.

Thirty Six
Killer

Agent Cardona sat in her car for a long time after she'd ended the call with the Sacramento field office. What she'd learned was disturbing, and she would've liked to share the information with someone. The thing was, the searchers already had their hands full trying to find their lost friend as well look for that baby, Jayden. And the sheriff's deputies were intent on capturing the kidnapper. Cardona couldn't see how it would help them to know that evidence from the storage garage proved conclusively that Matthew had killed Jayden's mother.

A rapping on her closed window made her jump and set her heart pounding. Apparently she'd drifted off. Some guy in a light-colored uniform rapped again with a set of keys.

"You there," he said, "you FBI?"

Cautiously she rolled her window halfway open.

"Yes, that's right." She was too startled to remember to introduce herself.

"U. S. Forest Service law enforcement," he said, gesturing vaguely at a dirty white SUV left blocking the entrance to the parking area. "Would have been here hours ago but evidently the roads out here've gotten moved around a lot and I couldn't find the place." He giggled nervously at his own joke.

"Mm-huh. So, how can I help you?"

"Well," he adjusted the weight of his belt, leaving the heel of one hand resting on the butt of an ugly-looking gun. "This is my forest, and my jurisdiction. Those guys over there," he said, now waving at the firefighting crew, "they said you're FBI and I'm inquiring as to your purpose in being out here."

"Assistant Special Agent Cardona," she said. "I'm here because there's been a kidnapping, and it appears both the kidnapper and his victim are out there in your forest." She'd decided it would be best to coddle the delusions of this megalomaniac, or at least that was her policy in the absence of back-up. "County sheriff's deputies are deployed down the road six or eight miles. Near the dam. They're moving in from that end, hoping to trap the kidnapper. I think that's where you want to be."

"Yeah? Nobody said anything about that."

Cardona couldn't think of an immediate response to his observation. "Possibly it's a secret operation?" she finally said.

The law enforcement officer's eyebrows shot up, and he gazed off to the distant west. "Okay then, I'll head down there." He gave her a half salute, trotted to his vehicle, and returned to the highway.

She went back to gazing around the parking lot, now silent as night journeyed toward morning. Most everyone had settled into sleeping spots. She still had misgivings about sleeping in her car if hungry bears might peel it open. She started the ignition and moved to the spot previously occupied by a CHP vehicle, as close to Jody's Subaru as she could manage. It would have to be a very slender bear if it wanted to try to get between those cars. Of course, a slender bear would be a hungry bear. She scrutinized the area again. Sharing her new information would have to wait until morning.

She climbed out the passenger side, shifted her official Crime Scene Investigation kit from the back seat to the trunk, and tucked it next to the duffel bag of supplies the dogs had found. If the bears wanted to tear apart the car to get those Slim Jims, they could have them, as long as they left her alone. She looked at the strange gathering around her. Seemed like most people were sleeping, or at least quiet. She crawled into her back seat, wadded her jacket into a makeshift pillow and was sound asleep five minutes later.

***

Frank had finished washing the dinner dishes and contemplated hanging the garbage from a tree as he'd told Cardona he would. Inertia got the better of him. Instead, he locked everything in Jody's car and hoped the wildlife would be deterred by all the other humans. He leashed up MacDuff and took him for a short walk. The dog seemed interested in much that he was sensing at the edge of camp, but he and Frank were still learning to read each others body language, so MacDuff did not exhibit any behaviors that looked like alerts to Frank.

Afterwards, the two of them curled up on sleeping bags inside the exercise pen, the radio pulled close so Frank would not miss any calls. He laid his cell phone beside his head. He might miss a ring, but MacDuff would probably nudge him awake.

The puppy was thoroughly enjoying this adventure. He'd been attentively watching humans moving around camp all evening. Only after a long time did the puppy lower his head to his paws and drift off to join his friend Frank in unsettled sleep.

Thoughts of his son, tied to a tree somewhere in the forest behind him, were already fading. He walked on with no idea what lay ahead, or what he might do when he got there.

His back was to the east, so he missed the faint thread of rising sun along the horizon. The moonlight faded and dipped behind clouds to the west. The trail clung to the bank of the creek for more than three miles before it flattened and moved away from the water and into a forested area to the south. It was harder to stay on the trail there under the cover of trees, and harder still to continue heading directly west. For a moment, Matthew thought about the compass function on his cell phone, but then he remembered he'd abandoned the phone days before. His steps became less certain, and he peered more anxiously around the darkened forest.

Without warning, radio static buzzed somewhere to his left. He jumped and almost fell into a gully, then held still, listening. The tired female voice coming over the radio was muted.

"SD-four-one-three, come in please." A pause. "Deputy Tarrazo, please respond. Four-one-three, come in please."

There was no answer. Matthew took three more steps toward the sound, dead pine needles crunching underfoot. He stopped, squatted, untied his shoes and set them beside the path. Crept closer, more quietly now, stopping for long pauses to listen between each movement. The radio, twenty feet or so ahead, had gone silent. It was possible someone had dropped a radio. Or were they there, watching, waiting until Matthew revealed himself and be would be caught or killed? He could not be caught. It wouldn't matter to anyone that Cecily had killed herself with her struggles. No one would believe him. If he were caught, he'd go to prison for sure. He had to get away, and time was running out. Overhead, the sky was almost imperceptibly lighter, daylight no more than an hour away.

Matthew peered under the shadows at ground level. Moved closer. Then he saw it. A heavy body lying on the ground. More an absence of light than a visible object. It could easily have been mistaken for a fallen log. The body did not move.

Matthew crept closer. From that distance, he could see two tiny lights shining from the middle of the body. A radio, probably, and maybe some other device. Some shiny part of the uniform twinkled a faint reflection. Matthew gripped his club, shifting it into position, his hands sweaty with fear.

***

Miles to the east, the rounded mountain of granite scoured by ancient glaciers gradually gave up the glow of moonlight as the pale rays of a rising sun appeared. The stone warmed, and as it did, the air over it lifted, pulling the cooler night air upward in a whisper of a breeze.

One red ember crawled the length of a dry pine needle. As the needle turned to gray ash it gave life to the ember. Reaching the end of the needle, the ember dropped to the soft grass. The tiny fire, never vigorous, would have finally died there, but for the slightest upward movement of warming air. A few blades of dry grass smoldered and shriveled, giving off less smoke than a single candle on a child's birthday cake. More gently moving air wafted, and the surrounding grasses glowed a deep red. A second pine needle, then a third began to smoke, then glow. Another puff, and the smoldering vegetation burst into a brief orange flame. The fire reached the soft grasses at the foot of the small dead pine where the doe and her fawn had been sleeping hours before. Heat and smoke rose along the dry bark, reaching for the fuel above.

Stirring and stretching with the arrival of morning, first one gray squirrel, then another sniffed the air. Chattering to their comrades, they watched the dead tree explode into flames. Throwing their tiny bodies across the expanses between trees, and screaming in alarm, they flew away from the fire. Alerted by the squirrels, two does and their families emerged from the darkness deeper in one narrow canyon. The still-spotted fawns blinked in the rays of the early sun and lifted their noses to the unfamiliar smell. The does herded their fawns away from the smoke. They stepped cautiously, because the scent of humans and dogs became stronger as they moved west.

East of the falls, a black bear sow dozed at the entrance to her den, hidden behind the brush on the slope overlooking the canyon. Inside, two twelve-week-old cubs, still much too young to leave their nest, slept peacefully. The sow lifted her snout. She smelled the smoke, and could also sense that it was moving away from her den and her off-spring. In a crack a few feet away, a drowsy king snake curled his cold body against the last vestige of warmth held in the granite. He wouldn't move again until the heat of the sun coaxed him out to lie on an open face of rock. Above them all, a golden eagle shifted in the top of the tallest whitebark pine and turned her head to watch the tiny burning pine tree send flying embers to the next copse of trees. She spread her wings and caught the current of rising air enough to float upward. With a dip of one wing, she circled, then soared over the creek, heading for another favorite perch on the western shore of Lake Nell.

Thirty Eight
Fire

Jody and Flag drifted left, to the edge of the creek, still rock scrambling, still searching. They were out of sight of Andy and Rose, tracking along the trail. The moon had set and the sun not yet risen, so the darkness became deeper, more dangerous for the searchers. Jody's radio buzzed to life with a call from Andy. They discussed stopping to rest soon. It was too treacherous to continue.

Andy agreed to meet at the trail in twenty minutes. He said he had one more place he wanted to check.

He followed Rose to the right of the trail. They stood at the mouth of a tapering canyon. The canyon's stone walls rose steeply on each side, and no light penetrated the shadows. Rose pulled Andy deeper into the canyon, her nose close to the dirt. Rose's alert signaled the presence of the baby, or possibly the kidnapper. Rose might even be alerting on Kris, since she had been given that scent as well. Rose knew which she smelled, but if her alert distinguished between the three, Andy was incapable of understanding. He hesitated just inside the black canyon, alone and unarmed.

"What's there, Rosie? Is someone there?" Rose wagged in reply, then stretched her neck out and gave a low whine. "That's it, isn't it, Rose. Somebody is there."

Finding targets was the best game for Rose. For every hour spent on an actual search mission, Rose and Andy spent at least ten hours in training, where there was almost always a successful find, lots of celebration and many treats. Andy rummaged in his pack and found the plastic box packed with liver treats. He gave her a couple.

He peered into the darkness beyond the reach of his light. Opening his eyes wider, he gazed beyond the whitish trunks of trees disappearing overhead. Rose, too, lifted her gaze to the darkness and her ears to the silence. If someone was back in that canyon, they were watching Andy and Rose in mute stillness.

The thin beam of Andy's headlamp dimmed to nothing only a few feet ahead, but it did present a clear bullseye should anyone be taking aim from deeper in the darkness. Andy stepped away from the canyon opening. He radioed Jody. "We're on target here," he said into the device. "Rose found someone, but I don't want to go in on my own. Meet me on the trail?" Since they'd come around a curve in the canyon, neither of them had been able to raise Frank on their radios, and they didn't know the frequency being used by the deputy sheriffs. They were going to have to handle this on their own. Tugging Rose behind him, Andy made his way to the middle of the trail.

***

Greg had spent his night exploring the side canyons, calling quietly for Jayden, and wandering west, slowly catching up with Jody and Andy. Ambivalent about hiking back to camp, and with his headlamp battery failing fast, he had convinced himself that he was doing useful work being on the lookout for any signs of fire, or possibly a dangerous kidnapper sneaking up behind the searchers. He only realized dawn was approaching when he saw Andy and Jody standing on the trail up ahead. He waved and trudged toward them.

They all sat down and pulled out water bottles and snacks.

"Rose alerted to someone in that canyon there," Andy pointed to the right. "Not sure who."

With a wave, Jody said, "Flag is onto Kris's scent over there." She hoped that's what Flag was scenting.

"So it must be the baby in the canyon," Andy said. "How about if the three of us go get him, and then we'll hike out to where we can radio Frank."

"I'm not going to give up looking for Kris," Jody argued. "You and Greg can check out Rose's find. Flag and I are going back to the creek." Jody dumped the last handful of kibble into Flag's folding bowl and the dog inhaled it almost before it hit bottom. To prevent her from racing away again, Jody clipped a short lead on her harness. The dog needed a break as much as the rest of them.

Andy's reply was defensive. "Rose whined and even pointed into that canyon. She's definitely found the target, but you can't see a damn thing in there, and one of us might get hurt." He glanced east, where the sun dawned. Full sunlight might be almost an hour away. "Those search teams on the ridge are probably getting ready to start down. We could wait until they get here. They'll have first aid and stuff."

"Even better if we could raise the deputy sheriffs on the radio and get them over here," Jody said. "If there's a kidnapper with a gun back there, we've done our job."

Flag raised her snout in the air and shifted to face east. She sniffed again, blinked and squinted. It wasn't until she let out a soft whine that the humans paid any attention. Flag stood and lifted her nose higher. She paced left, then right, trying to localize the direction of the scent. Rose stood and joined Flag, lifting her head too. Rose was not an air-scenting dog, but she could still smell whatever it was Flag had noticed. Rose barked. Flag walked to Jody and tried to crawl into her lap. The dog was signaling anxiety, alerting to something dangerous. The humans looked at one another, trying to interpret the dogs' unusual behavior.

Movement in the dim light at the side of the trail brought them all to their feet. Judging by the rustling in the underbrush and shifting shadows, it was several large bodies coming toward them from the east. A couple of the bodies broke into the lighter area on the trail. Deer, six or eight of them. The deer regarded the humans and dogs warily, milling anxiously. Jody pulled Flag to the other side of the trail, encouraging the others to join her. A deer could do serious damage to a dog with one flick of its powerful, sharp-edged hoof, and those deer looked like they were already agitated. After a moment sussing the situation, first one deer began to creep past them, then another, then all of them ran by the humans, stampeding west.

"What's that about?" Andy asked.

Jody shook her head, indicating she had no answer to his question. "You think that's what Flag and Rose were smelling? Those deer coming this way?"

"Possibly," Andy said. He looked at Flag, her snout lifted again in the morning breeze, her eyes squinting and tearing slightly. She crowded herself close to Jody's legs, almost standing on top of her hiking boots. "Or possibly the dogs are smelling the same thing that spooked the deer."

More movement in the shadows, and a cinnamon and buff-colored creature about the size of a cat emerged onto the trail. She didn't even sniff in their direction. Behind her long fluffy tail trailed three smaller versions of herself. The kits looked toward the dogs, but the mother continued padding resolutely toward the west, and the kits followed.

"What was that?" Andy asked. "A weasel? I've never even seen a weasel."

Jody wasn't sure either. "Some kind of a weaselly-type creature. Like a pine marten, or maybe a fisher? Whatever it was, that was just strange. Why would a reclusive animal like that bring her kits out where there are dogs and people?"

The humans felt themselves breathing deeply, trying to catch a whiff of whatever the dogs were scenting, and what might be causing the other animals to behave so strangely. The trees in the dark canyon were suddenly alive with small birds fluttering about in confusion. Several of them burst out of the canyon's mouth and pumped their wings hard, also going west. Whatever was happening, the humans were just standing there while all the other animals were taking flight.

Greg leaned back, stretching. He looked as though he was considering lying down in the grass for a nap. It was contagious, and Jody also yawned and stretched. They were all exhausted.

"Come on, you guys. I know we're all tired, but we can't stop now," Jody said. Greg looked longingly at the ground, then turned toward the east and yawned again. The dawning sun had just burst over the edge of the granite escarpment, sending rays along the trail.

"Hey," Greg said, "does that look hazy to you down there?" He pointed toward the eastern end of the canyon.

"Yeah, like, possibly like dust, or smoke, you mean?" Andy said, voicing what was dawning on all of their faces.

"Oh, yeah, definitely like smoke." Greg was trying to disengage his radio from its holster in such a hurry that he wasn't having much luck. "And it's coming this way. That's a fire. That's what all the animals are running from. Looks like it could turn into a big one too. Well, shoot," he said when he'd finally gotten the radio out and keyed on. "We've been out here all night. My battery's dead. How am I going to call this in?" Greg was becoming agitated. His first chance to show real responsibility on a wildfire and his battery was dead. He reached into his back pocket, hoping to find his cell phone. This close to the lake and a cell relay station, he thought he might be able to get a signal on that. He came up empty. His cell phone sat on the dashboard in his truck. He looked behind them. "Maybe if I run the whole way, I could get back to the ford before the fire cuts off the trail."

No one answered him. Jody and Andy had both pulled out their radios. Their batteries were also low, but they took turns trying to raise Frank. Even when a call sounded as though it had gone through, it wasn't answered.

"Frank must be sleeping," Jody said, trying again.

Thirty Nine
Mobilizing

Frank was not asleep. He had managed a couple of hours of rest, but been awakened by Cullison's truck pulling in before dawn. He tried to doze off again, and had almost fallen asleep when another vehicle arrived. Crunching footsteps came toward him, and MacDuff awoke, shook himself, and began a happy wiggling greeting. Frank cracked one eye to see the toe of a well-worn running shoe in front of his face.

"Good morning," a voice murmured.

Frank opened both eyes and sat up. It was Lowell, Kris's husband. Frank had never met Lowell, but he knew him instantly. He looked exactly like Kris: on the roundish side, fly-away curls, lots of freckles.

"Sorry to wake you," Lowell said. "Any word from Kris? I've got Bullet in the car. I picked him up from the emergency vet on the way up here. He's going to be fine after a good rest. Anyway, have you heard from Kris?"

***

Cullison had returned to the Eagle Meadow camp before dawn, then hiked out to the pass. From her perspective at the pass, not only had she seen smoke, she'd also seen a flaming tree. She radioed back to camp, alerting the fire crew waiting there. Racing into camp, she yelled instructions to anyone who would listen. The entire parking area erupted into action. Cullison's loud commands awakened everyone, and she began mobilizing her forces. She was on the radio first to dispatch, triggering the pre-planned response that, at dawn, would set into motion at least two air tankers to drop retardant.

"And get me a helitack chopper with a strike team on it. That fire is in a narrow canyon where ground crews might be more effective at cutting it off, if you can get them here fast!" She waved at sleepy firefighters as they stumbled from their bags. Frank and Lowell could only watch in wide-eyed amazement as the meadow burst into the controlled panic of firefighting activity.

Cullison yelled again into her radio. "Once they've off-loaded the crew, deploy that chopper at the lake. I'm going to need water drops inside that canyon, places the tankers can't hit." She scanned the meadow. "And send the mobilization team. It's time to turn this meadow into a real fire camp."

***

Frank's radio crackled with a weak signal. On her third try, Jody made a connection. He relayed what little he knew. Static and interfering traffic on their frequency cut in and out. Frank spoke again, more loudly.

"There's an active fire burning at the east end of the canyon, headed your way, fast! Get out of there! They've called in air tankers, helitack crews, I don't know what all, but you need to find Kris and get the heck out of there!"

"Roger that. Ten-four! Ten-four!" Jody called back. She turned to the others.

"Frank says we need to get out of here. Something about an attack."

Andy's eyes widened, and he took a long shaky breath. Jody knew he had a tendency toward claustrophobia, and all these fleeing animals were probably putting him on edge. "An attack?" he said. "What kind of an attack?"

"I might have heard that wrong," Jody said. "In any case, I heard the 'get out of there' part right. Let's step this up." She knew that her calm leadership and a structured plan would contribute more to a successful search than any amount of hurrying.

She was done with excitement. She only wanted her friends safely home. It was obvious no one was going back to camp by way of the ford. They would all have to head toward the trail's end at Lake Nell, trying to outrun the fire. But before they could do that, they had to come face to face with whoever lurked in the dark canyon. And they had to find Kris.

"Check your watches, everyone," Jody said. "I'm giving you ten minutes to get in and out of that canyon. Then I want you to check in with me again. We'll all move forward toward the lake. Flag and I will be over there along the creek, heading the same direction. Let's go!"

Jody watched as Andy pawed quickly through his pack.

"I'm looking for something I can use as a weapon," Andy said, "even a stick." Jody tugged her taser out of its pouch and handed it over. She had more important things to worry about than a dangerous kidnapper.

Even after she and Flag started again on the search for Kris, she could hear Andy and Greg calling to one another.

When they again confronted the mouth of the canyon, the dawning sun illuminated its interior ever so slightly, increasing the chance they might be able to see someone coming at them. Andy kept Rose as close to his leg as possible, at the same time, letting her take the lead as she followed her nose. The three of them took one step at a time, Greg swinging the large flashlight back and forth across the dim canyon interior.

"There!" Greg said. "I saw a flash, something white. It's near that tree at the end of the canyon." He pointed the weakening beam of his flashlight.

"Oh, yeah, I see it, too, in the tree."

"You guys got something?" Jody called.

Andy's excited voice came back. "Yeah! Over here, Greg. It's over here!" This was followed by several minutes of silence. "Okay, never mind, Jody. It was just another wadded diaper, stuffed into a hole in the bark."

"Hang on! I just stepped on something." Greg's voice this time. "Oh. It's an empty juice box. Sorry, I thought it was something."

"So," Andy said to Greg, the disappointment evident in his voice, "the baby was here."

"And now he's gone," Greg added, in a no less discouraged tone. He swung the light through the rest of the short canyon. Let's get out of here."

"Checking in!" Andy called when they were back out on the trail.

Jody's head popped up over a boulder creekside. "Roger that!" She glanced east where black smoke rolled toward them. Still no sign of Kris. Possibly they had time to check one more potential hiding place. "See what Rose thinks over there!" She pointed at the dark mouth of the next canyon.

Already the smoke hung thick enough to cause Andy's eyes to stream tears, and Rose went into a sneezing fit. "I don't know if she'll be able to track with all this smoke," he replied.

Jody waved and went back to her search. She kept going, and hoped that Andy would keep going, too. What else could they do, and where would they go if they quit? Keeping Flag on the shorter leash, Jody headed closer to the bank of the creek where the air was clearer.

Flag would work faster off leash, but she might be equally likely to do what dogs usually do when they smell smoke coming, which is to crawl underneath something. Dogs can sound the alarm when they smell smoke, but they usually need help getting away from a fire, since their inclination is to crawl under some nearby hiding place. Also, Jody was not convinced that Flag's scenting abilities might not be overwhelmed by the drifting smoke now beginning to fill the canyon. If Kris was somewhere stream side, Jody and Flag might be more successful finding her by searching visually, now that daylight was returning. Jody was surprised when almost immediately Flag went back to work, this time snuffling closer to the ground where the air was less smoky.

At that moment, Jody had completely forgotten about a possibly armed kidnapper in their midst. Adrenaline was driving her. She and Flag had to find Kris. She had to lead them all to safely escape the oncoming forest fire.

She opened her mouth to call Kris, but only a dry-throated croak came out. She was so tired. She pulled her whistle out and blew insistently, once, twice, over and over again.

Forty
No Dogs Allowed

Frank and Lowell sat near the camp stove, watching the activity around them and sipping the coffee Frank had coaxed out of his stove-top percolator. Agent Cardona stumbled over to join them, smoothing where her hair had settled in a lopsided bunch. She accepted the cup Frank offered.

"So, there is actually a fire out there?" she asked.

"Blew up early this morning. Check it out." Frank pointed at the black smoke rising above the ridge in a thick thread. "Our teams are okay so far," he added.

"We hope." Lowell said.

"They'll find her, Lowell. Try not to worry." Frank introduced the other two. They enjoyed their coffee while they watched a large tent being set up on the other side of the camp, and tables and chairs positioned under it. A shiny catering truck pulled in close, opened its serving windows, and those inside began to distribute styrofoam-boxed breakfasts.

After a bit, Cardona remembered about her news. "Oh," she said, "our teams have completed evidence recovery and the investigation at that storage garage where they found Cecily Tolliver's body, you know, the baby's mother. Matthew Tolliver's prints are all over her car, the duct tape, everything. All the evidence points to him as the murderer. This is all on him."

"So the guy out there with the baby, the guy our teams are searching for ... he killed his wife and kidnapped the baby?" Lowell asked.

"Well," Cardona glanced at Frank for confirmation before continuing. "Your teams are searching for the baby. The sheriff's deputies are supposed to be rounding up the kidnapper. And I requested an FBI SWAT team last night. Not sure why they're not here yet.

"Anyway, the same morning Jayden was snatched, Cecily Tolliver never reported to work. And the search at her apartment turned up nothing. Agents said the place looked like any apartment where the occupants had gone off for the day. No signs of an intruder, or a struggle. She and Jayden apparently just left. She dropped Jayden off at his grandmother's, and that's the last the grandmother saw of her daughter. The car found in the storage garage is Cecily's car."

"So what do you think happened?" Lowell asked.

Cardona shrugged. "Looks like Matthew was waiting for her, possibly at her car after she dropped off the baby. Talked her into driving him to the storage garage, tied her up, and left her."

"Tied her up and left her, like he wasn't planning to kill her?" Frank said.

"Well, here's something else interesting. Our agents found Tolliver's handgun under the seat in the car. If he intended to kill his wife, why didn't he just shoot her?"

Frank nodded, but his eyes were tracking the smoke build as it blew to the west. "Guy dropped the gun under there accidentally?" he said. "Or the wife carried the gun under there for protection? You'd be amazed at how many people think they're going to be able to fish a gun out from under a car seat in an emergency situation." He turned back to the other two. "I'm a police officer in my day job," he explained.

Cardona nodded. "All things considered," she said, "this situation is not looking good for Daddy Matthew Tolliver."

A gust blowing over the ridge top replaced the early morning fragrance of pine boughs and mountain misery with the nose-stinging scent of smoke. More than a few eyes teared as soft ashes began to fall. Frank gazed upward, anxiety furrowing his brow.

"Guess we'd better get breakfast going here," he said. Lowell's late-night stop at a market had yielded enough breakfast makings to make much better breakfasts than those being served in the boxes. Cardona tore open the paper cups and poured orange juice while Frank fired up both burners and got the bacon going. Lowell made himself useful by cracking eggs into an aluminum bowl.

"We could use some therapy dogs when the canine search teams return to camp," Frank said, flipping long strips of sizzling bacon. "I wonder if therapy dogs offer comfort to other dogs?" he added, just loud enough for Lowell to hear.

"Good question," Lowell said, smiling.

***

Frank had just served the fragrant bacon, eggs, and fried potatoes breakfast when a young man in a dirty white apron sauntered up and introduced himself as Denny.

"I seen you got some dogs here," Denny said in a belligerent tone, pointing his chin in the direction of MacDuff, inside the exercise pen. MacDuff stood at Denny's approach and shook himself, jingling the tags on his collar. He made a play-bow toward Denny.

Frank looked at Denny in silence. The young man's observation seemed too obvious to comment on.

"So, anyway, you got some dogs here," Denny continued, "and I'm here to inform you that if you come over to the dining tent for a meal, you cannot bring those dogs with you. No dogs are allowed."

Again, there seemed no obvious way to respond to Denny's edict. Clearly Frank was not in need of a pre-prepared, boxed meal from the dining tent. He was also not trying to sneak his dog into the tent. Frank stared at Denny, not knowing what to say. Cardona, figuring she had no stake in the discussion, filled her mouth with a bite of runny yolk on buttered toast and chewed. Lowell followed her example, remaining wordless.

Denny puffed out his chest and hitched up his pants. "So that's it, anyways. No dogs allowed in the dining tent."

Turning, he cut between cars and headed back in the direction of the food service area.

Cardona gave Frank a puzzled look. "What was that about?"

"Oh, he's just throwing his weight around."

"Well, yes, but why? I mean, we weren't trying to get into his precious tent with the dogs in the first place. And second, why would dogs not be allowed? I've always wondered. I know dogs are not allowed in grocery stores and farmers' markets, but why not? What do people think dogs are going to do?"

Lowell chuckled. "Shed? And those farmers' markets. Are people afraid the dogs are going to pee? Heck, a squirrel or stray cat probably peed right there an hour before the farmer set up his stall."

Cardona shared Lowell's laugh. She herself did not usually shop at outdoor food markets, but that's not to say she never would.

"You're probably right," Frank said. "I'll tell you though, if people had any idea how much disgusting stuff humans deposit everywhere they go, all over the produce, on the packaging ... Nothing stops a guy from sneezing into his hand, picking up a box of cereal, then putting it back for you to put in your cart later. And don't even get me started about public nose-picking."

"Yuck!" Cardona said. "Now I'm going to remember that every time I go shopping!"

"Think about it. That is how these search dogs can even do their jobs," Frank said. "They follow the trail of the disgusting crud humans leave everywhere they go. I'd rather have a dog sitting next to me at a meal than most humans."

"Why are there all these rules then?" Cardona said, "You know, about where dogs can go or not go? Why do people make rules like that if there's no actual threat to health?"

"People make rules because they can. Lots of people like to make rules, and most of the time the rest of us go along without really knowing why, or thinking much about it."

Cardona shook her head. "When you consider those search dogs working in the canyon right now, risking their own lives trying to save that baby. I don't know, but it doesn't seem right."

Frank was especially embarrassed to have had the confrontation with Denny happen in front of Lowell, whose dog slept a medicated sleep on the back seat of his nearby car, and whose wife lay somewhere unknown and possibly injured after volunteering herself and her dog to search for the lost baby.

"No, it doesn't seem right. But this is what really breaks my heart," Frank said, nodding at his puppy. Cardona turned to see MacDuff still watching as Denny worked his way through the parked cars. The dog was wagging his tail, still hoping Denny would come back and play.

***

While still out of sight of the bustling camp, the embers had crept around the end of one canyon and into another, growing ever closer to larger sources of viable fuel. The sun-warmed rising air of morning gave it the breath it needed to reach pine trees riddled and weakened with bark beetles. Rising almost gleefully along the trunk and to the top of one dead tree, at long last, the fire exploded into the nearby copse of dead trees. It leapt as though with delight from one patch of dry brush to the next dead tree, growing stronger with every conquest.

Tucked between branches where Jayden had once lain, the plastic cover on a soggy disposable diaper melted into tree bark, and the wet, cotton-like filling released white steam.

***

A tall plume of black smoke snaked up through the early morning sky, clearly visible from the lookout tower. But Charlie had not seen it, and thus had not called in a report. Even when the fire ignited a broad-limbed oak tree and erupted into a roiling dark cloud, Charlie snoozed on. Unaccustomed to the

Thirty Seven
A Breeze at Dawn

Matthew walked quickly through the moonlight, stumbling only as the moon moved to the western horizon and its light grew fainter. He had crossed the creek to the south bank at the place he'd seen the old guy going over. The slope on the south side was steeper, a thin deer trail the only path. Traveling west, he hoped to find the junction of the two-lane highway and the dam at the end of Lake Nell, and catch a ride there. He knew that few cars traveled the mountain road, and even fewer at night. Still if even one car passed, surely they would pick him up. He knew this plan faced dubious success, but he had no other.

The helicopter had flown through the canyon earlier. On his trip to the ridge top to collect his duffel of supplies he had seen all of the people and dogs crowded there. "Supposed to be a wilderness, not crowded with people," he muttered, but no one heard his complaints.

The tumbling creek masked the rhythmic sounds of Matthew's footsteps. He clutched the heavy steering wheel lock more tightly. With his lowered brow and a four-day-old beard, he looked like a guy who wouldn't hesitate to crush the head of anyone who unwisely attempted to interfere with him. In fact, he had already done just that not more than a few hours ago, using the club on that first hiker with the dog. That was before he'd seen that the place was crawling with hikers.

As he walked, he swatted one palm with the club. Dizzy, he tripped more than once and nearly slid into the creek. He stopped to wipe his brow. In the faint light of the setting moon, his skin was gray. Whatever plan he may have had at the beginning was no more. He only knew he had to get away.

alcohol he'd treated himself to the night before, Charlie dreamt of happier days shared with his wife and boys. He remained blissfully unaware of the danger filling his eastern horizon. The escape route from his mountain perch would be cut off by walls of flame if he slept much longer.

***

Jayden lay at the base of a pine tree where his father had left him. He drifted between sleep and unconsciousness, oblivious to the smoke contaminating the air around him, not yet awakening to fear of the oncoming fire. Beside his sleeping form, a small rodent, a chickaree, disturbed from her usual rounds by the smoke and fleeing creatures in the forest, investigated the crumpled brown sack. The baby presented an unfamiliar and possibly dangerous presence to the chickaree, but hunger drove her to scratch at the sack. The fingers of Jayden's hand clutched momentarily in response to some faint brain activity. The chickaree looked up, then went back to gnawing resolutely on the paper bag.

Not far away, Ted's gaze penetrated the shadows, watching Jayden, the chickaree, and the bag. There was no sign of the returning enemy soldier. Ted crept forward, never shifting his eyes from the tantalizing paper bag.

Forty One
Controlled Frenzy

Eagle Meadow buzzed with frantic activity in response to the growing fire. Pilots and crew at the Bald Mountain air attack base were scrambling. Pulling on jackets and juggling helmets, they ran toward air tankers loaded with tons of fire retardant and water. Already in the air was Cal Fire's OV-10 Bronco fixed-wing tactical aircraft. That aircraft did not carry retardant, but would serve as the lead plane to circle over the fire. Assuming a command and control mission, this plane would direct the air tankers to their targets. The two additional aircraft, the S-2T air tankers, would soon be pulling in low over the fire and dropping their loads. Staggering their drops by twenty minutes, the plan was to keep up a steady barrage drawing lines around the fire as long as it took to confine it inside the canyons surrounding Turtle Creek. That should halt any danger of progress toward the small stand of cabins at the lake's edge.

The motor warmed up on the pride of the U. S. Forest Service's firefighting arsenal, their helitack copter. Capable of delivering nine highly trained wild land firefighters and their equipment into the remotest locations imaginable, the Bell 212-HP was built, and its crew trained, for missions exactly like the one presenting itself in the Lake Nell watershed that morning.

Smoke filling the deep canyon would make landing close to the fire's advancing front too dangerous. Rappelling into the canyon from the granite wilderness to the east would require advanced climbing skills. The determination was made to deliver the strike team onto the shore of Lake Nell. From there they could hike the six miles or so double-time while carrying as much as seventy pounds of equipment each. They'd go directly to the leading edge of the fire, where the tankers would have already laid down layers of retardant. They'd take a stand there, where they could at least steer the fire away from the cabins. Preservation of human life was the first priority, then structure protection. The lives and homes of wildlife came in a distant third.

The possible presence of an armed kidnapper was not considered in formulating this plan, and was never communicated to the firefighters. It was the job of CalFire and the Forest Service to suppress the forest fire. Some other agency was responsible for dealing with the kidnapper.

Cullison had set the seasonal firefighters to work clearing brush and felling small trees to create a second driveway into Eagle Meadow. Truckloads of ground crews would be arriving soon, followed by more catering vans, flatbeds carrying portable toilets, tents, cots, and everything else the firefighters might need. Depending on how big the fire got, and how long it went on, there might even be a retooled semi-truck trailer providing shower and laundry facilities. At the far edge of the meadow nearest the trailhead sign, Cullison had the crews set up a long table ready to hold the maps they'd need to plan their attack. She moved the public service affairs officer to that location and set her second in command to work filling out computer forms on the seat next to her. When the fire camp became fully functional, those tables would form the center of the Incident Fire Command Base. For now, and at the fire's present size, Cullison would serve as the designated Incident Fire Commander, and this would remain a District Incident. The base would provide all administrative and logistical needs at the center of a fire camp that would resemble a small city. If the fire escaped the canyon, burned structures, or ignited multiple fires on several fronts, Cullison and District Ranger Russell would let the big guns take over and call in a Type II Incident Management Team from the Forest Supervisor's office.

A space large enough to accommodate a medical tent was staked off next to the command base. Immediate first aid could be provided there for everything from cuts and burns to smoke-triggered headaches.

The community response volunteers had erected a much smaller but similar camp on the other side of the parking lot, near the shade cover and exercise pen that had been set up for the dogs. In addition to their own toilet, they had a tent area and a folding picnic table. They would share the catered meals with the firefighters.

In a nod to the possible presence of an armed kidnapper, Cullison had ordered everyone other than fire crews out of the canyon and off the trails, so for now the community volunteers milled aimlessly, poring over maps, trying to listen in on radio transmissions, and chatting amongst themselves. There was a discussion going on somewhere behind Frank about the idea that community volunteers should relocate their operations to the lake end of the trail where, it was argued, the baby might be more likely to turn up. The flip side of that argument was, if the baby were going to be brought out of the canyon by others there would be no need for the volunteer searchers at all and they should simply pack up and go home.

Once she had set all of this activity into motion, Cullison took up her position at the incident's radio, monitoring the imminent arrival of the air tankers and firefighters. The tankers would drop a couple of loads of retardant before any ground crews arrived at the edge of the flames.

Every firefighter had, at one time or another, taken a direct hit of fire retardant chemicals. Most brushed off any concerns about the long-term consequences of such exposure. The evidence is clear that, due to their presence in clothing, bedding, and building materials, the blood of every person in the developed world is already contaminated with flame retardant chemicals. Still, the jury remains out on the safety of that exposure.

"We're going to have to make retardant drops on the wildlife in that canyon, even though I don't want to do that," Cullison said to her second in command. "No way around it.

Got to get that retardant down before the fire crews get there. After the tankers knock down the flames, it'll be easier for ground crews to spot where their efforts might make the most impact."

Frank watched the activity on the other side of the parking lot, and noted the command table being set up. He turned to Lowell.

"Could you staff the radio for a few minutes? I need to go talk to that woman in charge." Lowell didn't look altogether like he knew what he was doing, but he shifted over to sit in front of the quiet radio. Frank approached the uniform now at the table unrolling maps.

"Ma'am? Are you the incident commander here?"

"What do you need?" she asked, glancing at his now-disheveled civilian attire. Only the canine search and rescue patches on his orange vest distinguished him from the community volunteers.

He held out his hand. "Frank Morelos, ma'am. My dog and I are with the canine search teams?"

"Oh, yes, well, no searching will be going on in that canyon this morning, son. We've got a fire filling up the east end and blowing down toward the lake. Where are you folks searching anyway? I heard there was possibly a father and his son on the trail out to the lake? They'll come out of there quick enough on their own with the smoke blowing down that way. My guess is, we won't need any searchers in that area, and I've got air tankers headed in now in any case."

Frank could feel his heart beating faster. He might be the new kid on the team, but if he didn't slow this woman down, his friends and their dogs were going to be in serious danger, if not from the fire, then from the aggressive response to it.

"That's what I needed to talk to you about. We've got two search teams with dogs already in that canyon. They've been there all night looking for an injured woman. She's the third team member. And if I'm not mistaken, your guy, Greg, is also down there with them."

"So that's where my fire prevention tech got to. Why the heck didn't he call in this fire?"

No one had informed Cullison of the presence of people already in the canyon. The fire management officer's job was to mount the response to forest fires. Anything else was pretty much static. Cullison shook her head slowly upon hearing the news that she'd ordered air tankers over—what?—four people?

"How many people have you got down there?"

Frank enumerated on his fingers. "There's two search teams. That's two humans and two dogs. Then there's Kris. She's the missing search team member. Your guy, Greg. And they all went in after this kidnapper, who I guess must still be down there, and his victim, the baby he kidnapped. Then, down closer to the lake but still somewhere along that trail I assume, are about four to six county sheriff's deputies."

"Holy cow." Cullison dropped her forehead into a palm. "Here, help me unroll this map. You can show me where all these people are."

Maps and spatial tasks in general were not Frank's strong suit. Jody had taken the map with her that was clearly marked with x's, the trail highlighted with a fat yellow line, and the pencilled grid. This one now spread out on the table was just a mass of light green and white patches, overlaid with millions of faint gray curving lines. If he knew how to read those, he would know how to spot the ford across the creek where Andy and Greg met Jody last night. That would at least give him a place to start. He asked the woman to help him find that spot. From there, he pointed along the north side of the creek.

"I've been in radio contact periodically," he said. "They are moving steadily but very slowly along this trail. Searching the creek banks for Kris and still using the tracking dog to look for the baby. There's been no contact with the kidnapper, but that's who the sheriff's deputies are pursuing."

"How close to the lake are they now?"

"I have no way to know. They may not even know."

"Well, I would say they are probably making faster progress now. Smoke is filling that canyon and every living thing in there is moving toward the lake."

"Yes," he said. "They might be moving fast, except we have one search team member who's presumably injured. The others won't leave her behind. They'll find her first. Even after they find her, she might not be able to walk. Or, they may be trying to evacuate her by returning across that ford and up that way. You can't drop a whole load of retardant on them."

"Would you rather they get caught in the fire? They'll survive a retardant dump, but if we let the fire go, the smoke alone will kill everyone in that canyon."

"But ... " Frank didn't want to back down, but he could hear the static of a transmission coming in on his radio. Glancing over, Frank saw that Lowell was looking confused. Staffing that radio was Frank's main responsibility. He hadn't heard anything from Jody or Andy in an hour. This had to be them.

"Gotta get this," he called to Cullison as he dashed the short distance to his radio. The transmission was faint and garbled with a lot of other traffic on the frequency. Whoever was calling must be a long ways away and behind granite. And with a dying battery.

Cullison went back to poring over the map. She drew a finger along the line representing the creek near the ford where the tankers would do their first drops. She got the attention of her second in command. "If retardant drops can stop the fire here," she tapped the map, "that'll give ground crews from this meadow a pathway to hike right down near the leading edge of the fire. They can cut lines here, and here," she pointed. "And stop the fire from blowing the length of the canyon. But with all the people already in the canyon, we're going to have to hold off."

She picked up her radio, already squawking with numerous transmissions, and tried to find a clear frequency that district dispatch would pick up. Once connected, she asked dispatch to relay a message to hold off on the retardant drop on the first pass.

"That only gives you an additional twenty minutes," her assistant said. "You've got to sort out the locations of almost a dozen people already wandering around in that canyon. Better think fast."

Minutes later, the truck bearing the first ground crew pulled in and the firefighters aboard jumped down. They tugged on heavy jackets, reloaded water bottles, grabbed hand tools and chainsaws and were headed out the trail at a trot within ten minutes. Even at that pace it would take them almost an hour to get to the pass on foot, and another to get safely down to the creek. The tankers should have dropped several loads by then. Tankers were great for fire suppression in a broad expanse, but there was nothing as effective as a highly trained ground crew for making sure a fire was well and truly out. Watching the crew disappear out the trail, Cullison leaned back, yawned, and checked her watch.

"Those crews made a good response time considering the sun's only now coming over the tops of the trees," she said.

A steady stream of new arrivals began to fill the fire camp. District Ranger Russell showed up to help with incident command responsibilities, bringing along with him the rest of the district management team. Media trucks filled in the center of the parking area, and two more arrived just after dawn. They fired up generators and ran wires, and the public information officer got ready to give a morning briefing. The whine of another transport truck crunching through the newly constructed driveway interrupted the activity in the meadow. Heavily laden firefighters rolled off and got ready to join the battle.

Forty Two
Bitter Smoke

In the canyon below, the fire made the most of the quickening breeze, invigorated by dry brush and dead trees riddled with pine bark beetles. In a last gasp of irony, thousands of the quarter-inch long black beetles scuttled frantically in all directions before being caught in the flames, crackling, and dropping to the ground, dead.

Indifferent to the turmoil it caused, the fire grew in all directions, stopped only in the east by the granite escarpment, where it sent roiling black smoke toward the bear's den. She pulled her head inside, and blocked the entrance with her body, keeping the smoke from reaching her young. She and her cubs would survive. Many of those running through the canyon that morning would not be so lucky.

In an enthusiastic burst, the fire raced the length of one ravine, exploding on both flanks, throwing billows of flame over one another, climbing toward the sky. All the fuel in that canyon was exhausted in a matter of minutes, and the fire hurtled west, claiming everything in its path in an inferno of yellow-white flames and black smoke.

***

A commotion erupted in the entrance to the parking lot as a roll-back tow truck pulled in, showing lots of chrome and tricked out with multiple light racks. The CHP officer sauntered to the truck and held a lengthy conversation with the driver, which included a fair amount of waving and hand gestures. After vehicles had been cleared out of the way, the tow truck got turned around and the BMW was loaded onto its flat bed. It rumbled out of the lot, the CHP vehicle trailing along after, headed for the highway patrol's secure lock-up in Jamestown.

In her role as the agent responsible for evidence recovery, Cardona could have gone along to secure the chain of evidence, but she found herself reluctant to leave the scene. More evidence might reveal itself as the search proceeded. She'd heard no word from the FBI SWAT team she had requested, and she was concerned about ensuring an agency presence if the kidnapper was successfully captured and his victim recovered by someone else.

A swirl of smoke and wind blew through the camp at that moment, heightening tensions, inciting a burst of activity. All attention was focused on amassing resources and gearing up to fight the blaze in the canyon. Tracking down and detaining the kidnapper had taken second place to the more immediate threat of a forest suddenly on fire.

The SWAT team might be out there somewhere already, searching for the kidnapper. They might even be in the path of the fire. Cardona checked her cell for messages, finding nothing, then moved closer to Frank's radio, hoping for news. She helped herself to a fresh cup of coffee and hardly even noticed when a fleck of ash dropped in and floated on top.

***

Jody followed Flag as fast as she could scramble over rocks and damp sand at the edge of the creek, holding tight to the dog's lead. They were making steady progress to the west and the confluence with Lake Nell. Even with the haze of smoke clearly visible around them, Flag was air-scenting again, interested in something downstream. She held her tail at a half-staff position. Kris or someone had to be nearby. Jody scanned both banks of the creek, and even tried to peer into the depths of the rushing water itself, looking for anything submerged or snagged.

Flag gave a sudden jerk forward, nearly pulling Jody off her feet, and the dog yelped a happy tone, her tail gyrating wildly. Jody could see nothing but more rocks up ahead. She reeled Flag back to herself and unclipped the dog's leash. Instantly,

Flag was off, leaping between rocks to a place Jody couldn't see. Flag reappeared and clambered back to Jody, turned and ran back, again wiggling into the hidden spot. Even without seeing her, Jody knew Kris was there, and judging from Flag's behavior, it was a live-find. Jody stared at the spot as she scrambled toward it, and a moment later, Kris's head appeared from between two rocks. Wads of bunchgrass and dry brush clung to her matted hair and fell around her shoulders as she slowly sat up. Flag danced on the rocks nearby. Kris shook her head, watching the dog in apparent confusion.

"Oh my god," Jody said as she finally reached Kris's hiding place among the rocks. "I thought we'd never find you! What happened? Why are you hiding? You're six feet at least from the creek. How did you get here? Thank god for Flag. I'd never have found you here." Jody brushed the vegetation away that had been piled over her friend. She took a deep breath. "Are you okay?"

"I'm ... I'm not sure ..." Kris said. "Where's Bullet?" She surveyed her surroundings, one hand caressing Flag's neck. "Where is he?" she asked again, her voice beginning to rise into a panicky range.

Jody decided to wait on the whole story. "Bullet's fine. He's fine. It's you we're all worried about. I want to hear what happened, but right now we have to get out of here. There's a forest fire coming. Can you walk?"

Her eyes still unfocused, Kris gazed into the distance, only then noticing the air, yellow with smoke and thick with the scent of burning trees. "You found me, Flag," she said, using the baby-talk tone that dogs love so much.

"Good dog!" Jody said, dumping out a handful of treats. Flag had more than proven her value on this mission, but there was no time to celebrate, and no one but the handlers to witness her success. Jody wanted to reinforce and reward Flag properly for her find, but now was not the time. She had to get Kris up and moving. A gust brought the rapidly approaching heat and the crackle of breaking branches.

Her eyes rolling in sudden terror, Flag broke away from the women, running from the sounds and smells of the fire. Desperately, Jody recalled her frightened dog. Flag responded to years of painstaking training, returned in a cower, and allowed Jody to clip the lead onto her harness.

"Help me, please," Kris said, trying to get a grip on a nearby rock and raise herself. Between the two of them, Kris was able to get to her feet. Jody drew Kris's arm over her own shoulder and lifted. At that moment, Flag jerked on her lead, nearly spilling the two women back onto the rocks. Jody planted her boots, gritting her teeth with the pain in her ankle. She tried to control the weight of her friend against the dog's efforts to pull away, terrified she would have to let one of them go.

"Heel," Jody commanded, trying to keep the desperation out of her voice. Flag returned to her side, letting the lead go slack. Looking like wounded soldiers returning from a ghastly battlefield, the two women and the dog stumbled and climbed their way to the trail. Once they were moving, Jody could see blood soaking the side of Kris's head.

Forty Three
Tankers Overhead

Deputy Hogan stared in horror as a massive fixed-wing aircraft bore down on him, seeming to float atop the early-morning mist rising off the lake. From his perspective, that plane was going to crash directly into the rocks where he was perched. He would die in a fiery ball of fuel. Briefly the image of his official portrait printed large on the front page of his hometown newspaper flashed. He would be a hero, serving honorably in the line of duty. Then his consciousness snapped back to the present moment. Dying a hero was small comfort compared to knowing he would not only be dead, but would probably also die an excruciatingly pain-filled death.

Hogan turned away from the approaching plane with its thundering roar, and tried to scramble off the wet rock. One foot slipped. The other got caught for a half-second between rocks. He turned, trying to free his shoe. It came loose suddenly, and he slid toward the creek. He scrabbled frantically to escape the tumbling water, the entire forest now shaking with the booming of the plane's engines. Icy water soaked instantly into his socks, triggering him to reflexively pull his knees to his chest, and springing his body off the rock. He rolled to a stop, something hard lodged against one shoulder. Afraid to stand, fearful the low-flying plane might slice him in half, he remained curled with a rock stabbing his shoulder. He felt, rather than saw, the plane pass harmlessly overhead.

He sat and shook his fist at the departing tanker. "Damn fool!" he yelled. The tanker pulled up and out of the canyon, the sound fading. Hogan tipped his head from side to side. He might never hear again. Even now with the plane rising above the escarpment to the east and banking north, already a half mile away, the only sound in Hogan's head was the ear-splitting roar. He tapped one ear, but felt rather than heard the sound. Had the plane actually been loud enough to split his ears? Could he continue to be a deputy if he had been deafened in the line of duty? Shaking, he stood up.

Both shoes were soaked and the tips were badly scarred from his mad scramble across the granite. Other than that, his hearing loss, and a sore shoulder, he seemed to be unharmed.

Without moving his feet, he keyed on his radio and tried to raise any of the other deputies. The only connection he made was with the deputy stationed at the vehicle parked near the entrance to the highway. She reported only that she had also been unsuccessful at reaching anyone else. She had seen a couple of fisherman near the other side of the dam. At least she thought they were fishermen. They'd waved hello, but the mist rising off the lake was too thick to see much else. She had no idea what had become of her partner, Tarazzo, or the other deputy, but no one was answering their radios. Hogan told her he would head back to her position.

He took a step, and one wet leather shoe gave a squeal. Another step, another squeal, and a crunch from the twigs and dead leaves underfoot. Instead of rejoicing in the return of his hearing, he thought about all the noise he was making. If there was still a kidnapper lurking in this forest, all that noise was going to alert that guy to his presence. There was no way to surprise anyone, should anyone be in this vicinity, with all of this squealing. He felt less and less like a hero. He would have to be satisfied with getting home safely, and if his family couldn't respect him, he would have to deal with that when he got there. Hogan pulled out his phone, opened the compass app, and looked ahead through the otherwise directionless forest. He noted the lighter bark of one tree to the southwest, sighted on it, and began walking toward it. He figured if he walked far enough to the southwest, he would eventually run into the lake, or the highway. He wouldn't be a hero, but he would at least survive.

***

Jody couldn't tell if Kris was fully conscious. She trembled as though cold, and Jody worried her friend might be going into shock.

"I'm so sorry," she said. "I never should have let you go off on your own. I must have been hopped up on adrenaline, excited about finding that baby. I'm so sorry I let you go."

Kris didn't seem to be listening, more focused on staying on her feet. "Don't worry, Jody. Here you are now. You found me, you and Flag."

They stumbled together onto the flat trail. Jody helped Kris discard her torn and soggy jacket, then slipped her own across Kris's shoulders. Kris's boots were wet too, but some things would have to be tolerated. Together, the two of them moved as quickly as Kris's stiff and still somewhat dazed condition would allow. They had almost made it to the curve in the trail where Andy and Greg should be waiting when the rumbling sound of the approaching air tanker set the forest around them shaking. It appeared suddenly, its wings seeming to fill the canyon from one side to the other. Jody and Kris crouched to fold Flag into their arms and cover the dog's sensitive ears. The three of them clung to one another as the plane lifted overhead and began to bank north.

Up ahead at the mouth of another canyon, Andy was curled in a similar protective posture around Rose. She at least had long floppy ears to cover the delicate parts inside. The plane passed, and when everyone stood again they spotted one another. Jody helped Kris forward to join the guys, shifting Kris's weight to Andy's shoulders when she got there.

As the sound of the air tanker faded, a long, agonized scream erupted from deeper in the side canyon. The scream stopped abruptly. Rose barked once, then Flag and Rose both pulled hard into the mouth of the canyon. It was hard to say whether they were alerting to a find, or only trying to get away from the choking smoke. Their handlers peered into the canyon, searching for a possible target and for the source of the scream.

***

Deep in the canyon, Ted had been crouching beside the paper bag, disappointed to find only crumbs inside a graham cracker box and a peanut butter jar filled only with water. The baby lay silent and still on a dirty blanket at the base of the tree. Someone had tied a strap of the baby's overalls to the tree. Probably that enemy soldier was keeping this baby captive. Ted stroked the baby's cheek with one callused finger, but there was no response to his touch. The baby was either sick, or already dead. Ted dampened a corner of the blanket with water from the jar and wiped some of the dirt off the baby's face.

There, under the trees, there was no context for Ted when the roaring began and then grew louder. The forest trembled as the air shook overhead. The sense of a monster approaching was all around him and on top of him. It would surely crush him. Ted opened his mouth and screamed.

Whether it was the roaring plane overhead, or the scream, Jayden's arm gave a startled twitch. Ted's scream stopped in amazement. Maybe the baby was alive. Ted thought he saw the eyes open slightly, but then not. He bent his hairy face closer, but could detect no further movement. After almost a full minute of watching the baby, Ted realized the roaring sound was fading. All he could think about was escaping, but then another thought dawned. Ted had no use for a baby, but this baby might be valuable in trade for something he did want. Although possibly not if the baby was dead. Carefully, Ted curled himself over Jayden and began working at the knot securing the tiny child to the tree. Ted listened for breathing as he leaned over the baby, but couldn't hear anything.

***

Rose barked again. "She's onto the target," Andy whispered. "The baby is in there."

"Come on, Andy," Jody said. "There's something in there for sure, but it can't be the target. Rose can't be smelling anything. The smoke is too thick. She's just trying to hide from the fire."

Kris settled it, reminding them all of possibly the most important lesson in canine search and rescue. "Trust your dog, Jody. Trust the dog."

They crowded more closely together. Silhouetted against the hazy sunlight at the mouth of the canyon, they stepped forward, deeper into the darkness.

Forty Four
Gunshots

Like Ted, Matthew was under the trees and had no context when the plane roared overhead. A shadow briefly cut off what sunlight did penetrate the tree cover, and he could only assume the authorities were coming after him. His desperation to escape intensified. Matthew peered through the gloom at ground level, seeking the shape of the body he'd seen. He watched for movement, and considered the possibility that this might be a cop lying in wait for him. There were no more radio sounds. Matthew took another step toward the body, searching the shadows ahead.

The shiny part of the uniform continued to twinkle a faint reflection, but nothing moved. Matthew crept closer, acutely aware that, even prone, the man was much larger than himself. Matthew shifted his club from hand to hand as though that would even the odds. This was definitely a cop. He leaned over the prone deputy. The guy was lying still, but not snoring. Either dead or unconscious. He had a gun in a holster. Matthew thought he could really use a gun. He reached toward the deputy's holster and fumbled with the strap holding it closed.

Just behind a slight rise, Hogan's flashlight faded and died, leaving him feeling even more alone. At least the sun was finally beginning to show itself, although not so much under the trees. He tried his radio again but it gave off only a short burst of static before dying. It had either taken a dunking when he fell into the creek, or its battery was depleted. He turned his back on the rising sun and walked again, one shoe still squealing with each step. As he crested the rise ahead, a ray of light broke through the trees, illuminating a piece of the forest floor maybe a hundred feet ahead. He saw something moving there. It was a man, leaning down. Hogan squinted, peering, creeping forward. He unsnapped the restraining strap on his holster. The guy was too far away to hit with a taser. In a flash, the scene resolved itself into meaning. There was a deputy down, his uniform now visible in the sunlight, and a guy leaning over him. Looked like the guy was trying to steal the deputy's gun.

Hogan drew his weapon. "Hey, you there! Step away from the deputy! Put your hands where I can see them!"

Matthew looked up and froze. He was blinded by the rising sun and could not see the source of the disembodied voice. Was it another deputy? Armed? He heard footsteps coming toward him.

"I said, step away! Freeze!" Hogan shifted to take aim. His movement brought him into a patch of light, and Matthew got a good look at the gun aimed directly at him, ready to fire. His mouth went dry.

Pure terror motivated Matthew at that point. Terror of going to prison for killing Cecily. Terror of being shot. Terror at that horrific roaring. Logic and reason shut down, and terror triggered his actions. He had to get away. That was all that mattered. Matthew took off running, dodging randomly between trees, trying to stay out of patches of sunlight. Twigs stabbed through his socks, but he didn't have time to stop and get his shoes.

When Hogan saw the guy fleeing, not obeying the order to freeze, he went into fury mode. He had a deputy down, and from all appearances, this guy running away had done it. He fired, and the guy kept going, ducking behind trees. Hogan fired two more times in anger, not really aiming. The tree cover was too thick. He could hear the guy running, but he couldn't see him well enough to get a good shot off.

Hogan holstered his weapon and ran to Deputy Tarrazo's side. The gunshots had startled Tarrazo into semi-consciousness. He was moaning, trying to roll over. A twisted ankle, a bad fall including a blow on the head from a hunk of granite, and he'd been sidelined for most of the night. Hogan determined that Tarrazo was injured, but basically okay.

Hogan muttered that he would get help, and be back as soon as he could. He took a good look through the trees. If that guy kept going in the direction he was headed, sooner or later he'd run right into the vehicle and deputy stationed on the jeep track. They could corner him there, or at the lake when he came up against that dam. Hogan took off again, after the fleeing guy. That guy had injured his deputy and had to be the kidnapper. Who else would be out here in this forest, and who else would try to steal a weapon right off the body of a fallen law enforcement officer?

***

Ted saw the platoon of enemy soldiers coming. Aided by dirty and broken fingernails, he'd finally gotten the knot loose and picked the baby off the ground. He had started to make a sling to carry the baby, but the blanket was beyond saving, even for his standards. Too dirty and soaked with urine. He tucked the baby securely under one arm, abandoned the paper sack, and dashed behind a thin cedar. The platoon kept coming. They had dogs with them. Only one of them was armed, his rifle slung over his shoulder.

As the soldiers grew closer, what had looked initially like a rifle resolved into an ordinary shovel. Ted stared, and as he did, the figures began to look like ordinary hikers. There were two dogs with the hikers. One of the dogs looked right at him and barked once. Those people were probably looking for this baby. Possibly, Ted thought, he could trade the baby for one of those dogs. A dog would be a much better treasure than a sick and nearly dead baby. Ted took a deep breath and prepared himself to negotiate. The people watched in silence as he emerged from behind the tree.

Even once Ted and his burden became visible, it was hard to discern what was there. Most of Ted, including his ragged short pants and formerly blue shirt, were the color of dirt. The mass of dreadlock-like graying hair covering his head and most of his face gave him more the appearance of a wild animal than a human. It was the reddened face of the baby in his arms that arrested everyone's attention. Could this grizzled apparition be the kidnapper? The baby's father?

They froze in place, all except Rose. Her tail wagged gently, and her ears dropped in greeting. She glanced up at Andy. This was the scent she had been following. Here was the target. Without breaking his gaze from the bizarre creature emerging from the shadows, Andy unzipped a pocket on his pack and extracted a handful of jerky treats to reward Rose.

Ted made a slight gesture, as though to hand the baby to Jody. He pulled the baby back, and stretched out one grubby hand toward Flag's leash. His meaning was clear. He wanted to trade the baby for the dog. Jody stepped back. He offered the baby again. Jody stepped back again, behind the others.

"No," she said. Stunned, she realized the child must be the kidnap victim they had all risked so much to find. But who was this guy? She could not imagine who he was, or how he had gotten the baby.

Someone started to speak, but the fire chose that moment to unveil its threatening presence. With a boom, a large dry and dying pine tree exploded into flames out on the trail, firing blazing embers in every direction. Clouds of black smoke spilled toward the searchers and blew into the narrow side canyon. In seconds, the group could feel the heat pulsing closer. Without a word, Ted tucked Jayden under his arm like a football and ran out of the canyon to the west. The handlers and their dogs surged after him, toward the hope of safety on the shore of the lake. Andy had one of Kris's arms over his shoulder, and Jody got her other side. Between them they made a three-legged-race sort of progress. Even that wouldn't have been possible if both dogs had not been pulling ahead on their leashes.

Greg glanced back at the fire, squelched a thought that he should go back and fight the inferno himself with his shovel, and joined the retreat.

Coming up fast behind them, completely ignoring the people and dogs, another small herd of deer appeared, escaping the flames.

As they ran, Hogan's sudden gunshots echoed and reverberated within the confines of the steep canyon rock walls. That made the gunshots sound much closer than they were. The ragged band skidded to a stop and looked at each other in confusion. The shots came from somewhere up ahead, nearer the lake. Gunshots ahead, fire chasing from behind. The deer had also halted, milling, uncertain, their eyes wild with fear. After a few moments, the deer trotted forward, skirted the humans, and resumed their flight. Gunshots were scary, but relatively unknown. Fire was a primal fear, imparted to them through many generations of forest-dwelling ancestors.

With a long, loud whimper, Ted's fragile grasp on everyday reality suffered a final implosion. He had to run. Someone else could take this baby. He thrust the baby toward Greg, went into a defensive crouch, and took off zigzagging back toward the fire. His figure disappeared into a cloud of dense black smoke as they watched in horror.

Forty Five
Help!

"Hey!" Andy yelled. "Oh, geez! That guy's nuts. What's he doing? We've got to go after him!"

"I don't think so," Jody said, shaking her head.

"But he'll die if he runs into that fire!"

"Maybe, but he knows where he's going, I think. He has to have another way across that creek, a crossing we don't know about, and another trail to the ridge top. We'll all die if we try to go after him, and I'm not letting any of us get into trouble again. Just let him go, and have faith that he knows where he's going."

"Hey, guys?" Greg called. He'd dropped his shovel and was cradling the baby. Holding Jayden's head in one hand, he gazed with concern into the baby's face. "I think this little guy is really sick." The others gathered around, keeping a wary watch on the trail behind. For the moment, they seemed to have outrun the fire. Greg laid the baby on a bed of soft grass at the trail's edge and began to pull off his wet and smelly clothes. "Does anyone have any clean water left?"

They passed around water bottles. Kris eagerly emptied the bottles she was handed. Jayden let the water dribble across his cheek and shifted his head away. The last half bottle was shared between Rose and Flag, who had to be persuaded to stop pulling away from the wind-driven smoke long enough to drink.

When Greg got most of Jayden's clothes off, his bloody welts, open blisters, and angry rashes were revealed. Slowly, Jayden opened his eyes and stared wide-eyed in eerie silence at the man hovering over him. Jody quickly dug the first aid kit from her pack and broke it open. Together, they smeared antibiotic gel on the cleanest of Jayden's injuries.

Jody considered trying to bandage Kris's head, too, but getting her out of the canyon to medical care as the fire and smoke drew closer seemed more important.

"Andy," Jody said, "try to get Frank on your phone. I think everyone's radio batteries are dead. Try to get him on the phone. That's our only hope."

Andy pulled out his cell phone, juggled Rose's leash, and tried to make the connection with Frank. "Frank! Frank! Are you there? Can you hear me?"

Between the sounds of the creek, the roar of fire, and the last rumble of the departing air tanker, it would have been hard to hear anyone on the other end of the line. "I think I'm getting a reply, very faint," Andy said.

"Frank! We found Kris! We found Kris!" Andy glanced at Greg and Jayden. "And the baby! We found the baby! We're running to the lake! Get us a helicopter, Frank! Get us out of here! We need a medevac! Get us out of here! Frank? Over?"

In one of those sudden moments of quiet, they all heard Frank's tiny voice coming through the phone.

"Roger that!"

***

Lowell hovered over Frank's shoulder as the call ended. "Well, thank goodness for that!" he said. "I mean, if they want a medical helicopter then she must be alive, right? She's probably just in shock from being out there all night."

"Yeah, that makes sense, Lowell. We'll get them up here as quick as we can, then we'll know for sure.

Frank turned some dials, hailing forest service dispatch on the radio. He could have run over to the incident command desk forty feet across the parking lot, but they seemed increasingly disorganized. Dispatch would be the quickest way to get a rescue helicopter out to the lake to pick up his friends. Or dispatch could arrange for a medevac copter to pick them all up and take the injured to medical attention. Andy had not said who among their group was in need of emergency medical attention, the nature of their injuries, or even how many of them might need transport to a hospital. Frank also had no idea how many patients a medevac copter could carry.

Dispatch agreed to radio for a medevac copter to be sent to the ridge top. The fire presented too much danger to risk a landing at the lake. The transmission was interrupted by the roar of another air tanker going in low over the canyon. Frank had to ask dispatch to repeat the welcome information that a helicopter was already en route to the shore of Lake Nell to drop a strike team of firefighters near the front edge of the fire. The copter crew would be instructed to wait for Jody and her group before starting water drops.

Frank turned to Lowell. "Can you get one of those community response people? I need to tell them the search is over. We've got that baby, and we've got a rescue copter extracting the searchers out of the canyon and a medevac copter coming. We're going to need that space. The sooner those folks clear out, the better."

The community response team began to break up camp and pack gear. With any luck, they would clear out the space and be gone before the two helicopters needed to land at Eagle Meadow. Lowell and Frank went to work setting up an area, lowering the shade structure, and securing anything that might blow away.

Cardona was on her own radio passing the news to the Sacramento field office that the kidnap victim had been recovered. She was instructed to return to the office at her earliest opportunity, and leave the apprehension of the kidnapper to the SWAT team. She disconnected, quickly gathered her gear and said her good-byes. Reluctantly, she backed her vehicle around and headed out. Ahead of her by only a few minutes, the community volunteers had already bugged out, towing the trailer with their portable toilet behind them.

There was a burst of activity among those clustered in the fire camp as a third air tanker drew near, this one coming from the north. The tankers were spreading wide swaths of retardant on the sides of the fire, steering it in an increasingly narrow path toward the lake, where it might be pinched to death before it could spread. The incoming tanker would drop its load along the canyon wall and at the edge of the ridge top, just missing a direct hit on the fire camp. Everyone began to seek cover.

Lowell, Frank, and MacDuff dove into Lowell's car, snuggling up to Bullet on the back seat.

Forty Six
Crowning Flames

Greg still fussed with the baby. "You know the best thing for this diaper rash is to leave it open to the air," Greg said, almost to himself. Quickly, he unbuttoned his dirty uniform shirt, pulled his tee shirt off and gently lowered it over Jayden's head, leaving the baby's body mostly open to the air. "There, that should make him more comfortable," Greg said. The boy was a cute little guy, and almost the same age as Greg's oldest. Greg offered Jayden the water again, but the baby had faded back to unconsciousness. Lost in his own thoughts, Greg didn't even hear Jody when she first called.

"Greg! Come on, Greg, we have to go now!" Jody said. "Just pick him up and run! Everybody, run!" Her commands were punctuated by crackling in the pine branches behind them. The air was filled with electricity as the fire sucked every ounce of moisture from the trees. Needles shriveled and curled just before the hiss as they exploded into flames. Black smoke swirled around the trail. The hot air rising toward the treetops pulled cooler wind in from below, igniting new fires all around, leaping toward them. The forest was alive with birds and small animals, those that could fly or run, bolting for the shore of Lake Nell.

The heat was so intense, Jody could almost feel blisters forming on the back of her neck. This was more excitement than even she wanted. Moving as fast as they could, the little group safely negotiated the next curve in the trail. Then abruptly the sky was filled with another tanker coming in, preparing to drop its load of red retardant. This time the drop would be nearly on top of them. Jody shoved and pulled everyone under the overhanging branches of a trail-side tree.

She tucked Rose, Flag, and Jayden into the middle. The others hunched tightly over them, covering ears and eyes as best they could. Jody crossed her fingers that the tree they huddled under would not be the next one to explode into flames.

The plane roared overhead, drowning out every other sound. A fine red mist began floating into the canyon, much of it falling on the trail. The searchers continued to crouch together, the sound of the plane fading as it lifted up and out of the canyon, leaving nearby trees painted with red.

As the noise from the plane died away, the group was startled to hear a chortle coming from the center of their scrum. They eased apart and looked down. Rose had awakened Jayden by gently licking his peanut-butter-and-dirt encrusted face, setting the baby to giggling. If their situation had not been so dire, the sight might even have evoked laughter. As it was, they shared a quick smile, then prepared to continue their flight.

Greg hoisted the now more alert toddler onto his shoulder. Andy wrapped an arm around Kris, and the little band headed off again. Jody slowed, then hesitated at the sound of something loud approaching from the east. Sounded like a cattle stampede coming right for them. Then, from around a curve on the trail ahead, they came. It was a stampede all right —a stampede of about nine heavily laden firefighters resembling giant alien creatures. Yellow coats reaching to mid-thigh, matching pants with broad reflective stripes, helmets with flaps covering necks, and pull-down plastic face masks. They all had respirators dangling around their necks, ready to cover noses and mouths. Every one of the firefighters carried huge packs looming behind their heads, tarps and fire shelters lashed on top. Chainsaws, axes, and shovels hung from the packs. They jogged up to and around the searchers, hardly slowing, only one or two indicating they'd seen the searchers at all.

Flag cringed, wrapping her leash around Jody's legs. Jody wondered if the dog even knew the firefighters were human.

The tanker had laid down a swath of retardant to slow the fire for the firefighters. This strike team was headed in to reinforce and secure a fire line. The hope was to prevent the monster from tearing toward the lakeshore, leaping over canyon walls, and devastating the forest surrounding Lake Nell and possibly beyond. Even now, tall spires of flame rotated high into the sky, creating fierce winds and tornados of fire. It was hard to imagine how nine firefighters would have much of an impact. Amid the surrounding roar, another tanker approached, flying so low it hardly cleared the horizon.

The last firefighter in line stopped, tipped her head back and lifted her plastic mask. She looked at Jody.

"Copter is waiting for you on the shore. About quarter of a mile. They won't wait long with this fire coming, though, so go!" She pointed.

"Roger that! Thank you," Jody called, her voice barely a croak. She turned to the others. "You hear that? They're waiting for us with a helicopter. We have to get over there fast." They all huddled again as the next tanker came directly overhead. It held its load of red retardant until it was past them, but the firefighters still jogging along the trail would take a direct hit. The fire spit and hissed like a ferocious cat, and the heat billowed out again, slamming Jody hard in the back.

They started again, limping, hobbling, and carrying one another toward the lake. After a few more steps, Kris came to the end of her endurance. One knee crumpled under her and she went down. Andy still held one elbow, but Jody had lost her grip.

"Kris! Kris, you've got to keep going! We're almost there, Kris, please!" Jody wasn't even sure Kris was still conscious. "Does anyone have more water?" Jody thought about taking the time to pull off her pack and dig through the first aid kit for an ammonia capsule to wake up Kris, but that wouldn't restore her ability to walk.

Jody looked at the others, helpless to save her friend. Greg was already holding a silent and staring Jayden. Rose was so frightened by the fire, she was pulling Andy off the trail toward the hollow at the side of a fallen log. Andy had a hold on Rose's harness and was pulling the bloodhound forward, but the dog weighed almost as much as Andy. If they could just get moving, the dogs would run with them, but as the fire drew closer, both dogs were panicking, looking for any hole to hide inside.

Everyone's eyes were stinging, making it hard to see in the smoke-thickened air. Flag sneezed several times, and Andy started coughing and couldn't stop. A crashing erupted at the trail's edge and two huge bucks burst from the underbrush, their eyes rolling wildly. They surged toward the humans, very nearly plowing Greg and Jayden over in their rush. Then they were gone, down the trail toward the lake.

A "crack" rang out from overhead, and chunks of flaming wood rained around them. The fire was crowning, the tops of trees exploding, towering flames reaching into the sky. There was no way mere humans could out run that monster, and the helicopter, their only hope, would escape while it still could. They were out of options.

"Kris, please!" Jody dumped her pack, preparing to haul Kris's semi-conscious weight on her own back, despite the pain in her ankle. She heard pounding footsteps approaching. Two firefighters had left their packs at the side of the trail and come back to help. They scooped Kris into a sling formed by their arms and took off, Kris sitting between them. The rest of the group fell into line behind, doing their best to keep up.

Forty Seven
Trapped!

At the east end of the canyon, the fire leapt above the edge of the escarpment, reaching over, threatening to take off across the granite shelf. Flaming pinecones and embers of ash exploded over the edge as the fire created its own windstorm. Standing a full mile to the east, the backcountry ranger watched the billowing smoke fill the sky, and stomped on the red embers landing around him. He'd already called the smoke in to dispatch and requested a crew of firefighting smokejumpers. The granite itself formed an effective line, preventing the fire from moving aggressively in his direction, but the smokejumpers would need to to hold the line and keep blowing embers from carrying the fire across the granite to the eastern forests.

***

Miles to the west, Charlie had finally awakened to towers of smoke. He couldn't believe he'd slept so soundly. He used to be able to fall asleep drunk and still wake up in time to go to work.

Through the window, he could see the tanker that had awakened him almost disappearing into the smoke. Soaring red flames crowned through the trees at the lake's shore, sending embers in all directions. He called the smoke into dispatch, but of course they already knew, and a full scale attack had been mounted. Dispatch said nothing about the long delay in Charlie's report.

He went out to stand at the railing, the air filled with enough ash and smoke to make his eyes burn. Across the lake where the fire raged down the canyon a red-and-white helicopter sat on a patch of grass and rocky beach. Through his binoculars he could see splashing at the lake's edge where large animals were escaping the flames by fleeing into the water. Enough wind was blowing this direction, carrying hot ash and embers, a secondary fire could easily be ignited on this side of the lake, cutting off any escape for him. The fire could be on top of him within minutes. He could try to run, probably useless at this point, or he could at least make himself useful by watching for smoke from those spot fires and calling them in to dispatch. With luck, they could get a bucket of water on any secondary fires before they engulfed his lookout tower. He might die there, but he'd rather die there than at the bottom of the steps from a heart attack triggered by a panicked attempt at escape, or worse, halfway down the mountain trapped in his Jeep. He decided to stay where he was and accept his end, whatever it would be. He went inside the glass-walled cab and closed the windows against the smoke.

He started a methodical circuit of the cab, searching in all directions for any sign of spot fires springing up around him. When his cell phone signaled an incoming call, he assumed it would be dispatch looking for an update. He answered without looking at the display.

"'Lo?"

"Pop? Is that you, Pop?" Charlie pulled the phone away from his ear and stared at the display. It was his youngest son.

"Mark?" Charlie said, beyond surprised. "Is that you, Mark?"

"Pop! Are you okay? There's a big fire out that way! We saw it on the Cal Fire website. Where are you? You're not still out there in that tower, are you?"

Charlie was pretty sure the tears streaming down his cheeks were caused by all that damn smoke. "Son," he said. "I'm okay. I'm doing my job. You know these firefighters. They'll keep it away from me." His voice quavered. "Or they'll come get me if it gets bad."

"Pop! Get out of there as soon as you can. David is on his way to pick me up now. We'll be at the fire camp by dinner time. Wait for us there, okay, Pop?"

Too choked up to give much of an answer, Charlie said, "Okay, son. Okay. I'll get there if I can. It'll be good to see you boys."

"Yeah, Pop, it's been too long." Charlie couldn't believe what he was hearing. After all these years, and all the bad feelings.

"And, Pop?"

"Yes, Mark?"

"Well, it's just that ... well, I love you, Pop."

"Love you too, Mark, and David too. I'll see you both soon."

Forty Eight
Running!

Matthew ran faster, crazed to escape the gunshots. Even running away from the fire, he could smell the smoke. His lungs burned as they sucked in the oxygen-depleted air. He was not accustomed to running even under the best of circumstances. At high elevation, in a gunfire-fueled panic, and in his stocking feet, he was lucky to be making any progress at all. He knew the highway was ahead somewhere, and was aware of the possibility that he might be running right into a trap.

Matthew could hear the deputy gaining on him from behind. His desperation kicked into high gear. After everything he'd done, he could not let himself be caught now. It might be too late to save Jayden, left far away in the woods, but he had to save himself. He'd seen movies; he knew what prison was like. He would die before allowing himself to be caught. He kept running, trying to formulate a plan, trying to keep cover between himself and that deputy with the gun trained on the back of his head.

Up ahead, the flashing lights on an SUV came into view. There'd be more deputies there with the vehicle, Matthew had no doubt. He dodged out of what he imagined would be the line of sight from the vehicle and veered left, closer to the highway.

In fact, the sheriff's SUV was empty. Hogan's partner had made his way back, and joined the deputy assigned to watch the highway. Together, they had trotted down to overlook the lake, alarmed by the stream of tankers flying low. The early morning mist had lifted, and with the sun now glinting off the lake, they could see movement at the other side of the dam.

Looked like guys in black tactical gear, weapons on their shoulders. They waved, but weren't sure if the other guys saw them.

***

Cardona cruised the winding mountain highway slowly. She didn't dare drive any faster, what with the wildlife dashing across the road. She'd very nearly totaled the car fifty feet outside the trailhead parking lot when the largest deer she had ever seen crashed through the brush at the side of the road and leapt right in front of her car. He'd stopped, gazed at her with terrified brown eyes, shook his four-point rack, and leapt away to disappear into the brush on the other side. Now, every few feet, some other wild animal raced across the road in front of her. Every four-footed creature, even tiny chipmunks, an opossum with babies on board, a bobcat, and a whole pack of coyotes were leaving their homes in the canyon, racing away from the smoke and flames.

Her car crept around another curve and she saw something else running at the edge of the road. It took a few seconds for her to register that this was a two-legged creature. He turned frightened eyes toward her car and seemed to spurt ahead even faster.

Matthew had broken through a line of underbrush and suddenly found himself leaping onto the asphalt of the highway. Running there was much easier than through the forest, but he was also in clear view of anyone who might be driving along the road. Sure enough, not more than a minute later, the sound of a vehicle approached from behind. Matthew's chest was on fire trying to get enough of the smoke-filled air into his lungs to keep going. The muscles in his thighs were cramping painfully, and his socks, heavy with blood from the cuts on his feet, were sliding off. He took a quick look back and saw the black sedan now creeping toward him. He couldn't make out decals or lights, but to Matthew, it had cops written all over it.

Cardona allowed her car to roll forward and took a quick look at the driver's license photo of the kidnapper the Sacramento field office had circulated. This had to be him, even with the thick dark stubble of beard. She stopped her car close behind, and threw open the door. With one foot already out, she fumbled with the parking brake and prepared to pull her weapon.

"Stop! FBI!" she ordered. The guy leapt the embankment and dodged into the forest north of the road. "Stop! FBI!" she called again, but the sound of his crashing through the brush grew fainter. She couldn't leave her vehicle in the middle of the narrow highway and pursue him on foot. She slid into the driver's seat and let the car drift forward, watching the edge of the trees. The lake should be just ahead, and this area was supposed to be patrolled by those sheriff's deputies. Tolliver had to be headed into a trap.

The deputies at the dam looked up at the sound of a large body crashing through the forest in their direction. They were getting used to the deer coming this way, but this sounded bigger. Deputy Hogan burst through the trees and stopped. He'd expected to find his prey cornered at the edge of the lake. Instead, he found his officers waving gaily at someone on the other side of the dam.

Forty Nine
The Dreadful Caldron

Carried in the arms of the firefighters, Kris was first to reach the helicopter. Never was a sight so welcome as the view of the helicopter waiting for the searchers on the shore of Lake Nell. The fire had reached last season's dry grasses close to the water, the wind from the helicopter's rotors making swirls of fire in the taller deer grass. Kris, now barely conscious, was tucked in first, laid carefully on the floor and covered with a Mylar blanket. She had probably suffered a concussion and was likely going into shock. Leaning against the copter Jody, tried to take the weight off her own throbbing ankle. She arranged Flag and Rose at Kris's feet, lashing their leashes to the seat as far from the doors as possible. No one needed a panicked dog leaping out an open doorway while in flight. Greg tucked Jayden into his own seat, his head lolling to the side, his rag-doll body held upright by the shoulder belt tucked behind his head. The other adults clambered aboard, and the helicopter took off before Andy's last foot had even left the ground. Horrified, Jody watched the paint on the copter's body blister and bubble as the vehicle swung up and out over burning grasses.

***

Cardona continued to cruise the two-lane road slowly, searching the shoulders and shadows under the trees for any more sign of the kidnapper. Up ahead, the road took a sharp left hook beside the dam and turned downhill. With just enough room to get most of her sedan off the highway there, she parked and trotted uphill toward the dam. At the corner where dirt and granite boulders had been piled to construct the dam, she skidded to a stop at the canyon's edge, gun at the ready. She looked into the steeply dropping abyss on the downstream side of the dam. Water came through the spillway high above, and dropped a hundred feet to a pool and the river below.

A shout echoed from her right and above. Matthew Tolliver, still running to save his life, burst into view on the narrow top of the dam and kept going. Looked as though he was going to try to make his escape by running all the way across. Cardona might have had a shot from where she watched, but at that moment the silhouette of another man appeared on the dam and took a stance, his weapon aimed at Tolliver's fleeing back.

***

All three deputies standing at the dam saw Matthew break into view at the same time. He vaulted over a hunk of broken granite and took off sprinting along the top of the dam. The guy was really flying. His face was swollen and purple with exertion, and they could all hear his ragged and frantic breathing.

Hogan's partner lurched forward and made a grab as the suspect went past. He succeeded in startling Matthew into a stumble briefly, but Matthew regained his footing and continued running. In frustration, the deputies could only watch as he ran past, just a few feet away. Hogan, still holding his weapon, raised his arm.

"Hogan! Stand down!" The woman deputy's voice rang out. Hogan had taken a stance, his handgun aimed directly at the back of the fleeing kidnapper, his finger on the trigger.

"What are you doing, Hogan?" she called, "Shooting an unarmed suspect in the back?"

Hogan dropped the gun to his side and shook his head in her direction, stomping his foot for good measure. "Well, shit," he said. He was just so damned mad. That guy had caused everyone so much trouble. Somebody should shoot him.

"Let it go, Hogan," she said.

He slid to sit on the concrete, looking after Matthew's running form. There was movement in the background, and his eyes shifted focus. Figures in black were gathered around the other side of the dam, three or four of them. They loomed large, dressed in shiny helmets and tactical gear.

"They'll get him at the other side," she said. "That's a SWAT squad. I'm not sure whose, but they'll get him."

Hogan didn't want some other guys to get the kidnapper. He wanted to get the weaselly little twerp himself. He'd earned the takedown, damn it. He slammed his fist into a thigh and muttered in frustration. As he watched, the guys in black positioned themselves at the other side of the dam, military-type weapons trained on the kidnapper. Hogan's partner called him off the dam, out of the line of fire.

Matthew kept racing. He didn't seem to see the officers lying in wait for him.

The sheriff's deputies had gotten used to the recurring roars of air tankers over the lake that morning, but the chopping of helicopter rotors coming directly toward the dam took everyone by surprise. The bird was circling from the northeastern shore of the lake around to line up for a landing at the Eagle Meadow fire camp, a course that took them low and directly over the dam.

***

Matthew knew there were at least two cops behind him when he looked up and saw a helicopter bearing down. Twenty feet in front of him, the top of the dam opened up in a spillway, now flowing with spring runoff. The gap looked to be about eight feet wide, a jump he could easily have made if he'd been wearing his shoes, and hadn't already been exhausted. There was no choice. He had to keep going, make the leap, and disappear again into the forest on the other side. He pushed off with a back foot and went flying.

Deliberately not looking below, he focused on his intended landing spot. Airborne, halfway across, he spotted the tactical squad taking aim at him near the trees up ahead. There was the slightest hesitation, a faltering in his forward progress, as if he could stop himself in mid-air. Except for that, he might have cleared the spillway, but he didn't quite. His leading foot found no purchase when it came down, and his hands found nothing to grasp. His body hit the wall of the spillway a few feet down, then continued to slide, bouncing off the concrete of the chute as gravity pulled him over.

***

Overhead, riding in the helicopter, Jody bent her neck, watching Matthew dashing across the dam. She tapped Andy on the shoulder and pointed out the scene. Together they watched in horror as Matthew attempted the leap, then slid down the chute. As the copter cleared the dam, Matthew's body caught the sunlight for a moment as it spun into space. They lost sight of it then, until the splash far below in the pool at the bottom of the spillway gave it away. Jody could see several people, possibly law enforcement, watching as Matthew's body flew out of sight.

***

Cardona had the most stunning and horrific view, looking up at the spillway chute from the road's edge. Matthew's body bounced like a rubber doll as it careened off the concrete and spun in wider gyrations, falling. The water coming through the spillway scattered in millions of droplets, each one catching a single ray of colored light. Together they formed an arching rainbow that only Cardona could see, the black figure that was Matthew sailing through the exquisite beauty of the shifting and airy colors toward the gorge below. There were rocks at the bottom, but all Cardona saw was Matthew's body disappearing into a dreadful caldron of swirling water and seething foam.

Fifty
Red Sky

The air ambulance was already waiting when the much larger forest service helicopter with its precious cargo landed at Eagle Meadow. Lowell held Bullet, his hip wrapped tightly in an elastic bandage and purple vet wrap. He nestled the dog close to Kris for a moment, once she was transferred to the air ambulance, so both could see the other was safe. The emergency medical techs hooked Kris up to monitors and intravenous tubes. The family of three had a happy although brief and subdued reunion.

Jayden was readied for transport in the same ambulance. He had his own emergency medical technician, but there were no family members to celebrate his return. Greg gave Jayden a quick kiss on his sunburned forehead, and reassured him he would see his grandma soon. No one knew if that would prove to be true. As they prepared to leave for the faraway hospital, Kris reached out and stroked the baby's soft curls.

Jody, Andy, Frank, and Greg watched and waved as the air ambulance lifted off. The search mission was over, all search team members were either safe or being cared for, and the whereabouts of the kidnapper and baby were known. Still, it wasn't quite the end. They had gear to pack, paperwork to complete, and lives to resume. They sprawled on the ground or sat in folding chairs near the exercise pen while Frank produced mounds of scrambled eggs and paper plates loaded with bacon from his small camp stove. Andy roused himself long enough to make a visit to the fire camp dining tent and ferry an overflowing basket of freshly baked biscuits to the weary searchers.

There were long stretches of silence while the tired group watched the activity on the other side of the parking lot. More ground crews arrived, geared up and took off to fight the fire.

"How are they getting to the fire?" Jody wondered. "The fire is past the ford already, and there's no other way across the creek." The words were hardly out of her mouth when a ground crew that had gone out earlier trudged back into camp, followed closely by the crew that had just left. The fire had expanded so rapidly, there was no way to reach it on foot from this location. The public address system crackled to life and Cullison made the announcement that the whole camp would need to be moved to another site.

Greg sprawled on the ground next to Rose, petting her soft bloodhound head.

In a brief pause between vehicles rolling out of the lot en route to the new fire camp, Cardona's sedan returned and parked. She joined the group and Frank handed her a cup of his hot strong brew. She looked shell-shocked, and didn't even check the coffee for swimming bugs or ashes. They all knew how Matthew had met his end, but no one else had had quite the view she'd seen. Quietly they shared their stories.

"So is that the end of it?" Greg asked Cardona. He had curled around Rose and both were looking sleepy. "Case closed, kidnapper dead?"

"Well, we haven't recovered his body yet." Cardona said. "The SWAT team is trying to get down there now."

"That's a fast moving stream below the dam," Jody said. "Unless the body got caught up somewhere on the bank, it might float for a long time downstream before washing up." The group was solemn while they contemplated that image of Jayden's father. "You might eventually need one of our underwater human remains detection dogs to find him."

"I'll keep that in mind," Cardona said. "In the meantime, to answer your question, as long as his body remains unrecovered, Tolliver will be charged with unlawful flight to avoid prosecution and a federal arrest warrant will be issued by the United States District Court." For a moment, she sounded like she was reading from an official manual again, escaping into bureaucratic lingo.

Greg listened, and also slipped closer to a blissful state of unconsciousness. He laid his head on the dog's haunch, still caressing her head. Perhaps he could talk the wife into adopting a dog instead of having another baby.

Andy poured Flag a bowl full of fresh water and all the kibble she could eat. The dog began vacuuming both bowls clean. Jody hobbled to the privacy of her own vehicle, eased off her boot, and unwrapped the swollen ankle. From the size of it, and the pain, maybe she should have caught a ride to the hospital, too. It was a sure thing she wasn't going to be driving herself off that mountain.

She settled into the seat and scrolled slowly through her phone's list of text messages and missed calls. Her desire for search and rescue excitement temporarily quenched, she punched in a number and waited for the connection. Romance might be about as exciting an adventure as she was willing to tackle after her long night in the forest. Her call went to voicemail.

After her meal, Flag was enjoying a nap, snuggled up near, but not on top of MacDuff. Abruptly, both stood and Flag's tail came to alert as both dogs stared under the shadows of the nearby trees. Their noses had caught something strong enough to waken them, and now Flag was signaling her alert. Andy stood and wandered toward the trees while the others watched. No one was in the mood for yet another emergency.

It was Ted. The fragrance of bacon had overridden the scent of fire surrounding his makeshift home, and he had come to investigate. Frank waved him to join them, but Ted's inner state would not permit such a risk. He did accept a paper plate that Frank loaded with eggs and bacon and Andy carried to him.

***

The sky was suddenly filled with the sound of multiple helicopters, each ferrying bulging red bags of water. Steamy white smoke billowed around everyone left in camp as the water fell, dousing sections of the raging flames. The forest belonged to the fire now, and those doing battle with it.

Dear Readers,

Thank you for reading *On Scent*. I hope you enjoyed it. I appreciate your support! Please consider posting a review on your favorite book-related web site. If you liked this story, your friends would probably also enjoy hearing about it.

To learn about upcoming books, including a possible new adventure featuring Jody and Flag, and my Estela Nogales Mystery series, and to leave me comments and questions, please visit my web page at www.cherieoboyle.com.

Sincerely,
Cherie O'Boyle

THANK YOU

To everyone who read earlier versions of *On Scent* and tried to warn me: Karen Phillips, Karla Kroeplin, Pamela Beason, Marilyn Reynolds, and Joan Waters; to my loyal if sometimes doubtful critique group, Linda Townsdin, Michele Drier, and June Gillam; to an anonymous literary agent and Hallie Ephron who provided brief but pithy appraisals of sections, and to all those who encouraged and assured me that a story about a kidnapping/canine search and rescue/forest fire would make a great suspense, thank you!

To the professionals who graciously provided their expertise, SacMetro Fire Captain and canine handler, Chris Berquist, FBI Special Agent (ret.) George Fong, U. S. Forest Service District Ranger (ret.) Karen Caldwell, the late Sacramento Sheriff's Department Canine Search and Rescue team Patti Pearson and CJ (Shiner's brother), and Sacramento Animal Hospital Veterinarian Jennifer Koncz, thank you all for your valued assistance. Please know that I take full responsibility for any misinterpretations and/or fictional enhancements I committed.

Printed in the United States of America

****

O'Boyle, Cherie
On Scent/ written by Cherie O'Boyle
ISBN 978-0-997-2028-8-5

Cover design by Karen Phillips, www.PhillipsCovers.com

Made in the USA
San Bernardino, CA
24 June 2019